Forged in Peril

Forge Brothers Security
Book 1

Kendra Warden

Fearless
Faith Press

Chapter 1

The man eased his foot onto the gas pedal and rolled slowly up the incline, struggling to see the edges of his garage door through the darkness and the driving rain.

As he made his way through the gaping mouth of the door, the fly-encrusted tube light on the ceiling flickered, mocking him.

He should have changed it weeks ago, but he had no time for things like that. Not with the hours that his career demanded.

When he got his promotion, he would install new lights in the garage, clean the leaves out of the gutters, and repair the hole in the screen door that led onto the back porch. That was what he told himself.

He smiled at the thought as he listened to the door lowering behind him, shutting out the sound of the heavy raindrops pounding against his driveway.

His future would come, sooner or later, and whether or not he had more time was irrelevant. His higher paychecks would be more than enough to pay someone to do those sorts of things for him.

He opened the door of the car, and the grin fell away from his face just as quickly as it had come.

A man was standing there.

No, two men, but their faces were nothing but shadows in the dim light.

Before he knew what was happening, he felt rough hands against his chest, shoving him back down into his seat. He struggled against the assailant, but the man was stronger than he expected.

His heart was racing now, panic building as he struggled to force air into his lungs. He wanted to scream, but the sound caught in his throat.

He heard the man who was holding him down say something in Spanish over his shoulder, and the other replied. He struggled to think, to remember anything at all about the language that he hadn't studied since high school, but his mind was blank, consumed with the sound of the blood pulsing in his ears.

He watched as the man outside the car passed his companion a long coil of rope.

"*Gracias*," the strong man muttered.

The prisoner felt his hands being wrenched out in front of him, rope wrapping around them like a choking snake. The more he tried to shake free, the tighter his captor pulled the thick cord, pinching his skin until it burned.

He swore, and the man swore back in Spanish as he attempted to kick at him.

"Let me go! Do you know who I am?" he sputtered, the words finally breaking free of his lips. "Do you know who I work for? I'll kill you, and your friend. I know people. Dangerous people that you don't want–"

The other man leaned into the car just enough to fit the silvery barrel of his gun through the gap of the door, his finger poised against the trigger, waiting.

The prisoner stared at its round black mouth, imagining the bullet rushing through the chamber, his tongue going dry.

He let his hands be tied, and he no longer tried to kick as the strong man did the same to his feet.

The men were speaking to one another now in rapid Spanish, and he tried to listen, forcing himself to peel his eyes away from the gun and to look at their shadowy faces instead.

"*Chica*," he heard one of the men say amid the rush of unfamiliar words. The other man said it, too, and he could hear the disdain in their voices.

He laid his head back against the seat, closing his eyes, desperately searching his brain for which *chica* they could be referring to.

There were a few contenders, but he couldn't recall any latinas.

"I'm–I'm sorry," he stammered, looking down as the man leaned over his feet, tying the final knots. "I didn't know who she was–that she had people who cared, you know, a girl like that? Just a girl, just a *chica*, like you said. It didn't mean–"

In an instant, the man at his feet had retreated out of the car, and his friend with the gun had taken his place, leaning in toward the driver's seat.

The gun was close now, the sight of it enough to shut him up, even before he felt it being pressed against his forehead, slipping on the sweat that had accumulated there.

"You will shut up now," the man said in English, each word drawn out slowly as he held the gun in place.

After what felt like a very long time, the man with the gun pulled back again, allowing the strong man to finish the task at hand.

The prisoner only watched as his numb, bound hands were roped to the steering wheel. He couldn't move so much as an inch, and even if he somehow managed to get loose, they'd shoot him if he tried to escape or to scream for help over the sound of the rain.

He'd seen enough movies to know that he was supposed to start crying now, or perhaps to wet himself with fear, but his mind felt almost as numb as his limbs did.

He watched as though he was somewhere else entirely, witnessing the misfortune of someone else, some other man in some other car.

The man with the gun was outside the window now, staring at him, the gun still raised.

The strong man was tinkering with the button that controlled the driver's side window, opening it just a couple of inches before stepping out of the car again.

He disappeared out of the prisoner's line of sight for a moment, returning with a green rubber hose and sticking its end through the gap he'd created along the top of the window. He nodded toward it, as though his handiwork pleased him, and carefully leaned into the car again.

Once more, the prisoner considered screaming,

or even speaking, but the momentary courage fell away, replaced by a paralyzing curiosity.

He stared as the man pulled a roll of duct tape from the front pocket of his pants and began taping up the gap that surrounded the end of the hose.

The guy with the gun leaned in around the edge of the door again, letting the barrel fall casually against his side.

"There's no need to be worried, man. It's painless," he said, shaking his head. His face was still hidden by shadow, but his words sounded almost cheerful, as though he was doing his prisoner a favor.

The strong man jostled him out of the way and reached for the key, which was still waiting in the ignition, and at last, the prisoner understood.

The man turned the key and the car rumbled to life, a plume of gray smoke pouring in through the hose.

"No, no, no, don't do this–"

Before he had even managed to get a single sentence out, the man had retreated into the safety of his garage, slamming the door behind him.

The prisoner stared through the window, watching as his captor coughed over and over.

The thick smoke filled his vision, obscuring his view of the men.

They would be gone soon. Perhaps they were already.

He tried to scream, but only coughs came out, his lungs burning as the thick smoke stole away the last of the clean air that remained in the car.

But it wasn't the smoke that would kill him.

He closed his eyes, feeling more and more tired with each passing minute, and he remembered that carbon monoxide could put you to sleep forever.

All for a *chica*.

Chapter 2

Bristol

The engine shuddered as Bristol pressed her foot against the gas pedal.

"Come on, Boris," she said, glancing down at the RPM gauge with a sigh. "Not now. Do this at lunch or something."

After a few more seconds of protest, the car shifted into third gear at last, though Bristol had little doubt that the stubborn old Ford Taurus would indeed pull the same stunt later.

It had been several weeks since the transmission had started to act up, but unless she went to her mother for yet another favor, Boris was just going to have to survive a couple more weeks. As long as her new company was keen to pay her on time, she figured they'd make it. At least, she hoped so.

She reached down and took hold of the travel mug of green tea resting in the console, careful not to let the temperamental lid pop free as she took a small, careful sip. The taste was familiar and comforting, despite the uncertainties of the day ahead, and she was thankful that she'd stopped for it at the Screaming Peach Cafe on her way out of Silver Grove.

The small coffee shop was owned by her mother's old friend Iris, and the cozy, somewhat dated interior was almost as familiar as the mobile home she'd spent most of her childhood in.

She'd intended to grab only the tea, having scrounged together just enough change from the bottom of her purse and the cupholders of her car, but Iris had insisted on feeding her a full breakfast platter on the house.

Supposedly, it had been offered in celebration of her new job, but Bristol knew better.

Gossip traveled fast in Silver Grove, and her moving back in with her mother somehow qualified as newsworthy. Bristol wouldn't have been surprised if half of the sleepy town knew the precise, humiliating balance of her checking account by now.

She took another long drink as she merged onto the freeway, thankful that the Monday morning traffic was strangely light, even though she was heading into San Antonio closer to rush hour than she'd intended.

Still, she was thankful for her full belly and the accompanying encouragement that Iris had offered her. She hated accepting charity from anyone, but for the time being, she had been forced to let go of her pride more than once.

If taking a handout from Iris helped her to reach her goal of moving back into her own apartment a little bit faster, it would be well worth it.

As she settled into highway speed–Boris, thankfully, was still on his best behavior–she couldn't help but to let her mind wander to her old apartment.

Though she had moved out almost a month ago, she still half-expected to wake up there every morning, the sunshine shafting in between her lacy white bedroom curtains. Though it was tiny and overpriced, it was located right in downtown San Antonio, 'close to the action', as her mother would say, and her kitchen window had a view of the River Walk.

She had lived there for barely two years, but it had been long enough for it to feel like home, and now it belonged to someone else.

Bristol reached for the radio dial, turning up the volume as the weather reporter drawled on about the drizzling rain that was supposed to arrive in the late afternoon. She turned it off again immediately, her attempt to distract herself a total fail.

Now that Christmas had come and gone, she found the dull, cloudy January weather depressing.

"Maybe all of this is a mistake, Boris," she said, not caring how ridiculous it was to name and then talk to a car. She had a few friends in the city, but none that would understand her current predicament, and she had burdened her mother enough already. At least Boris didn't judge.

It was too late to turn back now, anyway. She was expected to arrive at Forge Brothers Security within the next thirty minutes, and she knew she'd need at least fifteen minutes to work up the nerve to actually go in.

Cameron Forge was going to think that she was crazy, taking him up on his offer after all of this time, but she could see no better way out of the mess she'd found herself in.

She'd just have to put on a brave face for the sake of her future.

Step one, get out of her mother's house.

Step two, save up at least part of what she needed to go back to school.

If she put her head down, she could achieve both of her goals in a year.

And if Cameron had a problem with her during that time, she'd just have to do her best to stay out of his way.

As she pulled off of the freeway ramp, she could see that the traffic was picking up as thousands of people poured into their offices, ready to tackle the week ahead. Despite everything that had happened, she couldn't help but to feel a twinge of melancholy as she passed the street that led toward the glittering office tower housing Dorling & Porter, Attorneys at Law.

For two years she had walked into that building six days a week, sacrificing the majority of her waking hours trying to carve out a place for herself as their top paralegal. She had put their clients and lawyers above everything else in her life, forgoing dinners with oft-neglected friends and Saturday morning coffee dates with potential suitors in favor of writing reports, filing paperwork, and preparing for court. And even after all that she had done to prove herself, it hadn't been enough.

One night, one lapse in judgment, one man's word against her own, and it was all over. Losing her career had been bad enough, but that wasn't all that had been taken from her. Not by a long shot.

Bristol tried to shake off the dark thoughts that threatened to consume her as she turned onto the correct street, eyes scanning the side of the street for a parallel parking space before she remembered that she'd been given an access code for the garage. She pulled around the back of the building, punched in the number at the gate, and slowly rolled down the underground driveway, pleased to see that the place was surprisingly well-lit.

It didn't take her long to find a parking spot in a secluded but bright corner, and though it was nearing seven-thirty, she was in no hurry to head inside.

Avoiding Cameron Forge while working at his company was going to be impossible, she knew, but she could afford to delay the awkwardness for just a little while longer.

Despite moving back to San Antonio two years prior, for the most part, it had been easy to avoid the Forge brothers. They lived in a different world than she and her mother did, and there were few places where their paths would naturally cross.

Of course, there were always exceptions.

After weeks of cajoling, Bristol's mother had nearly dragged her to a bake sale at her church in Silver Grove during her first Christmas back in town, which just so happened to be the same church that the Forge family had been attending approximately forever.

And, of course, all of the brothers had chosen to show up at the bake sale, including Cameron.

Bristol reached over onto the passenger seat, fiddling with the contents of her tote bag and trying not to remember what a jerk she'd been to him. He and his family had been nothing but kind to her, but she'd been standoffish–especially when he'd offered her a job in their security company's legal department as soon as he found out that she was finished with her bachelor's degree and paralegal program.

She could still imagine the way that she'd rebuffed his generous offer, telling him that she could take care of herself, and that she already had a job with a very prestigious local firm, thank you very much.

She cringed as she tightened the lid on her water bottle for the third time, not wanting to risk dousing the rest of the contents of her purse.

Dorling & Porter was prestigious, all right.

Prestigious enough to protect their own favored lawyers, no matter their conduct, and no matter the cost.

It had taken every ounce of humility Bristol had to write an email to Cameron's assistant the week before, asking if they were still hiring for any legal positions. At that point, she was desperate enough that she would have been thankful for a gig in the mail room, but she knew Cameron, and despite how she'd treated him, she was confident that he'd help her as much as he could.

So it had not been a surprise when she'd received an email back less than six hours later, telling her that their lead–and currently only–paralegal had recently gone out on maternity leave, and that they were desperate to bring in a competent replacement. He'd offered her the job then and there, without even asking for an interview.

Now, she realized that maybe talking to him beforehand might have made things a whole lot easier, but it was too late to do anything about it now.

With a final reluctant glance at her watch, she hitched her bag over her shoulder and climbed out of the car, pressing the lock button on her keys a couple of extra times, just in case.

"Not that anyone in their right mind would break into you, Boris," she said, glancing around to ensure that the garage was otherwise empty before starting toward the stairwell.

With any luck, most of the other employees would roll up in their BMWs or whatever they drove closer to eight, and no one, not even Cameron, would realize that the dumpy old Taurus with the mismatched fender belonged to her at all.

Cameron

Cameron yawned as he scrolled through his emails, trying to rub the sleep from his eyes as he forced himself to focus on the endless torrent of invoices, media inquiries, and junk mail that filled his inbox.

His coffee cup sat empty at his side, the cracked old mug proclaiming that 'God's mercies are new every morning'.

While he certainly believed that to be true, he also figured that said mercies would proceed just fine without him while he slept in.

This morning, however, that was not an option, and he figured that downing a couple of cups of hot coffee couldn't hurt.

Before he could rise from his desk to grab a refill, however, he heard a knock on the doorframe, and his brother Gabriel stepped into the office.

"Hey, Cam. Ready to see her again?" he asked, grinning.

His black hair was still wet from what had probably been a post-workout shower, and there was not even a hint of bags beneath his bright blue eyes, despite the fact that he'd almost certainly been awake before dawn.

Cameron suppressed the sudden urge to chuck a stack of Post-Its at his overly cheerful face.

"Ready to see who?" he replied, stretching his arms over his head as another yawn worked its way through his chest.

Gabe rolled his eyes.

"She'd better not make me regret letting you hire her," he warned, shaking his head.

Let him hire her? Last he checked, it wasn't Gabriel Forge Security.

Cameron decided it would be wise to keep his mouth shut on that topic. Gabriel was, technically, the boss—and more importantly, he was generally good at taking care of things. His control-freak tendencies could be annoying, but usually not worth starting a fight over.

"She has solid legal experience, Gabe," he said instead, shrugging his shoulders. "Two years as a certified paralegal in one of San Antonio's most well-known firms, and she got her bachelor's from Columbia before that. Her plan is to go to law school, get her JD, the whole deal."

Gabe leaned against the edge of Cameron's cluttered desk, raising a single eyebrow. "Is that what she told you when she went off to New York City and broke your heart, or was this a more recent discussion?"

Ouch.

At least his older brother had the decency not to

complain about his messy office for the umpteenth time. That was something.

"Irrelevant. That's all ancient history. She's perfect for the position, Gabe. You have nothing to worry about. And with Carly on maternity leave, the timing is clearly Providential."

"You asked her to start her leave early!"

Cameron didn't bother to deny it.

"Still. We were going to need to look for someone soon, anyway. You should be thankful that such a good candidate fell into our laps."

Gabe gave an exaggerated sigh. "Like I said before, I don't care if she's the best paralegal in Texas if she plans on breaking my little brother's heart again and damaging morale at FBS in the process."

"That's not going to happen. This is a favor to an old friend–yours as well as mine, in case you've forgotten–who also happens to be just what we need. That's all this is."

Gabe tapped his fingers against the black metal of the desk. He didn't look particularly convinced.

Nor was Cameron entirely convinced himself, but it didn't matter.

Whatever feelings came to the surface when he saw her again, he wasn't going to let his judgment be clouded.

God had made it pretty clear that what he thought he wanted wasn't in the plan, at least for now, and Bristol Chaplin showing up in his life again didn't change that.

Chapter 3

Bristol

Bristol took a final deep breath as she reached the first floor, pushing against the heavy stairwell doors with both hands. She forced herself to step through them and out into the hall, her plain black flats making an obnoxious slapping sound against the marble as she walked.

She rounded the corner, finding herself face to face with a massive reception desk, manned by a woman who she was certain would never be caught dead in anything but the most glamorous designer shoes.

"Welcome to Forge Brothers Security, how can I help you?" the woman said, giving Bristol a gleaming white smile. Gently smudged black eyeliner complemented her bright blue eyes, and her curly blonde hair bounced against perfectly-tanned shoulders.

If this was what all of the women at FBS were supposed to look like, she was in trouble.

Bristol plastered a smile on her own face, forcing herself to meet the beautiful woman's eyes instead of looking down at her own basic black skirt and white blouse. She hadn't even attempted any makeup more ambitious than a swipe of copper eyeshadow and some mascara.

She had always fit in well enough at Dorling & Porter–despite the wealth that the firm generated, most of the lawyers were more practical than fashionable–but this morning she felt completely out of place.

"Hello," she said. "I'm Bristol Chaplin. I was just hired in the legal department."

"Oh, wonderful," the woman said, still beaming. Bristol wondered if her cheeks ever started to hurt from smiling so much. "Well, I'm Grace Hinton. I'm kind of the office manager, kind of the spare receptionist. It's nice to have you with us."

The woman extended a perfectly manicured hand for her to shake, and a few awkward seconds passed as Bristol hitched up her tote bag higher on her shoulder and shifted her still-hot green tea into her other hand.

Grace's handshake was warm, and despite how intimidated she felt, Bristol couldn't help but to sense a genuine friendliness radiating from the woman.

"Now, if you'll just give me a moment to get you set up on our clock-in system, I'll have you on your way," she continued, sitting back down and tapping away at her keyboard with rapid-fire speed.

Bristol took a couple of steps back, trying to get a good view of the large reception space without looking too eager.

Huge glass doors led out onto the busy street in front of the building, with the words 'Serve. Protect. Redeem.' emblazoned above them.

The floor was smooth marble, and every detail from the light fixtures to the leather chairs in the waiting area made it clear that no expense had been spared. She'd been expecting as much, but still, she couldn't help but to be surprised at just how extravagant the customer-facing area of the private security firm was.

Thanks to her mother's gossip, she'd followed the development of Forge Brothers Security more closely than she'd ever admit over the last seven years, but seeing it in person was something else.

She could see no one else in the lobby at the moment–she doubted the place would be open to clients before nine–but down the hall opposite the elevators she could hear several women chatting and laughing together and the sound of heels clacking against the stone floor.

As usual, she couldn't deny the feeling of relief that swept through her whenever she realized that she was surrounded by other women.

It made her feel safe, and as Grace continued to type away, she felt some of the tightness in her chest beginning to dissipate.

There had been a time not so long ago that the sex of her coworkers wouldn't have crossed her mind, but things were different now, and all she could do was try her best not to let anyone else notice how uneasy she felt whenever she was alone with a man.

"All right, babe," Grace was saying from behind her computer, the lobby silent as the sounds of her keyboard ceased. "I've got your time card all logged in, and I'll make sure you get an ID badge before lunch so you don't need to be escorted through all of the doors. Security company, you know how it is."

Grace let out a laugh that reminded Bristol of tinkling glass, and she couldn't help but to give her a genuine smile back.

"I appreciate that, thanks a lot," she said, pausing as she waited for further direction. Before Grace could tell her where to head next, however, she heard a booming voice behind her.

"Bristol!" the man said, almost directly over her shoulder.

She spun around at once, and she was just in time to see Cameron's surprised expression as she dumped a half-full cup of hot tea all over the tops of her hands and down the front of her skirt, her metal travel mug making a thunderous crash as it fell against the floor.

Cameron

For several long seconds, Cameron stood perfectly still, unable to do anything but stare as the puddle of liquid seeped out across the lobby floor. Bristol was staring down at her soaked black skirt, holding up her reddened hands as though she wasn't quite sure they belonged to her.

Finally, he snapped into action, wanting to smack himself, not only for startling her but for standing around like an idiot when she had clearly been burned.

"Come on, there's a first aid kit in my office," he said, gesturing toward the elevator. Bristol followed without a word, and as soon as she was inside, he pushed the button for the third floor. She remained silent as the elevator slid neatly upward, her mouth a tight line.

Great first impression.

Burning a woman with scalding tea is always a memorable choice.

He cleared his throat, wanting to say something, but before he could come up with so much as a proper apology, the doors were opening in front of them. Bristol stepped through ahead of him, pausing as he directed her down the hallway leading to the left. Several people passed them as they rushed toward his office, including his brother Ben, who was on his way to the stairwell, balancing a tray of takeout coffees in each hand.

"Woah, woah, woah," he said, glancing down at Bristol, who was not only much shorter than he was but about a third of his weight. "What happened? Hey, are you okay?"

Bristol's face looked nearly as red as her hands as she gazed up at the big man.

Though Bristol had known all of his brothers when they were children and then teenagers, Cameron doubted that she'd expected the computer nerd of the family to turn into such a gym bro. Thanks to his sheer bulk he looked downright intimidating now, in his early thirties.

"I'm fine, just spilled a little tea. It's good to see you, Ben," she said, giving him a quick smile.

Ben looked around for a place to set down the coffees, and finding that no table had materialized in the hallway, gave Cameron a warning glance.

"You need to make sure she runs those burns under cold water for a full five minutes, at minimum," he said, his gravelly voice firm. Bristol gave him a funny look, but he didn't seem to notice. "That's the best first aid for a burn. Make sure you take the time before you worry about bandages or anything else."

"Okay, okay," Cam said, gesturing toward the stairwell. "I've got this, bro."

With a final grunt, Ben continued on his way, the paper takeout cups looking laughably tiny next to his bulky hands and arms as he shouldered his way into the staircase.

"Five minutes sounds like total overkill, but if he's still the smart one, I guess we should listen to him," Bristol said as they crossed the final few feet of carpet toward his office door. It was the first full sentence she'd said to him since her arrival, and despite his determination not to let her presence get to him, he couldn't deny the warmth that rose in his chest as he looked at her.

Despite her burned hands and ruined skirt, she was just as beautiful as he remembered her, perhaps even more so. Her light brown hair brushed against her shoulders, and her green eyes were striking against her pale, slightly freckled skin. He could tell that she was wearing a little makeup, mostly mascara and a hint of something glimmering and copper on her eyelids, but it was hardly necessary. The woman woke up gorgeous.

"He's definitely still the nerd of the family," he said, remembering just in time that she'd spoken and was expecting him to respond. "When he goes to the public gym, women are always trying to talk to him, impressed by the muscles, you know. And then he starts going on about the latest blockchain innovation or the present state of the NFT market and they realize just how badly they chose their target."

Bristol laughed at that, just as they reached the half-open door of his office.

"Well, I guess you should hit the sink before the burns permanently disfigure your pretty hands," he said in a rush, gesturing toward his private bathroom at the far end of the room, half-hoping that she wouldn't notice his awkward attempt at a compliment.

She entered the bathroom without comment, but after several long seconds standing there at the open door and listening to the sound of the running sink, he realized he couldn't exactly wait around like an idiot for the next five minutes.

He rushed over to his desk, settling into his ergonomic chair and rooting around in search of the first aid kit he'd stashed.

Over time, all of his desk drawers had become filled with all manner of random and pointless objects. After several minutes of digging through drawer after drawer, he drew the small red bag from beneath a stack of plastic sheet protectors.

He waited for several more seconds, wondering if he had time to make the top of his desk a little more presentable before Bristol re-emerged, but before he could decide, he heard her calling out to ask him if he had any bandages.

He let out a breath as he unzipped the first aid kit, relieved to see that unlike the rest of his office, its contents were well organized–likely because he hadn't had a chance to use this one yet. Selecting a roll of non-adhesive wound dressing, he strode into the bathroom, just in time to nearly plow into Bristol as she came out.

This was going well.

"I'm so sorry," he said, holding up the roll of bandages. "About that, and about earlier. I didn't mean to startle you."

"It's fine, Cam," she said quickly, giving him a pinched smile. Her eyes caught his for a long moment, and there was an expression on her face that he couldn't quite read. "Can you help me with my left hand?"

"Uh, yeah, of course," he said, cringing at the way his words came out in a stammer. Even now, as a grown man, she had a way of making him feel like a lovestruck teenager.

Even though he was more determined than ever to never feel that way about her again.

Bristol extended her arms in front of him, and he

wrapped the white cloth around her still-red hands, leaving her fingers mostly free.

"Well, I can still type," she said when he was done, wiggling her unpainted fingertips back and forth. "I guess you guys probably need to bandage yourselves up often enough, in this line of work."

He nodded, looking down at his own hands, which felt suddenly empty now that they were no longer brushing against hers. "Unfortunately, yes. Ben's the first aid dork, but all of us know our way around a med kit. It comes in handy."

Bristol smiled again, and this time, it actually looked genuine.

"Anyway," he said, running a hand through his dark brown hair, "you're not typing anything today. I'd tell you to go home until you heal, but–"

"–You know I'd never go for it," she finished. "And you'd be right. Honestly, I'm fine. I want to get started, though I guess I need to find a change of clothes."

As if on cue, Grace appeared at the open door of his office, a bundle of gray material in her hands.

"I had some sweats in my gym locker," she said, handing the pants to Bristol with an apologetic look. "Not exactly the most fashionable, but at least they're dry."

Cameron smirked at her. "But are they clean?"

"Obviously. Unlike you disgusting men, I prefer to keep my locker biohazard-free."

Bristol laughed, holding up the pants in front of her. "They'll totally work, so long as I can avoid being seen by any clients. Thanks, Grace."

"Any time," she said, giving Bristol another winning smile.

There was a long pause.

Cameron glanced over at Bristol, who was still looking at the sweats instead of meeting anyone's eyes.

He felt Grace poking at his rib with the end of a rather pointy manicured finger.

"Maybe you could show Bristol where she can change and freshen up," she said, furrowing her brows.

"Oh, right," he said, shaking his head.

"I'll just throw them on in there, if that's okay," Bristol said quickly. "I really do want to meet the lawyer I'll be working under as soon as possible."

Cameron nodded, and Bristol ducked into his bathroom once again, the door locking with a click behind her.

Grace was already staring at him, her arms folded across her chest.

"I'm glad the cleaning service handles the bathrooms," he joked. "It's a lot cleaner than my office."

"Don't change the subject."

"What subject?" he said innocently, lowering his voice and hoping that Grace would follow suit.

"You're so not over her!"

He felt his cheeks burning. He didn't need to ask how Grace had managed to find out about his and Bristol's history. Somehow, the woman always seemed to know everything about everyone. Including history of the ancient variety.

"I have no idea what you're talking about, Hinton. Anyway, you need to get back to work. I need flights booked for the Tijuana job."

"Okay, boss," she said with a wink as she headed for the door. "Whatever you say."

Cameron picked up a handful of papers from the middle of his desk before setting them down again a couple of inches away, lost in thought.

One thing was clear: if he was going to help Bristol by giving her this job, he was going to need to get a grip.

Chapter 4

Bristol

"We're basically dealing with criminal law. Lots of fraud cases, some blackmail and extortion, and the occasional stabbing or shooting to keep things exciting," the woman was saying, her cool tone betraying no indication of whether or not she was trying to be funny.

For the last several hours, Bristol had been following lawyer Jaclyn Mercier around the small legal office, trying to get a grip on exactly what sort of work her new position at Forge Brothers Security entailed.

Most of what she'd done at Dorling & Porter had been related to corporate and tax law, but Cameron had assured her when he'd offered her the job that her experience was more than adequate, and so far, Jaclyn seemed to be trying to convince her of the same thing.

"I've been studying some criminal law material on my own," Bristol ventured, trying to surreptitiously adjust the waistband of Grace's sweatpants for the fifteenth time. To her credit, Jaclyn had not commented on her bandaged hands or her attire when she walked in, but unfortunately, the pants were at least one size too tight around the hips and had been digging into her skin all morning. "First-year stuff, mostly, but I'm definitely willing to learn."

Jaclyn nodded. "Cameron told me that you plan to go to law school in the future. I think FBS will be a good place for you in the interim, you'll learn a lot here. Anyway, if you can gather up those files off of Melanie's desk, I'll show you where the file rooms are located. And yes, there's more than one, just to keep you on your toes."

The woman's words were friendly enough, but

once again, her tone and facial expression revealed little.

She was in her mid-forties, tall and blonde and pretty in a pale, almost fairylike sort of way. At the moment, she was one of only two current employees in the legal department, the other being a law student named Melanie who worked at FBS part-time as a clerk during the school year.

Despite spending a good chunk of the day mere feet away from her new boss, Bristol had struggled to gather any personal information about her. In fact, Jaclyn had seemed almost angry when she had asked whether she was married or had any children, and Bristol had decided that for the time being, she would stick to talking about the weather or the law.

She had, however, managed to learn that Jaclyn was new to FBS as well, having only arrived about six months prior. Apparently, she had replaced a male lawyer who had gotten married and moved to Alabama.

Once again, Bristol was relieved to be working with another woman, especially considering the small staff and the likelihood that she'd often be alone with her boss.

She couldn't help but to notice that, so far, Cameron's presence had not set off any alarm bells, even when he'd been close enough to bandage her hands.

It was strange for her to feel so at ease around any male, but she supposed that the Forge brothers in general were somewhat of a special case. She'd known them all since she was in diapers, and she'd known Cam most of all.

She knew him well enough to be absolutely certain that he was a good guy, and that was half of the problem.

Bristol sighed under her breath as she gathered up the neat files and stray papers from the top of what seemed to be the only desk in the main area of the office - the other two desks were hidden behind closed office doors, one belonging to Jaclyn and the other, she was told, belonging to her.

She could hear nothing but the sound of shuffling paper for several long moments as

Jaclyn rifled through several drawers of a nearby file cabinet.

She'd made her choice about Cameron a long time ago, so why did she find herself thinking about the past?

She could have stayed in Silver Grove.

She could have accepted Cameron's offer.

Instead, she'd told him that she wanted something more, that she wanted to get out of this town and to make something of herself.

It hadn't taken long for her to discover that what she really wanted was to become a lawyer-ideally, a respected public defense attorney who could pursue justice for those who lacked the means to do it themselves.

She had made it a good part of the way there. And if she could just stick it out at this job and save up some money for law school, she knew that she could make it happen.

So long as she kept her distance from Cameron Forge.

* * *

Bristol had planned to stay in her new office over lunch, using some of the time to start setting up her desk, but Grace had other ideas.

Now, she found herself at a corner table in the company cafeteria downstairs, surrounded by several people whose names she'd already forgotten. The place was bright and pleasant, like everything else she'd seen at FBS, and she could see why so many of the employees seemed to stick around for lunch instead of going elsewhere.

Someone had ordered pizzas to celebrate the end of a job that had taken Reilly and Asher Forge to Alaska last week, and she was thankful that for the second time that day, she hadn't had to pull out her wallet in order to eat. Especially considering that she'd left her sack lunch in her mother's fridge by mistake that morning.

She nibbled at a pepperoni slice, listening to the chatter around her and making the occasional comment when Grace politely attempted to draw her into the conversation, but on the whole, she was already looking forward to going home for the day. New places and people always overwhelmed her, and this job was no exception.

Her bandages and sweatpants didn't help with fading into the background, either.

"So, Bristol," one of her new coworkers was saying, giving her a friendly smile. He was a hispanic man who looked to be in his early fifties, and if she remembered correctly, he was one of the guards who usually handled the garage and basement areas. "How'd you come to join us here at Forge Brothers?"

She swallowed the bite of pizza she'd just taken, trying to think of a good answer that didn't require her to share her life story with a bunch of strangers.

"Well, I've been looking to continue my paralegal career with the future goal of going back to law school. With my interest in criminal law specifically, it seemed like a perfect opportunity."

The others surrounding the table nodded politely, most of them chewing their own pizza as she talked.

"You're right about that," Grace said. "Jaclyn sort of scares me, but there's no doubt that she's great at what she does."

"I'm curious about you, Grace," Bristol said, thankful for any excuse to direct the subject away from herself. "You seem to know the place inside out. How long have you been here?"

One of the other women at the table–she'd already forgotten what part of the office she worked in–chuckled. "Hinton's been here forever. She knows the place better than the Forge boys."

"Hardly. But I was one of their earliest hires. I dropped out of college sophomore year and spent a couple of years volunteering on mission trips. Eventually, I realized I'd have to actually make some of my own money, and my dad grew up with the matriarch of the Forge family."

"May God rest her soul," someone interjected, and Grace nodded.

"Amen. Anyway, I got in at the ground floor, as they say, starting out as an intern getting paid in free paper clips. And I sort of stuck around since then."

Bristol looked over the woman's polished outfit, including her expensive-looking jewelry and designer tote, unable to deny the feeling of annoyance that rushed through her.

It was clear that Grace couldn't afford to dress the way she did on an office manager's salary, and as admirable as it was that she'd spent time spreading the Gospel, it was a lot easier to do when you had family money to fall back on. For people like Grace Hinton, opportunity was offered at every turn. She only had to reach out and take it.

It must have been nice.

"I'm impressed with how big FBS has gotten so quickly," Bristol said, hoping the smile she had forced back onto her face looked genuine. It wasn't a lie–she was impressed–and despite her general dislike for the spoiled and privileged, Grace had been nothing but kind to her, and didn't deserve Bristol's ire simply for being born rich.

"You should have seen our first office," another man cut in, fiddling with the straw that stuck out of his soda can. "Trust me, I'm glad we grew out of it fast. And had the money to hire a few cleaners."

"It's true," Grace said, giggling. "Gabe could have afforded a better office from the start, obviously, but he wanted to do it on his own as much as possible. I can respect that."

Gabriel was the eldest Forge brother, and though Bristol knew that he had been the one to officially found the company, she hadn't realized that the company revenue was actually funding their current luxuries within just a few short years. Her respect for her wealthy childhood friends kicked up a notch or two.

"It took a little while for the rest of the brothers to come on board, though," Grace continued. "I got here before everyone but Gabe and Asher."

"Right," the guy with the straw said. "It took a little while for the others to see the logic of Gabe's plan. Cameron and Ben joined in year two, and Reilly–well, he's a cousin, but he still counts–held out until we moved into this office."

Bristol wished she could remember what the man's role was, let alone his name, but clearly he'd been there nearly as long as Grace had.

"And Jacob still isn't here, obviously," Grace added. "But maybe he'll complete the crew at some point."

Bristol wasn't surprised. Jacob was the second youngest after Cam, and he'd been getting into trouble with the law ever since they were in high school. She hoped he was doing better, but for the moment, she didn't want to pry for any more details.

"How's Forge & Sons doing?" she asked instead, taking a sip of her ice water. She'd have to ask Grace where she could get a green tea around here when lunch was over.

"Without the 'Sons'?" the garage duty guard chimed in with a grin.

She smiled back. "Exactly. I can imagine things must have changed a bit with Gabriel poaching the entire family to go into the private security business."

The Forge family had owned their multi-billion-dollar agricultural chemical and equipment business for over a century, and when they were kids, it had been always assumed that the brothers would eventually take over operations entirely. Clearly, the priorities of the younger generation had changed a lot since then.

"It's still going strong," Grace said, "but most of the day to day stuff is being handled by outside management. Of course, Gabriel Sr. is still the big boss."

She paused for effect, raising a single eyebrow.

Before Bristol could hear more of what she was about to say, however, she noticed Cameron striding toward their table, holding a tray stacked with several pizza slices.

So much for keeping her distance.

Cameron

Cameron ignored the open seat next to Bristol and slid in beside Grace instead.

The last thing he wanted was rumors about him and his former girlfriend to start swirling around the office, though if Grace already knew the story, it was probably too late. He considered asking Bristol how her first day was going, but decided against it.

He was her boss. If it had been awful, it wasn't like she was going to tell him the truth, anyway.

"Already gossiping to the new girl, Hinton?" he joked, picking up the topmost slice of pizza and taking a huge bite. Lunch hour was nearly over, and he had a meeting directly afterward with a potential new client. His late mother would have scolded him for eating like a barbarian in front of the ladies, but for the time being, it was all he had time for.

Fortunately, Bristol seemed to be paying him minimal attention, her body turned toward Bobby Ramos, the basement duty guard, who was getting up from the table to head back to work.

"Actually, yes," Grace said, giving the older man a wave as he headed off toward the hallway, dropping his empty tray off as he went by the counter. "I was just about to tell her all about how thrilled Gabriel Sr. is with the raging success of Forge Brothers Security."

Cameron laughed, hoping that Bristol and the others picked up on Grace's obvious sarcastic tone. "Just make sure that Gabriel Jr. doesn't hear anything about it, or we'll all have to listen to him complain for the next week."

Grace leaned toward Bristol.

"Gabe has daddy issues," she said in a stage whisper.

Cameron shook his head. "Pretty much. He doesn't think our father can forgive him for starting his own company and pulling everyone back from focusing on Forge & Sons, and it's caused some conflict."

"Haven't there also been some other issues going on?" Grace chimed in innocently as Cameron chewed another several bites of pizza.

There was a pause as two more people got up from the table and said their goodbyes. Lunch would be over in a few minutes, and if he made Grace or Bristol late, Gabe wouldn't be pleased, to say nothing of Jaclyn.

"I'm sure you already know as much as I do," Cameron deflected with a wink, beginning work on his final slice.

Truth was, he knew a little more. His cousin Reilly—who was, ironically, the closest to his father despite not being his actual son—had told him that there had indeed been problems at the company lately. But he'd also made him promise not to bring it up until Gabe Sr. had a chance to figure out what was going on, and he was going to let his old man handle things in his own way until he was ready to ask for help.

"I'm just glad that Mr. Forge is still able to run things like he wants to," Bristol added. "He's always been so passionate about what the company does. I admire that."

Cameron gave her a grateful smile, and just as she finally allowed her eyes to meet his own, he watched her cheeks going pink as a glob of bright-red pizza sauce slid down onto her sweatpants.

"Your skirt will be dry by now, anyway," Grace said quickly, getting up from her chair. "I'll go get it. I left it in the coffee lounge upstairs."

"I can get it," Bristol objected. She was trying to dab away the sauce with a napkin to no avail.

"Seriously, it's fine. I could use a coffee anyway. Want anything? Cam?"

Cameron shook his head. After the chaos of the morning, he figured that he'd better delay his next infusion of caffeine in case he ended up having to work late. Which he probably would, if the past month of post-Christmas chaos had been any indication of the workload that lay ahead.

" A green tea would be amazing, actually," Bristol said. "With milk, if you don't mind."

"Some things never change, huh?" Cameron said, giving her what he hoped came off as a not-too-flirtatious, but still teasing, smile.

"Nope," Bristol said. "Coffee is still disgusting, by the way."

Despite her cheerful tone and the smile that accompanied her words, he couldn't help but to notice that something had certainly changed about her, something subtle that he found difficult to place.

She leaned back in her chair, tossing the torn napkin onto her tray, and closed her eyes for several long seconds, giving him a chance to examine her face further without making her uncomfortable.

She looked more tired than he remembered, but then again, she was getting older. He couldn't survive on four hours of sleep anymore, either, and if Bristol's work ethic was as strong as it had always been, he doubted that she'd taken the time for much more than that the night before.

"Everything okay?" he ventured. "I really need to get back, if you're cool here by yourself for a few."

"Oh, goodness, sorry," she said, snapping back to attention, as though she'd been on the verge of falling asleep right then and there.

The cafeteria had largely emptied out, with only a few stray employees remaining dotted at their various tables. He was cutting it close for his meeting, he knew, but he didn't want to abandon a new employee in the lunchroom on their first day, even if that employee was Bristol. Perhaps especially not then.

"I'm totally fine," Bristol said. "You have things to do, don't worry about me. If Grace isn't back in like five minutes, I'm leaving, anyway. Jaclyn doesn't strike me as the kind of person who likes to be left waiting."

"Good observation," he said, getting up from his chair and gathering up both of their trays. "She's good for FBS, I think. She's tough in a courtroom, and when you're getting mixed up

54

with some of the most dangerous criminals in the city, that's the kind of lawyer you want on your side."

"Yep," Bristol said, sitting back again as he shuffled their garbage into one corner of the uppermost tray.

"Right," he said, not wanting to leave, but knowing he was about to overstay his welcome and end up late for his meeting in the process. "Have a good rest of the afternoon."

"You too," she said, no longer meeting his eyes as she gave him a tight smile.

That was his cue to bail.

He strode across the open space, his shoes squeaking on the gray tile.

As much as he hated to admit it to himself, even her small rejection stung a little. As he tipped the remnants of their lunch into the trash, he found himself lost in a time long past.

He remembered what it was like to be a lanky eighteen year old with dreams of a wife and a house full of kids, with an embarrassingly tiny diamond ring hidden in his pocket.

That rejection had hurt.

He hoped she'd found what she was looking for.

She was a good person, and she deserved happiness, even if things hadn't turned out anything like he'd wanted them to.

He risked a final glance at her over his shoulder as he ducked into the hallway.

At least she hadn't given up on chasing her dream.

It was more than he could say for himself.

Chapter 5

Bristol

Bristol took a final glance up at the clock on the wall of her office as she stuffed a stack of files into her tote bag, hoping that by tomorrow, she'd be free of the cumbersome bandages.

It was almost eight, but despite her general exhaustion and overwhelm, she didn't mind too much.

The afternoon had moved a lot more quickly than the morning had. When she'd returned from lunch, Jaclyn had spent another hour or two getting her up to speed, but after that, it had become clear that it was time to sink or swim.

Bristol smiled to herself as she slid a thick envelope in between her phone and the granola bars she'd helped herself to from the complimentary snack cupboard in the cafeteria.

Jaclyn was a typical lawyer, but she doubted she was going to prove as demanding as the masochists at Dorling & Porter.

Late nights were the norm there, especially for the lower level staff and junior associates. Here at Forge Brothers Security, though, she hoped that twelve hour days were more of an exception than the rule.

Jaclyn had assured her that mostly she was just behind, thanks to her former paralegal being on maternity leave, and that once the Pellman trial wrapped up later this week, they'd have a chance to catch their breaths.

In the meantime, she was thankful for the overtime pay, and the chance to impress her intimidating new boss.

Bristol locked her office and strode out into the main area of the legal department, passing the desk where their intern, Melanie, had sat until she'd left around seven.

She paused at Jaclyn's locked office door–she'd already headed home about thirty minutes before–and through the small square window she could see her boss's view of the gleaming lights of downtown San Antonio.

Her office wasn't quite as glamorous, and all she could see through her window was an alleyway, but it was still nicer than her office at D&P.

Besides, if she stuck to her plan, it would only be a few more years until she had a shot at moving up in the world–and the floorplan.

As she headed out into the various twisting hallways of the fourth floor, she was struck by how isolated the legal department was, especially when the cluster of offices around the corner were empty.

She pushed aside her unease as she made her way toward the elevator, clutching her overstuffed bag to her chest.

This was a security company, with twenty-four-seven guards, alarms, and cameras. She seriously needed to get a grip.

She was exhausted, and thoughts of falling asleep in her cozy childhood bedroom drove away her lingering anxiety by the time the elevator doors closed. She waited as she was whisked down to the first floor and the employee-access stairs that led to the basement and the garage.

As she stepped into the stairwell and started down, she could feel the cool air of the subterranean space prickling against her skin.

She reached into the side pocket of her bag, digging for her keys as she balanced the folded pair of sweatpants under her elbow. She'd insisted on getting the pizza sauce out and bringing them back to Grace as good as new, and fortunately, her benefactor hadn't objected.

She cringed to herself as she thought back to lunch hour. As a teenager, she'd hated that popular book with the teenage girl that fell apart at the mere sight of her way-too-old-for-her vampire boyfriend, and yet here she was, turning into a clumsy dork in the presence of Cameron Forge.

This was exactly why she'd left Silver Grove, and why she'd stopped going along with the script that every woman in her mother's church seemed to follow: snag a husband, have a baby, quit your job, stay home, and lose yourself to dirty diapers and playdates.

It wasn't who she was any more.

And a handsome face wasn't going to turn her back into the pathetic, weak person she'd been all those years ago.

Not a chance.

As she strode out into the garage and past the rows of mostly-empty parking spaces in search of the area where she'd left Boris, she was thankful once more for the bright lights that illuminated the large space. There were no dark corners, no shadows where some creep could hide out and wait for an unsuspecting woman to leave the office alone.

Still, she couldn't help but feel the familiar tightening in her stomach muscles as she looked around, wishing that she wasn't so alone.

There were no security guards in sight–she assumed they would be patrolling most of the building, not hanging around in one area all night–and the vast majority of her coworkers had certainly gone home hours ago.

She hummed to herself, the sound taking the edge off of the ominous silence.

"You're fine," she said out loud, forcing herself to sound as calm as she wanted to feel. She'd laughed when her therapist had suggested the idea, but now that she'd tried it, she had to admit it did help a little. "You can lock the door, start the car, and be out on the busy street in like two minutes. Relax, Bristol. Everything's ok–"

As she passed a large pillar, she stopped short.

Her facade of calm gave way to blinding, crushing panic.

Boris was parked there in the corner, but there would be no hopping in and driving off.

All four of the tires had been slashed more than once, leaving great black gashes in their sidewalls like claw marks from some huge beast.

Three words were scrawled across the entire side of her silver car, the bright red tone of the spray paint seared into her retinas.

SHUT YOUR MOUTH.

Bristol stood still, trying to force her lungs to take in slow breaths of air, but her body didn't want to cooperate.

She felt her hands shaking.

Her knuckles white against the straps of her bag, the documents inside no doubt crushed as she pulled her arms as close to her body as she could. She wanted to make herself a smaller target, and to find a dark corner of her own where she would be safe, but it was useless.

Just like it had been that night at the offices of Dorling & Porter, when junior associate Dillon Warrington had assaulted her.

She'd tried to push him away, and when that didn't work, she'd tensed up her body until her muscles screamed.

She could still hear the sound of him yanking his expensive leather belt through the loops of his pants, the buckle clattering against the floor, could still remember the way that she didn't bother to scream, because no one was there to hear her.

"I'm not going to say a word. It's too late for that

now," she muttered to herself. "Why can't you just leave me alone?"

She wanted to shout the words until they echoed through the expanse of the garage, but she didn't.

Surely he knew that she wasn't a threat to him.

But if he did, why would he terrorize her like this? How'd he even know that she was working here?

Half of the reason she'd taken the job was because FBS was largely isolated from the legal gossip scene. She thought she'd finally get to escape from the whispers, but this was worse than anything she'd experienced so far.

As she thought about the possibilities, she felt her racing heart begin to calm, and her chest rising and falling at a normal pace as her lungs filled with air.

Good. She had to make sure that the threat had passed, and she couldn't do that if she was frozen with panic.

As the pounding of blood in her ears subsided, it was clear that the garage was still as empty and silent as she'd first assumed.

For the moment, she was okay. She could think.

She walked around the car on all sides, finding no hint, aside from the obvious, that anyone had ever been there.

The doors were locked, just as she'd left them, and all of the windows–including the ones covered in those terrible red words–were unbroken. Even if there'd been something to steal, this wasn't a theft. Warrington or one of his friends wanted to scare her. It was the only thing that made sense.

She looked up at the ceiling overhead, and saw that the two nearby security cameras had been smashed to pieces. No surprise there, but she'd have to let security know if they didn't already. She sighed, reaching into her bag and taking hold of her phone. She'd call a cab first and then call the after-hours number for FBS once she was en route to report the damaged cameras. They'd just have to wait until the morning if they wanted her to give any more details or to report the vandalism to the police.

All she wanted was to be safe in her bed.

As she punched in the number and waited for someone to pick up at the taxi company, she considered the current amount waiting in her checking account, worried that a thirty minute ride to Silver Grove might send her into overdraft, but at that point, she had no choice. It wasn't like the bus could take her there, and her mom was working tonight, as usual.

Before the line connected, however, she heard the sound of the staircase door opening somewhere behind her, the sound echoing through the cavernous room.

She hit the red button to end the call, preparing to dial 911 if she had to, but to her relief, she could hear the deep, rolling voice of Ben Forge as he crossed the room.

She was relieved, but on the other hand, she knew that her chances of escaping without notice had just gone from slim to none.

"What in the name of–"

She stepped out from behind the car just as Ben and his twin brother, Asher, reached the row of parking spaces where she stood.

"Hey, Asher," she said, trying to keep her tone light. "I'd wanted to stop by and say hi today, but Jaclyn really put me to work."

He shook his head, ignoring her comment.

"What happened, Bristol?" he asked instead, rushing forward to place a hand on her forearm, his bright blue eyes filled with concern. Despite being Ben's twin, he looked nothing like him. While Ben was burly and redheaded, he was compact and blonde. If anything, they barely looked related at all.

Ben was examining the car just as she had a moment before, his green eyes flashing with rage. He had one hand on a pistol holstered at his waist, and Bristol had no doubt that he'd be willing to use it then and there, if he had to.

"I'm okay, guys," she ventured, trying to smile and not quite managing it. "He's gone. Probably has been for a while now. I'm fine. I really just want to go home. It's been a long day."

Asher shook his head, and Ben made a low noise in his chest that she assumed constituted agreement.

"We'll get you home, but first I'm calling Cam," Asher said, pulling out his phone. "He's still upstairs. We had a late meeting."

She tried to protest, but Ben cut her off. "You're safe now, okay? Just hold on."

She didn't have the energy to tell him that safety wasn't her only concern at the moment.

Once again, trouble had managed to find her, and once again, Cameron was going to jump in and save the day.

Just perfect.

Chapter 6

Cameron

"What? Here? Okay. I'll be there in two minutes," Cameron half-shouted into his phone, hanging up without saying goodbye.

He shoved it into his pocket and tore out of his office, not bothering to lock up behind him. He rushed down the hallway past several empty rooms, ignoring the doors to the elevators as he ran.

He took the stairs two at a time, glad to be heading down instead of up. Anger coursed through him, urging his body to move faster, though Asher had assured him that the scene was clear and that they wouldn't leave Bristol's side.

As he pushed through the heavy double doors and into the parking garage, he forced himself to slow to a fast walk, giving his burning lungs a couple of seconds to recover before he scared the poor woman all over again. He glanced over the space as he walked, noticing nothing out of place.

Whoever had done this was probably familiar with the basic after hours security protocols of the FBS guards. His men weren't the type to slack on patrols, but they only posted two guards on most normal nights, and it was a five-story building. Walking through it took time.

The vandal could have just gotten lucky, but according to his brother's report, he had done a good deal of damage to the car and two security cameras, and would have taken several minutes to complete his task. It was more likely that he'd known when the patrols would be taking place.

Cameron made a mental note to bring in additional men and change up their routine as of tomorrow. Until they figured out who had done this, his whole staff could be at risk, not to mention the further danger to Bristol herself.

Finally, he reached the far end of the parking area.

Ben and Asher both stood near the car, fingers resting lightly on their holstered weapons, but he hardly noticed them.

Bristol was leaning up against a pillar, staring down at the floor. He could see her hands shaking at her sides as he approached her. When she finally looked up at him, she was pale and terrified, her eyes rimmed red with threatened tears.

"Are you okay?" he asked, cringing at the words as soon as they escaped his lips.

Of course she wasn't okay. Some psycho just trashed her car in the parking garage of a security company, where she should have been completely safe.

She gave him a weak attempt at a smile.

"I'm fine," she said, drawing her arms over her chest. "It's Boris I'm worried about."

Cameron raised an eyebrow. "Ha. Boris the Taurus," he said, catching on. "I like it."

Her pretty smile broadened just a little.

"Are we going to call the police?" Ben asked no one in particular. Cameron ventured a couple of steps closer to Bristol, though he kept his arms hanging loose at his sides, not wanting to touch her and risk making her even more nervous than she already was.

"I'd rather not get them involved," Bristol said softly, her eyes retreating to her toes once again. Cameron noticed Asher about to speak and gave him a warning look.

This attack was personal, that much was obvious. And that meant that it was very possible that Bristol had some idea who was behind it, and her own reasons for not wanting to discuss the matter with police. If he tried to push her now, he'd risk scaring her off. If he and his brothers handled the matter in-house, however, he might be able to convince her to open up and accept help.

Fortunately, both Asher and Ben seemed to understand without another word that they shouldn't push it. Despite the amount of ribbing and bickering–and the odd near brawl–that went on between him and his brothers, he knew that they always had his back when it counted.

"I understand," Cam said. "If it's okay with you, though, I'd like to give our liaison at San Antonio PD a heads-up about the situation tomorrow. Allie won't get on your case, but at least there will be a quiet record if anything else ever happens."

Which it wouldn't. Not if he could help it.

"I guess that makes sense," Bristol said, though she didn't sound entirely convinced. Cameron didn't want to make her feel pressured into anything, but he had to put her safety first, even if she had competing concerns that were unknown to him.

"Allie Parker is solid," Ben put in, his usually gruff voice going gentle. "She's been our biggest ally in the department. If Cameron tells her to keep her distance, she will."

Cameron gave his brother a quick nod of thanks.

"Okay," Bristol said, meeting Ben's eyes and giving him a quick smile before turning back to

Cameron. "It's probably a good idea. In the meantime, though, I'm really tired. I'd just like to call a cab and go home."

"Absolutely not," Cameron said. "I'll drive you, and while I do, Ben and Asher will be here taking a more thorough look around and meeting with tonight's duty guards."

"And I'll see if I can salvage any security footage," Ben added, as Asher nodded in agreement.

"Thanks, guys," Bristol said.

There was a brief pause, and Cameron gave his brothers a look, hoping that he was able to adequately convey 'thanks, now get lost' without speaking.

Finally, the twins headed off toward the staircase, leaving him and Bristol alone with the ruined vehicle.

"Thanks for driving me home," Bristol said, still standing with her back to the pillar, as though she feared a sudden attack from behind. "I'd say no, but honestly, I'm pretty shaken up."

"Anyone would be," he said, gesturing toward the far side of the parking lot. She fell in wordlessly at his side, and he resisted the urge to rest a guiding hand gently on her shoulder. Everything about her body language screamed vulnerability, and he feared that even the most innocent physical contact might be misconstrued.

"I know you're tired," he started, pulling his keys out of the pocket of his jeans as they reached his forest green Jeep. "But I have a feeling it's gonna be hard to go home and sleep, and it might do you some good to talk about it."

To his surprise, she didn't blow him off immediately. Maybe she would tell him something about who was behind this after all.

When he moved to pull the passenger door open for her, she stepped ahead of him and took hold of the handle herself, climbing up into her seat.

"You could use a coffee and maybe some dessert," he added quickly before she shut the door, trying to ignore the beating of his heart as he walked over to his own side and got in.

"I hate coffee," she pointed out as he settled in behind the wheel and put the Jeep into drive.

"I know," he said, pulling forward until he reached the code-operated gate. "But I love coffee, and you love dessert. So it's a win-win."

"What kind of a weirdo drinks coffee at nine at night?"

"Me, apparently," he said, sneaking a quick glance in her direction before pulling out into the still-bustling San Antonio night. He could see the slightest hint of a smile tugging at her lips. "So, that's a yes?"

She let out a sigh.

"Honestly, I was exhausted, and I do have a mountain of files to look at before tomorrow, but I think I've gotten a second wind."

"Yeah, terrifying situations have a way of causing that. Better to go to bed when you're actually tired instead of laying in bed worrying all night."

"That's true. Fine. But I'm totally expecting some top-tier dessert after all of this stress."

"It's a deal."

Bristol

Bristol leaned back against the soft leather of Cameron's passenger seat as he wove through the downtown traffic, noticing just how nice his new Jeep smelled compared to her own old beater.

Not that it mattered any more. At this point it was no longer worth fixing, which left her without a way to work.

Great.

"So, where's your place?" Cam asked, not taking his eyes off of the busy intersection in front of him. She was glad to have an excuse to stare out the window as she answered, not wanting to let him see the blush rising to her face.

"I'm staying with my mom for a while. She's working nights and a lot of overtime at the nursing home, though, so I don't see her much. Being a personal support worker doesn't exactly pay that great, so I'm glad I can help her out a little with rent in the short term," she said, surprised at the defensive tone that she could hear in her own voice.

She hated the shame she felt about her living situation, but she couldn't deny it. After all that she had done to foster an independent life on her own, having to crawl back home to her mom was humiliating, especially sitting next to a man with millions in the bank.

"She's still in the same neighborhood, near the hardware store?" Cameron asked, omitting the fact that said neighborhood was in fact a trailer park.

"Yep, same place."

"That's perfect, then. My bungalow isn't far from there. I bought it last year, actually."

"Oh, nice," Bristol said breezily, trying to contain her surprise. She couldn't believe that he was still living in their hometown of Silver Grove when he could easily afford a great place in the heart of San Antonio.

"I like the small town life, I guess," Cameron explained without prompting, checking over his shoulder as he merged onto the highway. The traffic was easing up now that they had escaped downtown, and within a few minutes, they'd be surrounded by farmland. "Besides, it's still really close to the city, and it's home. I'm trying to convince a couple of the boys to move there, too."

"I guess I can see the appeal of leaving the big city chaos every night. I miss my old place, but it is a lot easier to sleep without motorcycles blasting by my window all night."

"One day, I want to buy a farm, and have some land of my own. I guess that part of the original family business rubbed off on me," Cameron joked.

She said nothing for a moment.

Cam had wanted to buy a farm of his own, with a country house like the one he and his brothers had grown up in, for as long as she could remember.

All he had ever wanted was to settle in, and all she'd ever wanted was to run. They were never going to work. They should have realized that, even as a couple of lovesick teenagers.

Cameron cleared his throat. "I, uh, thought that maybe we could stop at the Screaming Peach

Cafe. It's close. I haven't been there in a while, but I know you always loved it way back when."

If Iris was there, she'd be matchmaking them before they even sat down, but the sweet older woman's shift had probably ended hours ago.

"That sounds great," she said. "I was actually in there this morning. It's just as great as always."

They drove for a few more minutes in comfortable silence. Bristol looked out the window at the endless fields dotted with houses and barns. Though the sun had long since set, the moon was bright, casting a gentle blue glow over the countryside. It was beautiful, and despite the fact that she would move back to the city the first chance she got, she could certainly enjoy her time here while it lasted.

Finally, Cameron pulled onto the long stretch that was Main Street, and she watched as the houses moved closer together until finally they were in what passed as Silver Grove's downtown. He eased the Jeep slowly into the small parking lot of the Screaming Peach and turned off the engine with a click.

As they walked through the front door, listening to the friendly chime of the old-fashioned bell, she was surprised to see that the place was still fairly busy, even nearing closing time.

She could see a group of older women taking up most of the back right corner, several copies of a Francine Rivers novel piled on the table between them as they chatted and laughed with one another.

"I assume you want the famous peach pie to go with your green tea?" Cameron asked as he walked up to the counter. She hesitated for only a moment before agreeing, and waited as he ordered for both of them, resisting the urge to insist on splitting the bill. Her bank account would thank her.

The cafe had hardly changed in twenty years.

There were the same worn board floors, and the same painted white tables with their mismatched chairs, replaced only as necessary. Nearly a whole wall was dedicated to built-in bookcases that stretched from the tin-paneled ceiling to the floor, stuffed with hundreds of books and a decent collection of playing cards and board games.

It was the kind of place that made you want to stay, just like Silver Grove itself.

Bristol pushed that uncomfortable thought aside as she followed Cameron to a table near the front window, not bothering to try and carry over her own plate of steaming pie. For the moment, she was tired enough to allow him to play the gentleman if he wished.

"Thank you for this," she said, picking up her fork and taking a bite. The sweet peach and flaky pastry were perfectly prepared, and no matter how many times she ate the dessert, it never seemed to get old.

"You're welcome. This really is the best pie in Texas," Cameron said after swallowing a huge bite of his own. "Clearly I need to eat here more often. Ben is always telling me I need to bulk up, anyway. It would be a good excuse."

Bristol chuckled. "Ben looks like a computer-nerd version of Gaston from Beauty and the Beast. I'm not sure you could be as massive as him even if you ate five thousand calories a day."

She didn't tell him what she was actually thinking; that his toned, muscular body couldn't be improved. No, that was dangerous territory, and she wouldn't go near it.

"I caught him eating five dozen eggs for breakfast once," he said, giving her a wink. "Raw. With the shells."

She smiled down at her plate, quickly adding a huge bite of pie to her fork and stuffing it into her mouth before she started singing along about Ben being roughly the size of a barge.

She was thankful for Cam's company tonight, after what had happened, but she had to make it clear that on her end, at least, their reunion was all business.

Cameron took a few moments to work on his own pie, and she started in on her tea as she listened to the book club ladies laughing over in their corner.

Finally, he set his fork down.

"So, how'd you end up back in Silver Grove?" he asked, his blue eyes meeting hers.

She sipped her tea for a moment, savoring its warmth as she tried to think of how much she could share.

"It's not that exciting," she started, trying to hold his gaze instead of shying away. "I finished my undergrad in New York City, and then I realized scholarships for law school weren't so easy to come by. I took a paralegal course and figured that I could work for a while and gain some practical law experience while I saved up."

"And New York City was more expensive than coming back to Texas?"

"Pretty much. I applied to some jobs in Manhattan, and then Brooklyn, and then New Jersey, and I realized that if I was going to be making peanuts anyway I'd be better off closer to home, and to mom. So I started applying in San Antonio, and here I am."

She let the final words escape in a rush, wishing that he wouldn't push the subject, but knowing that he wasn't going to let her gloss over it.

"When I saw you a couple of years ago, you were talking about your fancy new job. I assume that was Dorling & Porter?"

His tone was light, but she could sense the hurt beneath his words. She hadn't been very nice to him on that occasion, even though he'd done nothing wrong.

"Yep. I was actually waiting to start, so it was a pretty stressful Christmas."

Not that it was any excuse for being such a jerk, but it was true. She'd been settling into her new place and trying to prepare for her first grown-up job, while dealing with the sudden reality of having her mother back in her life after years of doing everything on her own. She had hardly gotten to enjoy her favorite season at all.

"Well, I hope running into me and my gang of brothers didn't add to that too much," he joked.

"Of course not," she said quickly, certain that color was rising to her cheeks.

There was an awkward pause, and she clasped the warm ceramic mug with her still-bandaged hands, looking down into the milky liquid.

"Look, Bristol," Cameron said, taking a sip of his own black coffee. "I hate to bring this up, but I think you know what I'm going to ask."

"Why I left D&P?"

He considered this.

"Well, yes, I'm curious about that, too, but I meant about tonight."

"Oh."

Of course, he had no idea that the two answers were one and the same.

She tightened her grip until her knuckles went white, the steam rising against her already damp forehead.

"Whoever trashed your car clearly targeted you specifically. They wanted to scare you into keeping quiet about something. And it would be a lot easier to figure out what happened if we know what that something might be."

He leaned forward slightly, his eyes filled with concern.

A part of her wanted to open up to him then and there, to tell him everything that had happened that night, and to no longer have to carry the weight of such a terrible secret alone, but she couldn't bring herself to do it.

Not with their history, not with the fact that he

was now her boss, not with any of it. It would only cause more problems.

"I don't know, Cameron," she said, letting out a slow rush of breath. "I don't know what I'm supposed to be keeping quiet about, or who might be afraid of what I'll say."

She could hear her mother in her head, scolding her for lying, always ready with an admonishment from the book of Proverbs. At the moment, she didn't care what her mother or even God thought. The truth was out of the question.

Cameron's brows knit together.

"Are you sure?"

"Yes."

"I believe you, I just..."

"So believe me, and let it go," she said, the words coming out snappier than she'd meant them.

"I'm sorry," Cameron said, sipping at his coffee once more. "I do believe you. I'm just worried for you, that's all. I never would have expected you to be in any danger working at my company, and I feel responsible."

"It's not your fault," Bristol said, the sick feeling of guilt worsening in an instant. "You could never have expected it, and it isn't like FBS wasn't taking security precautions."

"Either way, we're going to figure this out, Bristol," he said, reaching over and touching the top of her fingers ever so slightly. She let him linger there, wanting to flee from his touch and wanting him to stay, all at once. After a moment, he pulled away, leaning back in his chair. "I promise."

She hoped he was right, though she knew that her refusal to cooperate would make things more difficult.

Still, her own questions continued to linger in her mind.

Why would Warrington be taking such risks when she'd already given up and left D&P? Hadn't he already done enough to protect himself from the consequences of his behavior?

Maybe she was wrong.

Maybe it wasn't Warrington at all, or maybe it was, but there was more to it than just that night.

For what must have been the hundredth time, she thought back over the past two years, trying to piece together anything she might have seen, anything that might have told a deeper story, but she came up empty.

For the moment, she was too tired to think, anyway.

It would be better to revisit this in the morning, and maybe Cam and his brothers could help, even with the limited information she was ready to give.

"I'm sorry for snapping at you," Bristol said quietly, finishing the final dregs of her tea.

"No, I'm sorry for pushing," Cameron said. "You've had a rough night. You didn't need me giving you the third degree. But I do want you to know that you can trust me. If you think of anything else that can help, I'm here to listen. No judgment."

She let his words hang in the air, wanting with all of her heart to believe that they were true.

He meant them, that much she was sure of, but holding back judgment wouldn't be as easy as he thought.

Not if he found out what had been done to her.

Cameron

Cameron drove as carefully as he could, taking a leisurely pace down the familiar roads that led toward Bristol's mother's home. She was falling asleep, her head resting against the window, and he couldn't help but to steal a quick glance in her direction every few minutes.

Her brown hair had gone frizzy, and he could see a small tea stain on her white top that he doubted she'd noticed. He smiled to himself as he took another turn, his headlights illuminating the quiet streets of Silver Grove.

Despite her attempts at prickliness, it was clear that she trusted him, at least a little. She had let her guard down enough to let him buy her a pie, and for the moment, it felt like a victory.

The only problem was that he needed to be keeping his guard up.

Aside from the small fact that she clearly wasn't interested in him anymore, the last time he'd fallen for Bristol Chaplin, he'd ended up broken.

And even after all of these years, he still struggled to let himself heal.

Too soon, he reached the trailer park and eased his way past the tidy chain-link fence, following the outer round toward the back lot where her mother's trailer lay.

She and Bristol had lived there since Bristol was in elementary school, ever since Gary Chaplin had run out on the both of them.

It was an older style of double-wide, and it could use a new coat of white paint, but the front porch table was always filled with fresh-cut flowers from the modest garden and the grass was always immaculately trimmed. Everything about the little house had always made him feel welcome and comfortable, for as long as he could remember.

He got out of the car quietly, not letting the driver's side door slam. He opened Bristol's door, hoping not to startle her, but she woke with a jolt, looking around wildly for a moment before figuring out that she was home.

"Thank you," she said, allowing him to close the

door behind her after she climbed out. "For the ride, and for dessert."

Cameron glanced around the area near the trailer, not seeing any sign of Moira Chaplin's car. "Your mom is working tonight, I take it?"

Bristol nodded and reached into her bag for her keys, raising no objection as he walked her up the creaking porch steps and toward the door. "Yeah, she's usually gone by now. She won't be back until I'm getting ready for work in the morning."

He nodded as she turned the key in the lock and pulled the door open.

"If you need a day off, take one."

"Not a chance," she said.

"Do you need me to stick around any longer, or do you think you'll be able to sleep okay?" He asked gently, hoping against hope that she would take his words exactly as he intended them–an offer to keep an eye on the trailer, and nothing else.

She shook her head, giving him a half smile, her freckled skin bright in the yellow glow of the overhead light.

"I'm okay now," she said. "Really. Now that I've had some time to let the adrenaline wear off, I'll sleep just fine."

He stepped back, resting against the vinyl siding of the trailer. "I'm going to keep my cell phone right by my bed with the ringer on full blast. Call me if you need anything. Please don't worry about waking me up, I'm used to it."

"If anything else happens, I'll call you and the police right away," she said, her tone firm. "Promise."

"Make sure you lock up well, including the windows and any sliding doors."

"Of course."

"I already hired a car to pick you up for work in the morning," he said, pausing for a moment as he noticed the scowl crossing her face. "I figured I wasn't going to convince you to stay home, so it's the least I can do."

She was so pretty, even when she was mad. Sometimes especially then.

"It's not necessary–"

"Bristol," he said, reaching up and rubbing a hand against his temple, "I'm not going to argue about this. You're my employee now, and your car was damaged on company property. I feel horrible that this even happened. Please, let me at least make sure you're not worrying about finding a way to get to work."

She crossed her arms over her chest, though he could see her expression softening. "Okay," she said at last. "I really didn't have any idea what I was going to do about my transportation situation, so I appreciate that. Thanks, Cam."

"You're welcome."

A beat passed between them as their eyes met.

He could hear the sound of the chime hanging from the corner of the porch, a cool breeze sweeping past them and making him shiver in his t-shirt. Bristol stepped back, retreating toward the warmth of the living room behind her.

"Well, goodnight," he said finally.

"I'll see you tomorrow."

And with that, she was gone.

He hurried toward his Jeep, trying to think about anything else besides the way her green eyes seemed to pierce right through him.

Chapter 7

Bristol

Bristol sat at her desk, her fingers flying across the keyboard as she typed up yet another of Jaclyn's endless handwritten notes. The first couple of hours of her day had passed rather quickly–she'd sat in on a Zoom meeting with Jaclyn and one of their clients–and now she had a few minutes to breathe as she tackled one of her job's more menial tasks.

Though usually Melanie, the intern, handled it, she didn't mind typing duty. As she listened to the sound of the keys clattering beneath her fingers, she let her mind wander, reflecting on the events of her first week at Forge Brothers Security.

Aside from the destruction of poor Boris, the rest of her first week at the office had been rather uneventful, though work had consumed most of her working hours. Things had indeed slowed down a little now that the Pellman trial had concluded, but Jaclyn already had her hard at work on several new projects, and she still went home long after dinner each night.

Not that she had anywhere else more exciting to be, anyway.

If anything, aside from the extra money, spending so much time at the office was helping her to settle into her new role more quickly than she otherwise would have. She found herself becoming more and more open to Grace's overtures of friendship, and she'd even gotten to meet Reilly Forge's wife, Lauren, who was currently heavily pregnant with their twin baby girls.

Cameron had for the most part kept his distance, but she ran into him at least once a day, and she feared she'd never get used to the reaction that she had whenever she saw him.

Even though she had no interest in letting him get any closer, her racing heart and sweating palms had a way of making her question her own sanity.

The corded phone on her desk rang out of the blue, and Bristol almost swore in surprise, managing to punch in a few keystrokes of gibberish on her laptop before she could reach over to lift the receiver.

"Forge Brothers Security legal department, Bristol speaking," she said, purposely ignoring the caller ID on the screen that made it very clear the formal greeting wasn't necessary.

"Hey, Bristol," Cameron said, sounding as cheery as the wintry sunshine pouring in through the window. "Are you busy right now?"

Bristol glanced up at the computer screen, hitting the backspace key a few times and finishing her sentence properly.

"I can get away from my desk if you need something."

No point in letting him know she was currently doing the work of an intern.

She heard Cameron give a slight chuckle, his voice still rich and attractive despite the phone line that separated them. "Well, in that case, we need to do something about your transportation situation."

Bristol's stomach twisted. Of course. She'd known that he would bring it up sooner or later, but she'd secretly been hoping he'd hold off until her first paycheck arrived. Until then, she could barely afford a bus pass.

"I know, I'm so sorry," she said quickly, winding the cord of the phone around her now-healed palm. "I've been taking advantage of the car service for long enough, I know, but to be honest with you, that car was only minimally insured, and I've been trying to dig up enough money to get–"

"Bristol–"

"–mom knows a guy, but his garage is out in Lytle, and I'm not sure when I can get Boris there. But there's the bus, and–"

"Please, I–"

"I know it's a nuisance, but I have been trying, and I'm sorry–"

Bristol heard a click as Cameron hung up the phone.

She replaced the receiver on the cradle.

For several long seconds she sat there, tightening the cord around her hand like she used to do in her mom's kitchen as a child, feeling like she might cry.

What exactly did he want her to say?

He had no idea what it was like. No clue how it felt to be left with no options, and no wealthy relatives to bail him out.

The longer the silence went on, the more annoyed she got. He had some nerve hanging up on her.

The phone rang in her hand, and this time, she swore aloud.

"Not done humiliating me yet?" she answered, not bothering to hide the fury in her voice.

To her surprise, Cameron laughed.

"It's probably a good thing that you don't drink coffee. You need to learn to take a breath," he said. He didn't sound angry, or even annoyed.

Her cheeks burned, and she said nothing, clutching the phone against her cheek. "Sorry for hanging up, but I was trying to get you to let me talk for two seconds."

She sighed.

"Okay. Sorry about that."

"Also, it would have been hilarious if Jaclyn decided to call you right before I did," he added, chuckling to himself again.

He had a point. This time, she hadn't even glanced at the caller ID before rudely accusing the person on the other end of embarrassing her.

"Anyway," he continued, "I called to tell you to get your jacket and to grab a tea, it's a little chilly out today. We're going to go car shopping before lunch. I already told Jaclyn I'm making an executive decision to spring you from your vitally important Thursday morning duties. Let's go."

Bristol was so surprised that once again she found herself holding the phone against her cheek, completely speechless as her fingers tightened on the black plastic.

"I can't afford a new car," she choked out.

"Your car was destroyed while parked on company property," Cameron said calmly. "Ergo, I will charge the company account to buy you another one."

"That's crazy," she protested, her face suddenly warm. "No, that's way too generous. A week of paid car service out to Silver Grove was more than adequate."

"I don't aim to be merely an adequate employer," Cameron said. She could almost see the smirk on his face. "And, for the record, neither does Gabe. We're replacing that car. I'll be up at your office in ten minutes."

Without another word, he hung up on her for the second time.

Cameron

Cameron inhaled deeply.

The January sun was bright, and the air had a fresh taste to it. The streets of downtown San Antonio were busy and cheerful, with small groups of people dotting the sidewalk and darting in and out of boutiques, probably still spending whatever was left of their Christmas money. Altogether, it was a perfect morning to escape the office for an hour or two.

The only problem was the stubbornness of the woman who currently walked beside him.

Well, beside him was a stretch.

Bristol trailed a couple of steps behind him as they made their way down the street, largely ignoring his attempts at making casual conversation. She'd made it clear that she didn't need nor want his charity, and he'd tried to make it clear that charity had nothing to do with it.

As her employer, he wasn't letting her take three buses to work every day until she could save up to replace Boris.

"It's just around this corner," he said after another long silence, gesturing ahead. "A family friend owns the lot. It's not a big one, so it should be nice and quiet, especially at this time of day."

He tried to sound confident, but he couldn't help but to notice that his words came out a little too firmly, a little too forced. No matter what he tried to tell himself, he longed for her to open up to him, and her subtle rejection, especially since the night he'd taken her to the Screaming Peach, bit at his pride.

"Sounds good," she said after a while, making a show of checking the flow of traffic in both directions before following him out into the crosswalk.

"Jaclyn will kill me if I steal away her new minion for too long, especially with Melanie out today, so I'll try and have you back no later than lunch," he continued, trying to find anything to say that would fill the silence.

Fortunately, before he had to think of anything else, they reached the lot.

It was a decent place with a variety of vehicles on display, everything from a brand-new Lexus to a collection of rust buckets hiding out near the combination office and service garage.

He caught the eye of the owner, Randy, who gave him a quick wave before continuing to chat with another customer. He'd already called ahead and let his dad's old friend know that he was coming, and he knew he'd have the run of the place, including any test drive keys he needed.

"So," he said, turning to give Bristol a bright smile as her green eyes roved over the selection, "What about a Jeep? They're super reliable, and they've got a bunch here."

Bristol crossed her arms over her chest, a gust of wind sending her brown hair whipping across her face. She stared at him for a long moment, giving him a half-smile that didn't reach her eyes.

"Honestly, Cameron, the fact that you can so casually have this conversation is something I can barely comprehend."

He stuck his hands into the pockets of his jeans. "Look, Bristol. I know my family has always had money, and that I'm extremely privileged not to have to worry about finances, even if FBS went under tomorrow. I'm not stupid."

"I never said you were," she said, the hint of a challenge in her eyes.

Neither of them spoke for a moment, and he caught her glancing over her shoulder before stepping out farther from the row of vans she had been standing in front of. He'd seen her doing the same on their walk, silently taking in her surroundings every few minutes.

He could hardly blame her after the damage done to her car, but the situation still frustrated him. She clearly knew more than she was letting on about who could be behind the attack, but he couldn't exactly force her to talk. All he could do was beef up security while she was in the office, and hope that whoever was threatening her would leave her alone.

"Anyway," Bristol said at last. "That Ford Focus over there looks like it's in decent shape. And it's a 2014 that still has reasonable mileage."

She strode in the direction of the car, not bothering to wait as he rushed to catch up.

"Absolutely not," he said as soon as he realized which vehicle she was talking about. It was a black hatchback and one of the cheapest cars on the lot, which was hardly surprising.

The back of the car looked as though it had been in more than one fender bender, and one of the front panels had been changed out entirely with a bright red replacement.

"It's got character," she argued, running her fingers over the roof of the car.

Well, at least they washed it before chalking the price on the windshield. That was something.

"That's one way of putting it," he said, unable to resist a smile as she leaned down to examine the worn tires with one eyebrow cocked. "What would you name it? Crocus the Focus?"

"Not bad," she said, returning his smile before schooling her features at once. "I'd at least like to test drive it before you write it off completely. Please."

He couldn't exactly say no, not without coming off as a total jerk.

"Be right back," he said, jogging toward the building at the far side of the lot. He looked over his shoulder as he pulled open the glass door, glad to see that there were only two other people on the lot aside from Bristol, and one of them was Randy himself.

He handed her the keys and got in the passenger side, glad to see that the inside had been detailed, though there was a lingering greasy smell that he couldn't quite place.

Bristol got in on her side and slid the key into

the ignition, but before she turned it, she frowned.

"What's wrong?" he asked, suddenly on alert.

"It's a standard. I've always wanted to learn, but as it stands, I have no idea how to drive stick," she said, her face breaking into the most genuine smile he'd seen from her all morning. "Alas, Crocus the Focus is not meant to be. But I'm still not getting a Jeep."

He laughed, and she joined in, the sound of it enough to loosen the knot of anxiety that lingered in his chest.

Goodness, he loved seeing her happy.

She pulled the key out and moved for the door handle, but he reached out and rested a hand gently against her arm before she could step out of the car.

"Whether or not I end up convincing you of the superiority of the almighty Jeep, there's no need to rush. Why don't you let me teach you for a few minutes?"

She looked back at him.

"To drive stick? Now?"

"Why not? The owner won't care, trust me," he said, trying not to let his nervousness show in his voice. Randy wouldn't mind, that much was true, but he knew that trying to crack Bristol's shell was always going to be risky. "Besides, most of our ops vehicles are standard, so it would be good for you to learn. For work purposes."

She gave him a funny look and sat back a little in her seat, her hand still resting on the door handle like it was an escape hatch.

"My goal is to become a lawyer, Cam. Not a security guard."

"I was thinking you'd be better suited as a security *operative*," he said, grinning. "That's where the real fun is."

"Ha! I'd be horrible. And like I said, I have other goals in mind."

"Bristol, have you ever considered that sometimes our goals change as we figure out God's plan for our lives?"

The words hung heavy in the small space between them, and it was all Cameron could do to keep his eyes trained on hers rather than on his feet.

"I could ask you the same question," she said after a moment, her tone impossible to read.

Ouch.

They sat there like that for several long seconds. The awkwardness was almost unbearable, but at least she hadn't bolted.

Memories of bygone years filled Cameron's mind.

He could picture so many sunny days just like this, driving around Silver Grove in Gabe's temperamental old pickup, Bristol's hand clasped in his until he needed to change gears. Despite the obstacles, he couldn't help but to wonder if the possibility existed that they could be that way again.

At last, she let out a breath and placed her hand on the shifter, fiddling with the worn plastic.

"I guess it would be kind of fun to learn," she said. "Besides, Jaclyn is going to have a fresh task list for me as soon as she gets back from her meeting, and I'm not exactly in a hurry to start on it."

"Attagirl," Cameron said, keeping his own fingers gripped safely against the arm rest, where there was no chance of accidentally brushing against hers before she was ready.

"Let's do this," Bristol said, stabbing the key into the ignition slot.

"Wait," he said, laughing at the look of sheer determination that had appeared on her face. "The first thing we're going to do is teach you how to work the clutch."

Chapter 8

Bristol

There was a knock at her office door, and Bristol looked up from her desk, thankful for the excuse to give her tired eyes a break from the dense contract she'd been reading for the last forty-five minutes.

She'd been right.

Jaclyn had returned from her meeting just after lunch time, dumped a pile of paperwork on Bristol's desk, and headed back out the door once again, probably to find even more nightmarishly boring legal writing that she needed her new paralegal to summarize.

Now, apparently, she was back yet again, though with it being so close to what was theoretically quitting time, Bristol hoped that she'd save her demands for the morning.

"Hey, Bristol, sorry to interrupt," Jaclyn said, leaning against the doorframe.

She was dressed in an expensive-looking cashmere sweater, a knit scarf, and heeled brown boots, and she held a black satchel under her free arm. She wore no makeup today, however, and Bristol noticed that without mascara her eyelashes were such a light blonde that they were almost invisible against her icy blue eyes.

"Not at all," Bristol said, smiling up at her boss. "Can I help you with something? I'll probably stick around here for a couple more hours, anyway."

Jaclyn gave a heavy sigh. "I appreciate your dedication, but you won't be staying late tonight, I'm afraid. Judge Hammerstein's people just called to let me know that we're now due in court tomorrow instead of Monday, and he's slotting our preliminary hearing in before his first trial."

Bristol's heart sank. She'd spent most of the day on disastrous driving lessons and a takeout lunch with Cameron before he'd finally managed to convince her to replace Boris with a much newer and fully mechanically sound Taurus.

She'd expected to have tomorrow and the weekend to finish her mountain of paperwork, not to mention prepare for the preliminary hearing. Had she known it was going to get bumped up, she would have let Cameron buy the ridiculous Jeep if it had meant getting back to work at a reasonable time.

"Well, that's not great," she said at last, resisting the urge to apologize for her light work day. Cameron was not only her boss, but Jaclyn's, as well. There was no point in getting in trouble when she hadn't been the one who decided to play hooky in the first place.

Jaclyn brushed a few strands of her long blonde hair out from where they had become tangled in her scarf. "Not exactly a lot of warning, I know. I hate to ask this, but I need you to be here by six thirty tomorrow, at the latest. I want some time to go over everything together before we get up there in front of Hammerstein."

Perfect.

Her first time in a courtroom representing Forge Brothers Security, and she'd be not only unprepared, but barely conscious.

"No problem," she said as Jaclyn let out a yawn, trying to convince herself as much as her boss. "I'll be here even before that, if I can. At least we won't have to worry about traffic."

"Not me," Jaclyn said, giving her a rare smile. "I usually walk, actually. My condo is just a couple of streets over."

Bristol smiled back. She'd had no idea until now where Jaclyn lived.

Though she felt as though she was beginning to gain the lawyer's trust, she really knew very little about her. Jaclyn Mercier was basically the polar opposite of Grace Hinton. Bristol got the feeling that no one else in the office knew her much better than she did.

"Well, I guess some of this stuff will have to be dealt with tomorrow afternoon and over the weekend," she said, gesturing toward the half-read briefs, open case law books, and typed passages waiting on her computer screen.

Jaclyn nodded. "I know there aren't too many hours left before morning, but secure these files, go home, and try to get some sleep. I'll see you bright and early."

Jaclyn gave a quick wave as she disappeared back into the main office and then out into the hall, the sound of her boots trailing away as Bristol began tucking away files and shutting down her computer.

A few minutes later, she pulled out of the parking garage in her as-yet-unnamed new car, thankful for the extra security detail that FBS had been posting all week. She'd also been parking closer to the stairwell entrance rather than in the more isolated corner where the vandalism had taken place.

Now that her car wasn't quite so out of place, she didn't mind the company.

As she made her way through the evening traffic and out onto the now-quiet highway that led toward home, she couldn't help but to enjoy the way the car handled compared to her old hunk of junk. She still felt guilty that it had been given to her, but ultimately, she was going to have to set her pride aside and be thankful.

She needed to be able to get to and from work with some level of independence, at least while she was living all the way out in Silver Grove, and especially on nights like this when unexpected demands came up without warning.

The radio was playing in the background, but she struggled to focus on the music. Whether she wanted it to or not, her mind kept wandering to the morning she'd spent with Cameron.

They had had fun–even she had to admit it–but that hardly mattered. As she'd explained to him, she had no interest in working in the security field long term, and once she became a full-fledged lawyer, she doubted FBS's tiny legal department would have room for her.

And she was not about to spend the rest of her life doing paralegal grunt work.

Though the criminal law experience that this job offered was helpful, it was the money she needed more than anything, and once she had what she needed, she'd be on her way. It was easy for Cameron to talk about God's plan–he already had so much of what he wanted, and unlike her, he wouldn't have to give it all up if he fulfilled his dream of getting married and starting a family.

A few minutes later, she turned into the trailer park and slowed the car to a crawl, keeping a close eye out for dogs, neighbors on an evening stroll, or any wayward children up past their bedtime. She frowned as she noticed that one of the older ladies who lived nearby, Alice, still hadn't gotten her rotting porch steps fixed. They looked like they were about to detach from the rest of the ancient trailer.

No, she wasn't interested in the sort of Divine plan she'd grown up hearing about.

The life that had been offered to her mother had probably sounded like a fairytale, too.

Her father had asked her mother's hand in marriage, paid the rent on their little marital apartment on Main Street, and given her a baby girl.

And not even a decade later–after her mother had spent her prime career advancement years at home tending to skinned knees and helping with schoolwork–he'd found a younger model and left, never to return.

She put the car into park and grabbed her work bag, taking her usual extra look around the lot and the nearby trailers to make sure that no one was watching her before climbing up onto the porch steps.

The younger model got the fairytale, and Moira Chaplin got to rinse bedpans for a couple of bucks above minimum wage, just enough to pay the lot rent on the trailer that the alimony settlement had been enough to buy. That's what following God's plan had gotten her mother.

No thanks.

Still, despite her anger at the circumstances her mother had been forced into, it was nice to be home.

Now that she no longer had to operate a motor vehicle, the tiredness seemed to overtake her body all at once. She hurried to get ready for bed, ready to follow Jaclyn's instructions and squeeze in as many hours of sleep as she possibly could before morning.

After turning on three separate alarms on her phone and setting it on the nightstand, she climbed into her old twin bed, pulled the warm blankets up to her chin, and closed her eyes.

Cameron

"Come on, bro," Cameron protested, jabbing a finger in the general area of Ben's ribs, "I can't even see."

The two of them were crowded around Ben's desk. Most of their staff had gone home already, but Ben had finally heard back from his contact at the security camera manufacturer. For the last two hours, they'd been trying to get something useful from the warped footage from the smashed cameras in the parking garage.

Cameron had waited around while his older brother worked, attempting to clean his own office to pass the time with minimal success.

"There's nothing *to* see yet. This is the old footage, from just after the last patrol. Bobby was on duty that night," Ben said, the tone of his voice so deep that the words reminded Cameron more of a growl than actual speech. "Look."

Cameron obeyed, leaning forward in his chair toward one of Ben's several computer monitors, squinting at the Monday evening footage from the FBS garage. Even if Ben assured him it was clear, he had to double-check for himself.

He could see Bobby Altman, an older hispanic male, finishing up his security sweep of the far side of the garage before heading back toward the stairwell.

Nothing strange about that.

Bobby had been working at FBS for several years, and he'd never been anything but trustworthy. Besides, other security footage placed him on the second floor when the spray painting and tire slashing had likely taken place.

"And this one," Ben continued, switching to another camera. Cam could see concrete walls and pillars, as well as the glow of security lights, but little else.

Ben continued to click through all of the camera angles one by one. There were cars in a few of them, including their own vehicles, but nothing suspicious.

"Okay, I get the point," Cameron said. "Show me the stuff from the smashed cameras."

Ben nodded, moving his huge hand on the mouse while tapping something on the keyboard.

"Whoever did this was very careful. He knew his angles and stayed out of sight until the last possible second, and then used a powerful flashlight to blind the lens until he could smash it. Probably with a bat, though one would think he would have smashed Bristol's car windows, in that case.

"Anyway, obviously, once he starts swinging, the footage stops pretty quick," Ben paused, rolling the mouse wheel and selecting another file. "But everything right before still made it onto cloud storage."

Cameron gripped the edge of the desk, eyes intent on the screen. "And was anything there, right before the flash?"

Ben looked pained. "Well, yes," he said tentatively, pulling up the new footage. Cameron felt his chest swelling with excitement as his brother hit play.

"–And no," Cameron finished for him, shaking his head as he watched the clip. It couldn't have been more than three seconds long, and even as

122

Ben slowed the speed, he could see why his brother wasn't more excited.

They could make out a person in what looked to be a hooded sweater, but thanks to the way the shadows fell and the location where he stood, they couldn't even estimate his height or get an idea of his race.

"I know," Ben said, sensing the disappointment that Cameron had not voiced. "I think it's probably a man, but even that I'm not positive about."

Cameron watched the footage several more times, coming to the same conclusion.

At that moment, there was a knock on the door, and Grace strode into the office without waiting to be invited, making her way over to Ben and peering over his shoulder at the computer screen.

Cameron suppressed a grin, watching the way that Ben tensed up when a few strands of Grace's bouncy curls landed against his neck.

The woman flirted with him shamelessly, and though it seemed obvious to everyone else in the office that the bubbly blonde set Ben's heart aflutter, he usually pretended to be oblivious to her advances.

"Oh, hey, Cam," she said, barely glancing in his direction.

"You're working late, Hinton? Has an asteroid struck the earth or something without me noticing?" he teased.

"Ha-ha," she said, sticking her tongue out at him. "As a matter of fact, I wanted to get a look at the jerk who scared my new friend. Mostly, though, I need to know if anyone in the tech wing is looking for any office supplies."

Cameron raised an eyebrow.

Grace was great at the important stuff, but was a master of procrastination when it came to things like replacing printer ink cartridges or, apparently, ordering paper clips.

"Now? It's gotta be almost eight o'clock. Besides, I thought you did it already. Like, weeks ago."

Grace winked at him before returning her attention to the screens. Cameron shook his head, chuckling under his breath. She was clearly here to talk to Ben, and as much as he enjoyed teasing her like the sister he never had, he wasn't going to get in the way of her flirtation.

"Don't worry about it, Grace," Ben said, reaching over and clicking off two of the screens. "I think we're pretty much done with this. I'll try and put together a short list before I leave and give it to you in the morning."

"Thanks," Grace said, bouncing a high-heeled foot back and forth as he talked.

"And make sure one of the security guys is around in the basement before you walk to your car," Ben added. Cameron could see the redness rising to his cheeks.

How sweet.

A few moments later, Grace headed out, her shoes clacking against the floor as she made for the elevator down the hall.

"She's so obviously into you, bro," Cam said as soon as she was out of earshot.

Ben ignored him.

"Get some rest. I'm gonna go do a pencil inventory, or whatever, and then I'm heading home too. I'll send this footage to this wizard I know in Thailand, but unless he can work a miracle, I think we'll have to admit defeat on ID-ing this scum."

Cameron ran his fingers across his five o'clock shadow.

Admitting defeat was the last thing he wanted to do, but this clue, at least, seemed to have led them to nothing but a dead end.

Chapter 9

Bristol

The ringing filled Bristol's mind.

It droned on and on, and she turned over in her bed, pulling the covers over her head and burying her face against her pillow

The dream she was having had started off with a nice walk through downtown San Antonio, but now the ringing noise coming from all of the cars nearby was rather distracting...

She sat bolt upright, feeling suddenly very much like she'd just been woken up by a bucket of ice water being dumped on her head.

She fumbled for the phone on her desk, which stopped ringing just as she got her fingers around the slippery rubber case.

There was one missed call from Forge Brothers Security.

She tapped in her passcode, messing up the first two numbers and having to do it over, her fingers shaking.

It was already well past seven-thirty, and she was supposed to be in court at eight.

Finally, she managed to navigate to the call log and hit the correct number, punching in Jaclyn's extension immediately.

"Bristol, I hope you're calling to tell me you're pulling in right now," Jaclyn said without preamble, her tone clipped.

"I'm so sorry," she said, pressing a hand to her forehead and trying to stem the tears that threatened to spill over. "I set three alarms, Jaclyn, and somehow–"

"Cut the excuses," Jaclyn spat. "Just get here as soon as you can. I'll try and stall Hammerstein, but he's not gonna be pleased."

Bristol swallowed a groan of frustration. "Okay. I'm coming."

She hung up the phone, realizing that her heart was racing. She forced herself to take a few breaths. She was already late, anyway, and panicking wasn't going to get her there any faster.

Besides, there was one thing she had to check.

She tapped at the phone's screen until she located the alarm app, and as soon as it opened, she felt her chest going tight.

There was nothing there.

She had selected three times that were close together for the alarms.

She could remember doing it the night before, and then double checking that all of the little sliders were slid to the 'on' position at least twice before she slept.

Did she somehow manage to not only turn off the alarms, but actually delete them in her sleep?

It made no sense. She wasn't exactly a morning person, but she wasn't quite that bad. And she'd been so anxious to get this right. She doubted her subconscious could have engaged in such an act of sabotage.

She sucked in a breath as she got off of the bed and put on a pair of socks.

If she hadn't done it in her sleep, what other possibility was there?

Her mom had been at work all night, and wouldn't be back until at least eight. Not that she would have tried to make her late for work, anyway.

She headed for the back of the trailer, passing her mother's room, the tiny bathroom, and the beat-up utility area that doubled as a laundry room.

She reached for the back door's chipped metal handle. It was unlocked and turned easily, and with a burst of courage thanks to the friendly light of the morning, she opened it out onto the small back lawn. Nothing was out of place.

Cameron had told her to keep locking the windows and doors until they found the vandal, and usually she did so anyway, especially since what had happened at D&P.

Still, she couldn't be absolutely positive whether she'd locked it or not last night. She'd been focused mostly on getting her alarms set so she'd get up in time, not worrying about a break-in.

It wasn't the nicest trailer park she'd ever seen, but it wasn't a bad one, either. Most of her neighbors were older ladies like her mother. There were a few young families starting out, and a couple of single guys who wanted room for their dogs and outdoor gear that an apartment couldn't provide, but that was it. No one she had ever had reason to worry about.

She went back into the house, taking another look around in search of anything that appeared to be missing, or out of place, but found nothing. Everything looked exactly as her mother always left it, and her room showed no sign that anyone but her had been in it.

This was crazy.

No one would break in to mess with a phone alarm, leaving everything else intact.

She'd tell Cameron about it when she got a

chance, but for the moment, she'd just have to let it go.

She brushed her teeth and dressed as quickly as she could, finding herself looking over her shoulder every few minutes, though of course, no one was ever there. She had no time to eat anything, but with any luck, she'd be able to find five minutes alone with a vending machine when she got to the courthouse.

As she opened the front door, she was relieved to see that her new car looked just as nice as it had the day before.

She looked up at the clouds floating overhead and said a silent prayer of thanks, still finding it hard to accept that Cameron and FBS had been so willing to incur such an expense for her benefit.

As thankful as she was, however, she didn't want to remain in their debt—especially now that she'd overslept and possibly cost the company a court case, or at least their counsel's reputation in front of Judge Arnold Hammerstein.

She climbed into the front seat and started the engine, hoping for a traffic miracle.

When she became a lawyer, she'd pay them back for the car.

Every last cent.

Chapter 10

Bristol

As Bristol followed Jaclyn into the privacy of the Forge Brothers Security legal department, she braced herself for the scolding that was to come. All morning, they had been focused on getting through the hearing, after having only thirty minutes to prepare as a team–and they'd only been given that extra time because, according to his clerk, Judge Hammerstein was going golfing that afternoon and was therefore in one of his better moods.

Jaclyn had said nothing about Bristol being late, but her body language and her colder-than-usual tone had made it clear that she was hardly impressed. Not that Bristol could blame her.

Though some looked down on paralegals, a good lawyer like Jaclyn understood the importance of Bristol's role, and wasn't afraid to give her responsibilities that had a real impact on the case at hand. And now, however legitimate or illegitimate the excuse, that trust had been wounded.

Before the two women reached Jaclyn's office door, the lawyer stopped and turned to face Bristol, a briefcase still gripped between subtly manicured fingers.

"Well, I think that went as well as it could have, considering," she said.

Bristol forced herself to meet her eyes as she nodded.

As if being late wasn't bad enough, the rest of the morning had hardly gone smoothly.

While trying to figure out a copy machine they'd commandeered in the courthouse clerk's office, Bristol had managed to print some files from a totally different FBS case and actually included them in Jaclyn's paperwork for the hearing.

It was a total rookie mistake that never would have happened had she been on time, and even if it had, one of them would have caught it well before Jaclyn ended up in front of the court, shuffling through papers in search of a file that didn't exist.

"I'm sorry, again," Bristol said, unable to bear the silence that had fallen over the room. "I feel terrible. It won't happen again."

Still, Jaclyn said nothing, and all she wanted to do was to run away.

Despite her mistakes, her boss really had done an excellent job, and she doubted that their client would face any negative consequences. Even Hammerstein had reacted fairly well, making a couple of witty comments as Jaclyn tinkered with the contents of her briefcase.

Still, she'd made her lawyer's job harder than it had to be. And Jaclyn's quiet disappointment was far more upsetting than any of the fits of anger she'd endured at Dorling & Porter.

"I'd like you to do a full look-over for the files for next week's hearing before you get to anything else, just to make sure nothing is off," Jaclyn said at last, opening the door to her office. "We won't get a second day of happy Hammerstein. Thanks."

Bristol nodded mutely, unsure of what to say, and then it was too late. Jaclyn's door closed with a gentle click, and she was standing there alone and feeling about two inches tall.

Without quite meaning to, she found herself walking away from her own office door, and toward the hallway. She'd look at the files soon enough, but for the moment, she had to catch her breath.

A few moments later, she was in the fifth floor lounge, sipping a comforting mug of tea and trying to calm the anxious butterflies in her stomach.

Just as she'd thought she had gotten ahold of herself, however, Grace Hinton walked through the door, and Bristol promptly burst into tears.

Grace stopped short, dropping one of her many designer bags on the counter and rushing over to give her a hug.

"What on earth happened?"

Bristol sobbed, trying to swallow the sound of her crying with little success.

She hadn't cried at work since her first couple of months at D&P. She'd learned to control her emotions, or so she thought, but Grace's kind face had been enough to crack the wall of protection she'd been trying to raise.

"I slept through my alarms this morning, somehow, and ended up extremely late for court," she said, ragged breaths clutching at her chest between words. "Worse, I screwed up Jaclyn's presentation files and made her look bad in front of the judge. I need this job, Grace."

Grace's brow furrowed in sympathy as she rubbed Bristol's shoulder. "It's okay," she said, her voice bright.

"Every single person in this place has screwed something important up. Once, I booked the wrong flight and actually sent Carter and Reilly to Sydney, Nova Scotia, instead of Sydney, Australia."

Bristol shook her head, imagining the chaos that would have probably ensued. At least she and

Jaclyn weren't responsible for handling operations in the field.

Still, Grace had a point.

"Admittedly, I've made worse mistakes than this. Like the time I knocked over an entire cup of coffee on one of the senior partner's desks at my last job and ruined about fifty documents."

"Honestly, that's pretty on brand for you," Grace joked.

Bristol tried to smile, but after only a moment, her face fell once again. She was thankful to have a friend here, but the job came first, and after this morning, she was going to do everything she possibly could to get back into her boss's good graces.

"I need to get back upstairs and get back to work," she said, wiping at her eyes with the back of her hand. "Jaclyn is already angry, and I don't want her to come looking for me and find me crying in the lounge."

Grace shook her head and strode over to where she'd left her bag, rooting through the huge pink leather sack until she located her phone. Bristol watched as she stared down at it for several long seconds, her long nails tapping away at the touchscreen.

"There. Jaclyn is officially taken care of."

She tossed her phone back into her purse and reached in again, pulling out a monogrammed cosmetic bag that would have easily fit every bit of makeup and skincare that Bristol owned.

"You have time to get yourself presentable before you face the rest of the day."

"Thank you, Grace," Bristol said, taking the proffered bag and moving to get to her feet. She didn't bother to ask what sort of crazy distraction Grace had come up with. If Cam's testimony was to be trusted, the woman was a bit of a miracle worker when it came to getting out of a jam.

"But first, we're going to have a chat."

Bristol sat back down, surprised at the unusual firmness in Grace's tone.

"Look, this is obviously about more than Jaclyn," Grace said. "It's been clear to me all week that something else is going on with you. I mean, who wouldn't be freaked out after that whole thing with your car?"

Bristol stared at the tabletop, gripping her warm mug with both hands as she tried to form a response.

She didn't want to admit it, even to herself, but Grace was right.

It wasn't a disappointed boss that troubled her. She was used to that. And it wasn't the possibility of failing at this job when she had nowhere else to go.

No. Neither of those things were enough to make her cry.

But having her car vandalized, and worrying that someone might have broken into her house in a deliberate attempt to frighten her and to mess up her life? Knowing that somewhere out there was a scumbag who would do anything to make sure his crime against her stayed buried?

Yeah, that could do it.

She waited, taking a few unreasonably slow sips of tea.

Grace was the office gossip, and everyone knew it. As much as she liked the woman, she wasn't sure she wanted to confide in her, and in any case, who was she to demand that Bristol give up her secrets?

Finally, she broke the silence.

"Did Cameron put you up to this? Look, I know you're trying to help, and I appreciate you distracting Jaclyn so I can get myself together, but I already told him that I don't know anything about the vandal. I just want to settle into this job without worrying about some stalker that has clearly gotten bored."

She felt a knot of guilt twisting in her stomach as she remembered the empty alarm app, the absence of numbers that she'd been so certain she'd chosen. However crazy it sounded, she knew she'd set those alarms. She knew it.

"I promise you, I haven't mentioned a word about anything to Cameron," Grace said. "Really. Not a word."

Bristol searched Grace's pretty face. She could see nothing in it that hinted at deception.

Or maybe she was just as good of a liar as Bristol herself had become lately.

"Honestly," Grace continued, winding a coil of blonde hair around a finger. "I see the way that you're always looking over your shoulder and the way you tense up when someone gets too close, especially the guys. Maybe they don't pick up on it, but I do. I'm more perceptive than I look."

Bristol bit at her bottom lip.

"You're scared, Bristol, and you have been since before your car was trashed. I saw it the very first time we talked, and I just want to know why. Maybe I can help."

The woman stared across the table at her, her blue eyes filled with compassion.

It was one thing for her to omit the truth, but to deny Grace's words now, she'd have to lie to her face.

Again.

One side of her was screaming, demanding she keep her shield raised, but another part of her just couldn't do it. The secrets were too heavy for her to hold them inside any longer.

"If I tell you about what happened, I need you to promise me you aren't going to share it right now. Not with Cameron, not with Gabe, not with Ben, not with anybody," Bristol said in a voice just above a whisper, glancing around the room to make sure it was still just the two of them.

"Your secret is safe with me. And besides, why would I tell Ben, of all people?" Grace asked, the hint of a smile tugging at the corner of her glossy lips.

"Even the most oblivious guy here knows the answer to that," Bristol said with a laugh as some of the tension poured out of the room.

She could do this.

Grace waited, her face solemn once more, and Bristol drew a breath and began to tell her all about that night.

At least a half an hour passed before she'd finished with her story, but she no longer cared if Jaclyn was upset with her.

Once she'd started to hand off some of the burden of her secret to someone else, she hadn't been able to stop. Despite the fresh tears that had sprung to her eyes as she dredged up the painful memories, she felt better than she had in a long time.

She felt free.

Grace had listened calmly, but now that Bristol was done, she had gotten up from her chair and begun to pace. Her heels clicked as she moved back and forth alongside the table, eyes sparking with anger.

"I can't believe it, Bristol. I just can't believe it," she kept saying, shaking her head. "Dorling & Porter has been operating here in San Antonio for at least a hundred years. What else are they hiding, if they were willing to cover this up?"

"I've asked myself the same," Bristol admitted. "But it doesn't matter. I tried doing things their way. I tried to play the game, and I ended up blacklisted. They made sure that I wouldn't be hired at any firm from here to Dallas. It's not like I can really take them to court. Even if I could find a lawyer willing to take on a charity case, and even if I could find a judge that wasn't in their pocket, it's still my word against his, ultimately. No one would believe me."

"I believe you," Grace said fiercely. "And I'm sorry."

Bristol leaned into the embrace that she was offered, and though she blinked quickly, she found she wasn't yet out of tears.

"Thank you."

"If it's okay with you, I'm going to look into Dillon Warrington's background, and see what I can find out. It's your word against his, true, but sometimes other factors have a way of moving the dial."

"You think you'll be able to find anything? I thought you were an office manager."

"That's my real job, yes," Grace said, waving a hand dismissively. "But I've picked up a few things while working here. Admittedly, if you want all the tea, Ben's the one to ask, but I'm not going to go to him until–unless–you're ready. No pressure."

Bristol felt the familiar anxiety twisting in her stomach. She couldn't believe that she'd told someone. Not even her mother knew the real reason she'd left D&P.

But that didn't mean she was ready to let anyone else in. Not yet, and perhaps not ever.

"I appreciate any help you can give, even if I'm not ready to bring anyone else in right now," she said. "And I'm glad that I can trust you."

Grace understood the question written in her eyes.

"You can, Bristol. I promise."

Chapter 11

Cameron

Cameron stepped out of the fifth floor elevator and headed down the hallway, unsurprised to hear the sound of Grace's bubbly laughter as he made his way toward the coffee lounge.

The FBS office manager worked hard for the most part, but the odd time that she disappeared without warning, it was easy to figure out where she was hiding.

"Hey, Hinton," he said as he rounded the corner, "reception is looking for you, and Ben–"

As he reached the doorway of the lounge, he stopped short.

Grace, he'd expected to see.

Bristol? Not so much.

"Hi," he said to no one in particular, his eyes flitting between the two women as he took in Bristol's red-rimmed eyes and Grace's unusually serious expression. "Is everything okay?"

"You startled me," Bristol said. "Sorry, I'm about to leave, actually. I know it's not break time, and it won't happen again. I just need to use the bathroom."

Without giving him a chance to respond, she picked up a huge cosmetic bag that must have belonged to Grace, and disappeared into the bathroom that adjoined the break area near the hallway.

"What on earth is going on?" he asked Grace, unable to conceal the hint of annoyance that had snuck into his tone.

"Nothing that I'm at liberty to discuss, Cameron," Grace said, raising a single eyebrow and plopping herself into one of the chairs.

"But–"

"She can speak for herself, and she'll do it when she's ready. Let it go."

There was something in her eyes that shut him up immediately.

Whatever was going on with Bristol, he wasn't going to hear about it from Grace.

At least she was opening up to someone, by the looks of it. It was something.

"Message received, boss," he joked.

"Good."

Grace reached into the depths of her cavernous handbag and withdrew a tube of pink lip gloss, reapplying it as she waited for Cameron to say more.

"Anyway," he said, clearing his throat, "I take it you're the reason Jaclyn is complaining to me about having to set aside important case work to–if I remember her exact wording–'play with Hinton's error-ridden spreadsheets and put in the legal department's highly urgent order for staples and trash bags?'"

Before Grace could respond, Bristol headed back toward the table. Her eyes no longer looked red, and her brown hair hung sleek at her shoulders.

"To be fair, she, like everyone else, is late getting her order in," Grace said, glancing over at Bristol with an approving smile. "I know it may not be groundbreaking stuff compared to, say, solving an impossible case in front of the judge by demystifying the chemical properties of ammonium thioglycolate, but it's an important part of keeping Forge Brothers Security running smoothly."

Cameron stared at her, wondering if perhaps he had in fact been hallucinating for the past twenty seconds.

Before he could ask what on earth Grace was babbling about—or remind her that everyone was late because she hadn't mentioned the order at all until five seconds ago—Bristol started to laugh. It was a real laugh, complete with what he would have probably called a snort, but in that moment, it was the prettiest laugh he'd ever heard.

"She's talking about Legally Blonde," she said after a moment, catching her breath. "And yeah,

Grace, that movie is totally realistic about what lawyers do. I highly suggest you quote it the next time you want Jaclyn to rip your face off."

"Anyway," Cameron said, shaking his head and glancing down at his smartwatch, "Jaclyn has been looking for you, Grace, and I suggest you see what she wants. And make sure that order is dealt with before the end of the day."

"Yes, sir," Grace said, tossing the cosmetic bag that Bristol had returned into her purse. She turned to Bristol with a questioning look, and, seemingly satisfied by her nod, she got to her feet. "See you guys later."

Cameron sat there across from Bristol, suddenly very much aware of how empty and silent the room was.

He didn't want to pry at whatever she and Grace had been talking about, but on the other hand, he didn't know how to force himself to go downstairs and head back to work.

Before he could figure out what to say, however, Bristol spoke.

"I have a lot to finish up this morning, and I'll

probably just skip lunch to do it so Jaclyn isn't kept waiting, but..."

Her voice faltered, and she looked down at the table, drawing an unsteady breath.

"But before I do, if you have time, can–can I talk to you for a second?"

Worry mingled with relief.

He wanted her to open up to him. He wanted to help. But why did she want to come to him now? Had Grace convinced her, or was she in more trouble than he thought?

"Let's go to my office, if you're comfortable with that," he suggested, his voice gentle.

"Probably a good idea," Bristol admitted, glancing up at the big silver clock on the wall above the espresso machines. "It's almost lunch. People will be coming in here soon."

Bristol said nothing as he guided her into the elevator and down to level three, but as soon as he'd closed the door of his office behind them, she sunk into one of the chairs, rubbing at her temples with her fingertips.

"First of all, I assume you've already heard everything about my being late this morning, if you spoke to Jaclyn," she said.

Was that all this was? Would she really call a private meeting just to apologize for a single late arrival?

"I heard, yes. Sounds like it worked out okay in the end, though. And as tough as she is, Jaclyn isn't going to hold a grudge. These things happen."

He paused for a moment, realizing that as much as he wanted to be gentle about her mistake, he also didn't want to seem like he was playing favorites.

"That said, I really do hope this won't happen again," he continued. "This place isn't exactly a nine to five job. Most of us have to put in late nights and early mornings, at least part of the time."

"I understand that," she said, the crushed look on her face almost enough to make him want to take back the scolding he'd given, however mild it was. "I'm used to long hours, and I can live with early mornings. I'm sorry," she said.

She looked like he wanted to say more, so he waited.

"But, Cameron, I didn't come here just to apologize. There's something else I need to talk to you about."

Her mouth was pinched, and her knuckles were white against the armrests of her chair.

"Bristol, what's wrong?" he asked, not bothering to conceal his alarm.

She didn't look worried about getting into trouble.

She looked scared.

She paused again, glancing around the messy room as though ensuring that her escape route was clear.

"I'm here," he said gently, leaning toward her just slightly, wishing once again that he could offer a comforting touch but not daring to get too close. "I'm listening, okay? Whatever it is, you can talk to me."

She waited for several long seconds, not quite meeting his eyes.

"I know that I tend to sleep through alarms, so I did everything I could think of to make sure I'd be up in time this morning. I set three alarms, for three separate times."

"Look, Bristol, this really isn't the end of the world," he said, regretting at once his attempt to prove to her that he wasn't giving her any special treatment. "I promise you, no one is going to remember this in a week."

To his surprise, her pretty green eyes flashed with anger.

"You said you'd listen. But maybe I shouldn't have come. You're right, it doesn't matter. I have work to do, anyway."

He heard the sound of her chair scraping across the floor as she shoved it back, attempting to get to her feet. To get away from him.

"Wait, wait, wait," he said, lifting a hand. "You're right. I'm listening."

She hesitated a little, her expression filled with a sadness that made him feel sick to his stomach.

"I don't know why I bother," she said, sinking back into the chair, defeated. "It's not like you're going to believe me anyway. I'm getting used to that by now."

He clamped his mouth shut, scared that nothing he could say would possibly come out right. Truth was, he had no idea what he'd said that had upset her so badly, but if she needed him to hear something out, he was willing to listen.

The silence seemed to fill the cluttered office.

Outside in the hall, he could hear happy chatter as several people passed his closed door on their way to lunch. His own stomach had been rumbling for a while already, but he could wait.

Finally, he heard Bristol letting out a long sigh.

"I'm sorry for snapping at you," she said. "I'm just frustrated, I guess. It's kind of difficult for me to expect you to believe me when I barely believe myself."

"What do you mean?" he ventured.

"It's going to sound crazy. I know it is, and I didn't want to tell you, but I've turned it over again and again in my mind, and I can't think of another explanation that makes sense."

Cam felt his heart beating a little faster.

Was she going to tell him who it was that was threatening her? Had she finally decided he was worthy of her trust?

"I know I set those alarms, Cameron. I kept trying to tell myself that maybe I made a mistake, or I woke up and snoozed through them, but it's not true. I'm certain of it. When I woke up to Jaclyn calling me this morning, they weren't just turned off, they were deleted from the app. Someone had to have done it, and it wasn't my mother or me. But nothing else was taken at the house. There was nothing to indicate a break in. It's like I was sabotaged by a ghost."

Once she had begun to speak, the words had poured out of her faster and faster, to the point where she sounded almost manic. And yet, she didn't sound crazy or paranoid.

To Cameron, at least, the possibility of a break-in, however unlikely, warranted further investigation. But there was one question that he still had to ask.

"Bristol," he started, trying to weigh his words carefully. She had opened up to him, true, but he knew he had to proceed with caution or she'd pull away again completely. "I believe you. Instinct is a powerful thing, especially in our line of work. Maybe you'd be a better security operative than you think."

She cracked a small smile at that, and he pressed on.

"But it would be a whole lot easier to investigate this if we had any idea where to start."

His words hung there, too late to take back, but this time, she didn't get angry at his prying.

"I wasn't entirely truthful before," she admitted, pulling her arms more tightly around her chest. "I'm sorry. The truth is, I've been holding something back, just as everyone suspected."

He opened his mouth to speak, but she shook her head, continuing.

"That's the truth. But it's also the truth that I'm still not ready to talk about it, for reasons that I'm not ready to talk about, either. I know that isn't what you want to hear, but as for today, that's what it is. Take it or leave it."

Her final words had a bitter edge to them, and her eyes were filled with a deep sorrow that made his heart clench in his chest. She was defensive for a reason.

Someone had hurt her, and he was going to find that person, even if he had to go in blind.

Before he could talk himself out of it, he got out of his chair and strode over to hers, offering her his hand.

She took it and he pulled her up to her full height, wrapping her in his arms.

This is stupid, Cam.

You're not being professional.

You're going to get hurt again.

The voice screaming in his head faded away, ignored, as he felt her warmth against him.

She didn't shy away, and he could hear a sniffling sound as she pressed against his chest, her tears dampening his gray t-shirt.

When he finally pulled back, he forced his eyes to meet hers, searching them, hoping that she could understand that there was so much more he couldn't say.

"Just like I said before, I'm here, and I'm listening. If and when you want to talk is up to you."

"Thank you."

Hating to let her go, he reached over and rooted around on his desk, finally locating a tissue box and handing it to her.

"In the meantime, I'm not letting you take any more risks. Asher and Reilly will watch your house tonight. If anyone breathes out of order, they'll be there to intervene."

He wanted desperately to do the job himself, but he knew it wouldn't be wise. His presence would make her feel suffocated. Chances were good that nothing would happen at all, and if something did, his house was mere minutes away.

She shook her head, wiping at her running nose. "That's totally unnecessary. They have more important things to do than sitting around a trailer park in Silver Grove."

"Evaluating risk is a big part of what I do. And right now, I say it's necessary."

"I admit it might be nice to have someone keeping watch so I can actually sleep. But I'm only agreeing to this for tonight."

He crossed his arms. "I can't promise you that. We need a chance to investigate. Give us the weekend, at least."

"I didn't come here to be helpless," Bristol said. There was an edge to her voice, a warning not to push her much harder. But he couldn't back down. Not when it came to her immediate safety.

"It's nothing to do with being helpless. It's our job to protect people. You're part of the FBS family now, and that warrants special consideration. Let us do what we do best," he said firmly, wishing he had the courage to voice the rest of what he was thinking.

Even if everyone else at FBS thought he was crazy, he'd still take care of her, no matter what it took.

Bristol

Bristol pulled the blankets more tightly around herself, trying desperately to fall asleep. She resisted the temptation to look over at the clock on her night stand, not wanting to be reminded of just how little sleep she was going to get before work tomorrow.

She'd stayed up far too late, and now that she'd finally made it into bed, her body was refusing to let go of the tension that had followed her throughout the day.

After her meeting with Cameron that Friday, she'd managed to get all of the case files double checked with time to spare. Despite the disastrous morning, she'd been given a chance to redeem herself as the day wore on. Jaclyn had needed a mountain of research done surrounding tax fraud law, and finally, Bristol felt that she was right in her element.

She'd brought most of the work home for the weekend, determined to get well ahead and to distract herself from the three-night-long stakeout taking place outside of her mother's mobile home. Today would be the last day, whatever Cameron thought.

She let out a loud sigh as she stared up at the paneled ceiling. Distraction had helped for a while, and she'd gotten most of the files finished with, but the lingering anxiety was enough to keep her awake.

For the fifth time in the last hour or two, she got up from her bed and peered out between the curtains, hoping that her face was hidden from view by the darkness of the room.

If she squinted, she could just see Asher and his cousin Reilly sitting in the front seat of a nondescript black pickup truck. She imagined them joking around and raising thermoses of coffee to their lips every few minutes as they fought the urge to sleep.

They had moved their truck each night. This time, they were parked far enough away to be able to see both doors of the house, next to a bunch of trash bins and an old wooden fence. The area was shielded by several trees, and it would be easy for someone to overlook the two men if they didn't already know that they were there.

Satisfied that no one was going to break in and mess with her alarms tonight, she padded back over to the bed and climbed beneath the comforter, closing her eyes.

This time, her thoughts drifted to Cam, and she was so tired that she didn't try to push them away.

She remembered the way that he'd pressed her against his chest as she cried, his firm muscles tightening around her body like he never wanted to let go.

Being alone with him didn't scare her.

If anything, he made her feel safer than she had in years. When it came to her physical safety, she trusted him completely.

But the safety of her heart?

That was different.

Even if they wanted the same things, which they most certainly didn't, they came from two completely different worlds.

When she pushed her emotions aside, she knew that the truth was obvious.

It was too late to go back to the way things had been all those years ago. There was too much separating them.

The warmth of his embrace was hardly enough to change that.

Chapter 12

Bristol

Monday morning came far too fast, but at least her alarms worked.

After hitting snooze twice, Bristol dragged herself from bed and headed over to peer out the window. The truck was gone already–as usual, the boys had probably cleared out around sunrise–and she hoped that they were heading home for some well-deserved rest rather than straight to the office.

She showered and dressed in a knee-length gray dress, pulling her hair up into a twist and clipping it into place. As she made for the fridge, she noticed a note resting on the countertop, and a flicker of anxiety rose within her.

As she read the messy handwriting, however, her worry was replaced with amusement.

> Cam told us to tell you not to eat breakfast. Didn't want to wake you, but we'll see you at the office later.
>
> Asher
>
> P.S. I (Asher) have volunteered Cameron to take the next watch. I need sleep, and he needs to do something other than bossing us around.
>
> P.P.S. Mean raccoon near compost bin. Can recommend a decent shotgun.
>
> P.P.P.S. Reilly has volunteered to use said shotgun.

She shook her head, smiling as she tugged on a pair of boots and grabbed her jacket, skipping her usual energy bar and thermos of tea.

She knew exactly which raccoon they were referring to. He used to hide under Boris's rear end, scaring her as she climbed in. Other times, he would walk around on the front windshield, leaving tiny footprints of dirt all over the car.

Fortunately, he had so far lacked any interest in doing the same to the car's replacement.

Still, before she ducked into the driver's seat and tossed her work bag beside her, she did her customary check around the back wheels.

The skies were clear today, and despite her lingering exhaustion, the day ahead held promise.

The traffic was calm, and she turned on the country station, getting lost in the hits of the early aughts that they usually played at this time of morning. They reminded her of her mother, who was probably listening to the same thing as she made her way in the opposite direction from her job at the nursing home.

She wished that she didn't have to work so much. By now, her mother should have been slowing down and nearing retirement, but instead, she did almost as much overtime as Bristol herself, with no end in sight.

When she reached the FBS building and headed into the legal department, she couldn't help but to smile in triumph. The student clerk was at her desk already, but she'd beaten Jaclyn to the office.

After greeting Melanie, she headed into her own office, shutting the door behind her.

Sitting on her desk was a still-hot green tea and a bacon and egg breakfast sandwich, as well as an almond croissant. There was another note beside it, this one scrawled on a takeout bag from the Screaming Peach Cafe. It said simply to check her phone, so she did so, just in time for it to ping with a new text message from Cameron.

She looked around the room, wondering if he was somehow watching her, before remembering that only the main legal department area had any security cameras.

Iris assured me that you'd want
bacon, not sausage, so
hopefully she's right. I still
think it's weird that you won't
even try coffee (Green tea is
more bitter! It makes no
sense!) but I suppose I'll have
to pick my battles.

Anyway, I just wanted to let you
know that I'm driving with
Reilly to Corpus Christi right
now. We have to secure a
safehouse for a VIP client, but
I'll see you tonight. I'll be the
one watching your house later -
Reilly and Asher need sleep,
and everyone else is busy. I
hope that's okay.

Have a good breakfast and a
great day!

Despite her annoyance that he wanted to
continue surveillance on her house, and the
unwanted skipping of her heart at the thought of
him being so close while she slept, she couldn't
help but to be touched by the gesture.

She glanced up at the clock. Jaclyn would be here soon, and she would want an update on the tax fraud cases. Bristol took her tea in one hand and unwrapped her breakfast sandwich with the other, determined to get everything eaten before her boss arrived.

Before she'd taken two bites of the steaming meal, however, Grace appeared at her door, giving only a quick knock before bursting in.

"I have good news and bad news," she said, sounding almost breathless, a gleam of excitement in her blue eyes. "Which one first?"

Bristol chewed the bite of food and swallowed, reluctantly setting the sandwich down on her desk next to the croissant. "Bad news first."

Grace pressed a freshly manicured nail–glittery purple this time–to her lip. "Actually, they're kind of the same news."

"Just tell me, Hinton," Bristol said, reaching for her tea and taking a sip before she lost her patience entirely.

Grace closed the office door behind her and slid into one of the leather chairs in front of the desk, her expression suddenly serious. Bristol felt her mouth going dry, and she quickly took another swig of tea. Whatever it was, she wanted to know.

"Okay," she said. "Dillon Warrington couldn't have been responsible for your car being trashed, or for the potential break-in at your house."

Bristol waited for her to explain, but already, her thoughts were racing. If he wasn't responsible, who was? Was it possible that it had been a coordinated effort, and that he was just keeping his own nose clean and letting someone else do the dirty work?

Grace's next words, however, left no room for that possibility.

"He turned up dead two weeks ago. Suspected suicide. Died of carbon monoxide poisoning."

Bristol set her tea down hard, the warm liquid sloshing side to side within the walls of the paper cup.

She could think of nothing to say.

All this time, she'd been looking over her shoulder, searching for him in every shadow, and now that he was gone, she didn't know how she should feel.

She couldn't quite bring herself to be relieved, and even though she'd hardly shed a tear for the man after what he'd done to her, there was a sadness that she couldn't shake.

There would be no redemption for Warrington now, no chance to seek forgiveness for the evil he'd done. He'd chosen another path, and there was no way back.

Bristol felt a shiver sliding through her.

Even though she hadn't been on the best of terms with the Almighty in recent years, she couldn't help but to be thankful for the faith that she still held within her heart, however weak it had become. Even in the darkest early days of the aftermath, she'd never pushed so far into hating herself that she'd considered taking her own life.

Apparently, for Dillon Warrington, the guilt had been too much to bear, and however much he had deserved to die, she wouldn't celebrate the fact that he'd taken matters into his own hands.

"Are you okay?" Grace said, reaching over and resting her fingertips along Bristol's forearm.

"I think so," she said, reaching out and ripping off a piece of her croissant before stuffing it into her mouth. Chewing was a distraction, and she was hungry.

"I think you need to consider talking to Cam, Bristol," Grace continued. "I know you aren't thrilled about the idea, but this is a big lead."

Bristol shook her head, swallowing the sweetness of the croissant before replying.

"How so? Our main suspect–really, our only suspect–is dead. How will that help us to figure out who's after me?"

"It could mean he's working with someone else. It could mean that someone is after him as well as you. Or it could just be a matter of taking a very obvious motive off of the table," Grace said. "Cameron and the boys know what they're doing, but they need more information."

Bristol bit her lip. Grace was right, she knew, but it didn't do anything to alleviate the terror that rested in the pit of her stomach.

"I can't do it. He'd never look at me the same way, not after what happened."

She hated the pathetic, pleading sound that she could hear in her voice, but she couldn't help it.

It was true.

She was pathetic, and however brilliant of an idea Grace thought it was, she didn't need Cameron to know just how weak she really was.

Grace's brow furrowed.

"Cameron isn't that kind of guy. You should know that even more than I do."

She did know it, and that was the problem.

Cameron was a good man. He went to church, he said his prayers, he kept himself in line. These days, he dedicated his entire life to helping others. He had every reason to judge her.

She'd proven everyone back in Silver Grove right.

She'd gone off on her own, and in the end, she'd gotten herself hurt.

"Just promise me you'll think about it more seriously, Bristol," Grace continued with a sigh. "I'm worried about you. We all are. If something else happened, and I knew something that could have prevented it, I'd never forgive myself."

Guilt mingled with her shame.

"Please don't say that," she said, brushing a strand of hair behind her ear as she stared down at the half-eaten croissant on her desk. "Look, I'll think about it. Maybe when I see him tonight, okay?"

Satisfied, Grace nodded, just as Bristol's stomach let out a hungry growl.

"All right, point taken," Grace said, her smile a welcome break from the seriousness of their conversation. "You need to eat before Jaclyn gets here, and I need to try and actually do some work."

Bristol ate the rest of her breakfast, but despite her hunger, she barely tasted it.

No matter how hard she turned the puzzle pieces over in her mind, none of them seemed to fit.

If Dillon Warrington hadn't been the person trying to hurt her, who was?

Chapter 13

Cameron

Cameron listened to the sound of gravel scraping against the tires of his Jeep as he pulled into the trailer park and rolled into a parking space.

He'd decided against taking one of the more discreet vehicles that they kept in the garage at FBS for undercover work. If the guy who was scaring Bristol knew where she lived and worked, it was highly possible that he knew about their history together already.

Though it might set off a local scandal, he figured that in the eyes of the culprit, it would be less suspicious if he made his visit look like nothing more than a social call.

He took a final glance around the front yard before killing the headlights.

It was already eight-thirty, which was later than he'd intended, but so far, nothing seemed to be amiss. After a long day in Corpus Christi, part of him wanted nothing more than to go home and sleep, but all of his brothers were busy tonight, and he wasn't ready to let the other security staff take charge. Not when it came to Bristol's safety, anyway.

He just hoped that she wouldn't take his presence the wrong way.

As he exited the Jeep, he saw the front door open, and to his surprise, Bristol's mother, Moira, emerged. She was carrying a pink bag stuffed to bursting, and wearing a hooded sweatshirt with 'Hug a PSW' emblazoned across the front in swirling pink letters.

Grinning, he rushed over and gave her a hug before she could react, glad that she was a little less jumpy than her daughter was these days. Laughing, Moira hugged him back before pulling away and giving him an appraising look, her eyes running up and down his jeans-and-sweater-clad frame.

"I haven't seen you at church in a while, Cameron," she scolded. "I hope you haven't forgotten to give some time to the Lord, nevermind that fancy business of yours."

Bristol opened the door of the house and followed her mother out onto the porch. She was still wearing the same gray dress she'd worn to work, but she'd let her hair fall at her shoulders and had added a cozy-looking, oversized sweater.

"Hey," she said, giving him a nod.

Cameron smiled over at her, forcing himself to refocus on his conversation with Moira.

"Fear not for my soul, ma'am," he said, tipping an invisible cap in her direction. "I'm still attending, but there's been a lot going on lately, and a lot of the time it's easier just to go in the city."

"Well, we've all missed you," Moira said, shifting her heavy-looking bag onto her opposite shoulder. "Especially those strong arms of yours when something needs fixing. Right, Bristol?"

She winked at him, and he couldn't help but to grin as he saw Bristol's face turning bright red.

"You're going to be late for work, mom," she said, reaching into the doorway and grabbing a travel mug. "And you almost forgot your coffee."

Moira took it, and Cameron noticed that it, too, was pink.

"Yikes," she said, glancing down at her watch. "That wouldn't have been pretty. It's kind of a necessity when you work all night," she added, turning to Cameron, who nodded.

"I know the feeling."

"All right, I'm outnumbered by coffee lovers. You'd better get going," Bristol said, gesturing toward her mother's station wagon.

Moira made her way down the porch steps and climbed into her car, and drove out toward the highway with a final wave.

Cameron stood where he was, sticking his hands into his pockets, unsure whether to bolt for his Jeep or to try and say something.

Before he could decide, however, Bristol spoke.

"Do you want to come in for a little bit?"

The words hung in the air for a couple of seconds too long as Bristol stood with her arm propping open the screen door of the trailer.

All of a sudden, he was no longer tired.

Was there a chance that she actually wanted him here?

"You sure?" he asked before stepping over the threshold.

Her gaze caught his own, and he looked down at her, wishing that he could know what she was thinking.

Finally, she nodded, giving him a smile that reached the corners of her pretty green eyes.

As he followed her toward the living room, he couldn't help but to notice that she was pulling her sweater more tightly around herself and fiddling with the ends of her hair.

Now that her mother was gone, she seemed shy.

At least, he hoped that was all it was.

The last thing he wanted to do was to intimidate her, or to destroy the small amount of trust that they'd built.

Which was why he'd wanted his brothers to handle this assignment, but there was nothing that could be done about it now.

He took a chair nearest to the door, and she sank onto the couch, leaving a vacant armchair to separate them.

"Is everything okay?" he asked after a few more uncomfortable seconds had passed.

Her cheeks went pink again, and she pulled the sleeves of the sweater over her fingertips, her thumb poking at a loose bit of yarn.

"I'm fine, sorry, just have some things on my mind," she said breezily. "Anyway, have you eaten yet? I made pasta and meatballs for mom, and there's still a bunch left. There's no way we're going to eat it all ourselves."

"I stopped at a drive-thru on my way back from Corpus Christi, but honestly, I could definitely eat again, if it's not going to cause any extra work for you," he said. "They charge like five dollars for a burger the size of a coffee lid these days. It's just not cutting it."

"I wonder how Ben can afford enough groceries to stay alive," she joked.

He chuckled, thinking back to the last time he had been in a grocery store with his largest, most gym-addicted brother. He'd spent more on a week's worth of food than Cam spent in a month.

Then again, Ben also lacked Cameron's habit of ordering takeout every day, but that was beside the point.

"He must have a side hustle I don't know about. You'd be amazed by how much chicken breast one person can eat in a week."

Bristol smiled and got up from her spot on the couch, gesturing toward the kitchen. "I'm just gonna heat that up. You can eat here if you want, or we can sit at the table."

"The table sounds great," he said, getting up and following her deeper into the trailer.

He noticed that some of the tension had gone out of her shoulders as she walked, and her fingertips were no longer tangled in the fabric of her sweater.

It seemed that her reluctance to let him get closer was fading away, but it did little to calm the confusion that reigned deep within his own heart.

A part of him wanted to get closer to her and to break down her walls.

But another part–the smarter part, most likely–knew that he was treading on dangerous ground. He'd walked into this same minefield before, and he'd ended up watching his dreams shatter all around him.

Could he handle it if it happened again?

He forced the thoughts from his mind as he took a seat at the cluttered formica table, watching as Bristol fixed him a plate of delicious-looking food and stuck it into the microwave.

"Sorry it's not the fanciest setting for your microwaved delicacy," she joked as she rifled through a drawer in search of a fork, not bothering to turn around. "This house is kind of a disaster area."

He glanced around the room. It was a little messy, and held the typical cluttered look of a small space that had been lived in for a lot of years, but it was hardly a disaster. It made him feel immediately at ease, like he could curl up on the couch with a book without worrying about messing up the throw pillows.

"Honestly, I think it's great," he said to Bristol's back. "It reminds me of how it looked back in high school. Sometimes it's nice when things don't change."

She paused with one hand on the door of the microwave.

Bringing up their shared history was risky, he knew, but he couldn't help it.

Being here, with her, eating a simple dinner of leftovers after Moira had gone to work... It was like going back in time.

He knew that she could feel it, too.

"Right," she said at last, bringing over the plate of steaming pasta and setting it in front of him with a glass of ice-cold soda on the side. "I can agree with that, I guess. I miss living in New York sometimes, or even in San

Antonio, but there's something nice about the way most things in Silver Grove tend to endure."

He paused to say a quick food blessing before picking up his fork, and to his surprise, Bristol joined him. He wasn't sure where she was with Jesus at the moment, but with a mother like Moira, he hoped that she hadn't strayed too far.

He didn't want to bring it up at the moment, though. Finally, things felt more comfortable, and he wanted them to stay that way, at least long enough for him to eat dinner.

"This is delicious, by the way," he said after his first couple of bites. "Thank you so much."

Bristol had always been a good cook, which made sense–her mother's cooking had always been legendary among the local kids, and he and his brothers were no exception, particularly after their own mother had died.

"You're welcome," she said softly, sipping at her own soda.

They sat there in silence as Cameron ate, but now, the quiet that stretched between them was no longer uncomfortable.

"So," she said after a few minutes, once his plate had nearly emptied. "How was your day, aside from the mediocre fast food on the way home?"

"It was okay, though poor Reilly had to stay down in Corpus Christi all night to babysit our client."

"Why does he need protection?"

"Got into online gambling, ended up borrowing money from the wrong guy, the usual story."

"Sounds like a movie plot."

"While a lot of personal security work is way more boring than people think, some of it is pretty much exactly like the movies," Cameron admitted, swallowing another bite of his pasta. "Especially when it comes to all of the stupid ways people put themselves in danger."

Bristol looked down at the table, and Cameron wished that he could shove his words back into his mouth.

Did Bristol have the same kind of story that so many of their clients did?

Had she gotten into drugs or gambling and ended up on the wrong side of a criminal's vengeful streak?

"But just to be clear," he continued, hoping his attempt at a save sounded natural, "no matter what mistakes our clients make, I'm in this business because I love helping people. Every victim deserves compassion and justice. No matter what. It's a blessing to be in the position where I can protect the vulnerable."

To his relief, Bristol's shoulders visibly relaxed once more.

Finished with the last of his food, he got up from the table and gathered up his dishes and cutlery. As he extended a hand to take Bristol's glass from her, however, their fingers touched.

Bristol glanced up at him from where she sat, her green eyes searching his own.

Without quite realizing what he was doing, he set the dishes back on the table and leaned toward her, extending a hand to caress the edge of her soft cheek.

But soon as his fingertips brushed her skin, she jumped back, sending her glass rolling across the tabletop before it shattered with a crash onto the floor.

Bristol

Bristol froze, staring down at the broken glass that now covered her mother's kitchen floor.

Pieces of ice were scattered across the linoleum, floating in what was left of her soda. She swallowed the lump that had risen in her throat, willing herself not to cry in front of him.

Again.

"Okay, let's get this wiped up," Cameron said after a moment, leaning over toward the counter and plucking the paper towel roll from its holder. "Do you have a broom for the glass?"

She nodded dumbly, forcing her feet to move in the direction of the small hall closet.

"Thanks."

His tone was light, but as he knelt to the floor and began mopping up the sticky soda and bits of dirt-encrusted ice, she couldn't help but to notice the tight set of his jaw.

He'd tried to kiss her, and she'd pulled away like she'd been burned.

She took hold of the broom and began to swipe at the glass, leaving a line of wet brushmarks behind.

"Sorry," she said in a desperate attempt to fill the sudden, terrible silence.

"It's fine, I just don't want you stepping on glass. I'll get a wet cloth and give it a final wipe when you're done."

She nodded again, not knowing how to tell him that it wasn't the sticky floor she was sorry for. In any case, seeing him show so much concern over something so trivial made her heart ache. The man had enough money to never have to wash a dish or do a load of laundry again, and yet here he was, making sure everything was just right.

Finally, he got to his feet, tossing the cloth into the hamper that sat in the hallway without needing to ask where it was.

All she wanted to do was to run away to her bedroom, pull the covers up over her head, and hide away until morning, but that was hardly an option.

She drew a ragged breath, forcing her chin up as he took a few tentative steps toward her.

"Dinner was wonderful, Bristol, even though I ruined the ending. I think I'd better get outside and start my watch."

She winced. He hadn't ruined anything. That was all her.

"No," she heard herself saying. "Wait."

He obeyed, resting one muscled arm against the wall and leaning against it, waiting.

"Look, Cam, it's–it's not what you think," she said, the words jumbling together as she tried to figure out how to explain feelings that she didn't understand herself. "It's not you. Goodness, it's not you."

She risked a glance up at him, letting her eyes linger on his handsome face, a face that she knew as well as her own, even after all this time.

"I love it when you're near me," she confessed, her voice lowering until it was nearly a whisper. "Even though I'm terrified, and you're my boss, and it's the worst idea ever, that's the truth."

He lifted his hand again, but before he could rest it against her cheek, he drew it back.

"So what is it, then? Did I move too fast?"

He looked so concerned that her heart somehow managed to melt even more. Despite all of the ways that she'd been prickly toward him, he still thought only of making sure that she was comfortable.

It was a gentleness that she hadn't seen from a man since... well, since she'd walked away from him the first time.

She drew a deep breath.

In spite of her fears, Grace was right. Cameron was a good man. Perhaps the best man she knew.

And he deserved to know as much of the truth as she could bring herself to share.

"This is going to sound stupid," she said, biting her lip.

"Try me."

His blue eyes burned into hers.

"My fears and what I want clash sometimes," she said, searching for the right words. "I wanted you to lean in. I wanted you to kiss me. But my body rebelled before I could think about it."

He waited for her to finish, and she wondered how much more she was ready to say.

"Being alone with men scares me. I told you it was stupid, but that's just how it is," she said, not bothering to hide the defensiveness that snuck into her voice. "When I saw you again, even that first day at FBS, I was surprised that I didn't feel that fear around you. Even when no one else was around. But tonight, here, with you in my house... I guess my body is still nervous, even if my mind—and even my heart—knows better."

She knotted her fingers in the hem of her dress, hoping that he would accept that partial explanation of her actions, at least for now. She needed a chance to catch her breath before she dared broach the topic with any more depth.

"That doesn't sound stupid," Cam said firmly. "It sounds like I was moving too fast and making you uncomfortable.

"Please, I—"

"I noticed that you seemed nervous when I first stepped onto your porch, and I should have backed off. Instead, I chose to pursue what I wanted, without thinking of why you might have seemed anxious. I'm sorry for that."

Before she could figure out how to respond, however, she heard a scuffling sort of sound coming from the back of the house.

Cameron stood up straight in an instant, his fingers moving for the gun at his belt before she'd had a chance to understand the potential danger she'd suddenly found herself in.

"Don't run. Go into your mother's room and lock it. Now," he said under his breath, his tone leaving no room for her to argue.

She obeyed, walking quietly on shaking legs until she reached the front end of the trailer and the yellow-painted door that led into her mother's modest bedroom. She went inside and closed it behind her as softly as she could, the click of the lock deafening in the silence.

She stood there for a moment, struggling to slow her breathing as a familiar panic took hold of her insides.

Should she hide in the closet? Under the bed?

She walked toward the small window, remembering that it was mostly hidden from the outside by a hedge, a fact that Cameron had no doubt taken into consideration when he had sent her in here.

Seeing only darkness through the glass, she decided that she'd rather stay out here where she had two potential escape routes, rather than hiding away where she might get cornered.

Time seemed to pass with impossible slowness as she waited beside the bed. For a while she heard nothing outside of the room at all, the seconds marked only by the hammering of her heart.

There was a thumping sound, and then another.

Without quite meaning to, Bristol found herself cowering on the floor, resisting the urge to cover her ears.

She didn't want to hear what was clearly a struggle coming from the living room, but she had to listen.

Should she go for the window? Should she try for a phone and call for help?

She wanted to force her limbs to move, to get out there and do something, anything at all, but instead, she found herself whispering urgent prayers, her face pressed against the side of her mother's bed.

Just as soon as the noise had come, it was gone again, leaving only silence behind.

She pressed her eyes shut, trying to keep her balance as she felt the blood pulsing within her ears.

"It's clear, Bristol."

A voice. His voice.

"You can come out."

Relief flooded through her, and as she stumbled to her feet and made for the living room, she thanked God that Cameron was alive.

Chapter 14

Cameron

Cameron rested his head against the cool wood of the kitchen island. Now that his adrenaline rush had ended, he realized that he was too tired from the momentary exertion to get to his feet, let alone to go and find Bristol.

Fortunately, she had heard his call, and a few seconds later, she rushed into the kitchen.

She looked as bad as he felt. Her face was pale and drawn, and her eyes were wide with fright as she sat down next to him.

"You're bleeding!"

He reached up to his face, and his fingertips came away red.

"I'm fine. It's just a scratch."

She said nothing as she got to her feet, rooting around in a nearby drawer until she found a first aid kit. He could see her fingers shaking as she opened the zipper, but after a moment, she found what she needed.

He gritted his teeth as she swabbed the wound with alcohol and taped a piece of gauze over top of it. The moment she finished, she sat back against the island beside him, rubbing at her temples with her fingertips.

"What happened? Are you sure it's safe now?"

He nodded.

"As far as I can tell, the intruder walked right in through the back door, though I assume it was locked," he said. Bristol nodded, and he continued.

"Even though my Jeep is parked right out front, it didn't seem like he expected to see me here, which is sloppy on his part, but it's not as though there's any shortage of dumb criminals out there. Anyway, as soon as he realized that he was walking into a fight he couldn't win, he took off."

He paused, refusing to meet Bristol's questioning gaze.

"Okay, and?" she demanded.

He cleared his throat.

"I tripped and hit my face against the corner of the table. Not my smoothest moment, I'll admit. While I was distracted, the guy got away."

He sighed. His brothers were not going to let him hear the end of this one.

Bristol's face, however, revealed only concern.

"Did you get a look at him, at least?"

"Not really," he admitted. "He was wearing a ski mask and a hooded sweater, and I didn't get enough of a look at his hands or his eyes to determine his race. All I know is that he had a medium build and height. I couldn't even see if he had a weapon, not that he got a chance to use it before the table attacked me. It could have been the same guy from the parking garage footage, but it could also be someone totally different. I wish I had something more concrete. I'm sorry."

The cut on his jaw smarted beneath the bandage.

Had he been out in his Jeep where he should have been, the guy wouldn't have gotten inside the house in the first place. He had to be more careful. He couldn't let his feelings for Bristol put her at an even greater risk.

"I'm just thankful you're okay," she said, shaking her head and pulling her knees into her chest. "I can't help but wonder what would have happened if he'd come just a couple of hours earlier, when my mom was here by herself. I can't let her get hurt because of me."

"None of this is your fault," he said, reaching over and resting a hand on her shoulder. "You need to know that."

She gave him a weak smile, and he let his fingers fall away.

She'd been so close to telling him more about what was going on with her. He could feel it. But the moment was gone now, and he wasn't about to push the issue.

Not for the moment, anyway.

Not when there was something more important he needed her to cooperate with him on.

"Anyway, we need to regroup," he said, ignoring the aching of his tailbone as he got to his feet and pulled out his phone. "I'm calling our home security guy in the morning to have him figure out if and how we'll be able to secure this house. In the meantime, at least until I can wrangle up a safehouse, you're staying at the FBS offices where we can protect you."

For once, Bristol didn't argue.

Bristol

"Okay, sounds good, mom," Bristol said, pressing the phone against her cheek. "I'll explain more in the morning, I promise. Okay. Love you too."

"How'd that go?" Cameron asked.

"She agreed to stay with a friend after work, but I'm not sure she realizes just how serious the situation is."

Cameron said nothing, his attention focused on the dark highway stretching in front of them as he drove toward the city. Bristol had grabbed pajamas, a tooth brush, a change of clothes, and a few things that she needed for work the next day, but that was it.

All she'd wanted to do was to get out of that house, and away from the prickly feeling that someone was watching her, waiting to catch her alone.

She shivered in the passenger seat.

"You cold?" Cameron asked, reaching for the dial that turned up the heat.

"A little. Thanks," she said, wrapping her sweater more tightly around herself as she waited for the vehicle's interior to warm up.

She was safe now.

So long as Cameron or his brothers were close by, she knew that whoever was after her wasn't going to be able to get to her.

And even if she didn't enjoy being dependent upon them, she'd rather set aside her pride, at least for now, than end up dead.

As she peered out at the twin pools of light in front of the car, she couldn't help but to be drawn into more pleasant memories. They had taken so many drives like this as teenagers in the Forge family's old farm truck, arguing over what to listen to on the radio. Bristol would always complain about the coffee cups Cam left behind, and he'd pretend to be mad about the hair ties she always left wrapped around the gear shift.

It had been another lifetime, and yet, as Cameron clicked on the country radio station and she settled back into the comfortable leather seat, the past felt so close that she could reach out and touch it.

"Honestly, Bristol," Cameron said after a while, turning toward the city lights that now lay within view. "I thought that you'd argue about staying at the office tonight."

Bristol smiled. Some things, like her tendency toward stubbornness, hadn't changed much.

"I couldn't handle being in that house alone all night, not after that."

Cameron nodded, stealing a glance at her after he had merged onto the still-busy freeway that led into downtown. "I just wanted to say thank you for trusting me, even when I've had to make decisions that involve disrupting your life."

There was so much that she wanted to say.

Ever since Warrington's attack, she'd become vulnerable just existing in her own body.

Feeling that same sense of violation while in the safety of her childhood home was a crossed boundary that she couldn't ignore or dismiss.

But before she could find the right words, they were pulling onto the street behind FBS that led into the parking garage.

"I do trust you," she answered at last, as Cameron tapped in his keypad code at the gate. "At least, I'm trying to."

He paused with the window still down, the cool night breeze making his dark brown hair flutter as his eyes caught hers. "That's all I want from you, Bristol. That's all I've ever wanted."

She felt her heart catch in her chest as he turned away, continuing down into the garage and toward his usual parking space.

After a quick detour to one of the supply rooms, they made their way to the third floor and found an empty office down the hall from Cameron's office.

"Does this work?" he asked her, flicking on the light. The two of them looked over the plain, carpeted space. There was an empty desk, a chair, an old filing cabinet, and not much else.

Bristol strode over to the huge glass window and surveyed the bustling streets of San Antonio, the lights from a thousand windows peering up at her. "This is perfect."

He quirked an eyebrow at her, but didn't argue, instead rolling out the sleeping bag he'd carried upstairs and setting out a pillow and an extra blanket, muttering something about how they needed to buy a couple of cots for emergencies.

Satisfied, he got to his feet. "I'll have one of the guys from the security rotation start early tomorrow morning so he can go check on your house. I'll make sure he grabs you some extra bathroom supplies and clothes, too, assuming you're okay with some twenty year old rooting through your closet."

Bristol smiled. "Nothing too scandalous in there, I'm not worried. Thanks."

"Are you hungry? We can order some food, if you want."

"We just ate!" she protested, laughing.

Cam stroked at his chin, pretending to be deep in thought. "It's been at least an hour. Maybe longer."

"The horror."

"What about dessert?"

She considered this.

"Yeah," she said. "Dessert sounds reasonable. Some nice sugar before bed. I couldn't sleep yet if I tried, anyway."

She felt the prickle of anxiety rising within her once again as he took his phone out of his pocket, already on the hunt for takeout.

She had come so close to being hurt again, and even though she knew that she was safe here in the office, she realized that she didn't want Cam to leave her side.

Not tonight. Maybe not ever.

She felt tears stinging her eyes as he looked over at her, his phone pressed to his ear. He was halfway through asking if she wanted cookie dough or brownie ice cream when he saw the sadness in her face.

"Okay, scratch that, I'll call you back with my order later. Sorry about that," Cam said into the phone, hanging up without another word and shoving it into his pocket.

He rushed over to where she stood, resting his hands gently on her shoulders, just as the tears began to spill over.

"Hey. Hey. What's wrong? What happened?"

She tried to swallow the sobs that strangled her throat, but she couldn't.

"It's okay," he said, reaching up and stroking her hair. "Shh. It's okay."

She rested her head against his chest, closing her eyes, willing her lungs to work properly again.

After a few moments had passed, she pulled back, gently this time, and tilted her chin up until his blue eyes met hers.

"There are some things I need to tell you," she said, forcing the words out before she could change her mind.

She was desperate for justice, and her colleagues at Forge Brothers Security could help her get it. She just needed to be brave.

"You can tell me anything," Cam said, reaching up and stroking the side of her jaw gently with his thumb.

She pressed herself into his chest again, drawing several slow breaths.

She was ready.

Chapter 15

Cameron

Cameron took Bristol's hand within his own and led her toward the corner where he'd laid out her sleeping bag, propping the pillow up behind her so that she could lean against the wall.

He settled in beside her, giving her a few inches of space, which she quickly filled, leaning against his shoulder as she drew several long breaths. He let the silence stretch out between them, not wanting to say or do anything that would make her pull away again.

He could almost feel the heaviness of her unspoken secret closing in around them, suffocating them both, a shadow that had been chasing her long before her car had been destroyed and her home broken into.

Whatever it was, he had to know, even if all it meant was that she no longer had to carry her burden alone.

At last, she spoke.

"I don't know if I ever really told you back then exactly why I wanted to get into law," she began, keeping her head against his shoulder so that she wouldn't have to meet his eyes. "I loved the idea of helping people to seek justice for their crimes, and even the idea of making sure that those who had wronged others would be treated fairly and get a worthy defense in court."

He nodded, saying nothing. This didn't surprise him, though she'd never exactly articulated it.

Bristol had always excelled in academics, and when combined with her love for helping others, it made sense to him that she'd find the law to be an appealing career option.

"Anyway, to sum up several very difficult years, that passion only grew as I did my undergrad in New York, followed by my paralegal program.

Finally, I had the chance to work on real cases, even if it was mostly as a grunt for a slew of cranky lawyers."

"Sorry if that hasn't changed much in your new job here," he joked.

She cracked a smile in return, but a moment later, her expression grew serious again.

"I loved Manhattan, but it's expensive, and soon enough it became clear that if I wanted to actually go to law school and take this job all the way, I'd have to live somewhere that allowed me to work and actually save up some of the money. I applied to firms all over the country, but in the end, I realized that honing in my search on Texas made the most sense. I hated how long I'd left my mom alone. When I heard back from Dorling & Porter, it felt Providential. Ha."

She paused, and Cameron's heart ached at the sadness that filled her eyes.

God bringing her back to Silver Grove made sense, sure, but He certainly hadn't wanted Bristol to fall victim to the evil that had followed, whatever it was.

Before he could tell her this, however, she pressed on.

"As you probably can figure out from the timeline, I ended up at D&P for about two years. There was a lot I loved about it, to tell you the truth. I got to work on a lot of complex case law and was handed a lot of responsibility. I dedicated more hours to the job than anyone else in the paralegal department and worked my way to a very respected position. It probably wasn't a healthy work-life balance–I know it wasn't, actually–but I was able to scrape together enough to pay for an apartment I loved. I even started socking away some money for law school."

She paused to take a breath, and he suppressed the question that rose within him.

After she'd sacrificed so much to make it to the top, what could have possibly been bad enough to make her give it all up and start over?

"Not everything was good," she said, glancing up from his shoulder and giving him a quick flash of a smile. "Lawyers, well, they tend to live up to the stereotype. Jaclyn Mercier is a total pussycat compared to most of them, especially the senior partners. I got used to being screamed at for the smallest mistake, to the point where I no longer bothered to cry, not even while hiding in the bathroom. Not to mention the fact that they expected me to drop anything in my personal life with about ten seconds' notice, or face, you guessed it, more yelling."

Cameron tightened his fists. "What a pathetic bunch of scum," he said, narrowly avoiding unleashing the several creative swear words that they most certainly deserved.

Bristol only shrugged.

"There were other things, too, little things that never quite added up. Sometimes I found files with irregular numbers, or billing sheets that were clearly filled out wrong, things like that. There were also some smaller companies that made zero sense for the firm to have as clients, yet kept showing up on their books. But that wasn't until later, when I had started to gain more of their trust and less of their rage, and by that point..."

She trailed off, looking down at her knees as her body drew a couple of inches away from his own.

He wanted to reach out for her hand, to pull her against him, to assure her that no matter what she was going to say, it wouldn't change anything about how he felt about her.

Instead, he sat still, staring out at the lights of the tall office towers and condos that lay beyond the window.

They were far enough from the ground that he couldn't hear the sounds of honking horns, sirens, or screeching brakes, and the only people left in the FBS building now would be the security guards making their rounds.

To him, it was peaceful, but for Bristol, nowhere felt safe. It made him feel sick, and he would do whatever it took to make sure that one day, she'd be–and feel–safe again.

"Sorry," Bristol said after a while, letting her head fall against his shoulder once more. "This is the hard part. The part I've been putting off."

"Don't apologize," he said, feeling the tickle of her hair brushing against his neck. "Take your time. I'm not going anywhere."

He wasn't. If she'd let him, he'd stick around forever.

The risk to his heart no longer mattered, not if it meant that he could make sure she was protected, treasured, and loved like she deserved.

"There was a senior associate named Dillon Warrington."

She paused, and Cameron breathed in the scent of her hair, trying to calm the anger that was bubbling within him. The tone of her voice was enough to make him hate the man already.

"I had worked with him off and on over my first year and a half at D&P, but in the last six months, I got assigned to him more and more. At the time, I didn't think much of it, but now it's pretty obvious that he must have been requesting me. He was on track for partner, if the office gossip was to be believed, and from what I could tell he had some sway with the big dogs.

"Anyway, working with him was no big deal, at least at first. If anything, he was one of the more pleasant lawyers there. He was very good at his job, and I quickly realized that the partners, for once, weren't really playing favorites. He was young and hungry, and he'd proven himself in a relatively short time, at least in terms of the legal field."

Bristol paused again, and Cameron looked down at her as she shifted her weight against him.

Instead of pulling away, as he'd expected, she had moved even closer.

Without a word, he placed his arm around her shoulders, drawing her to him, and she sunk into his chest, so close that he could feel her breaths against him.

"Sorry. This is where the story gets rough. I know I need to spit it out, but it's so hard to make myself say the words."

"Would it help if I promised not to react?" he asked.

She shook her head.

She was quiet for a long time, and when she finally spoke, the sadness in her voice almost broke his heart.

"Just promise me you won't let go. That you won't push me away. Please."

He swallowed, his throat suddenly thick.

"I promise."

"There were a lot of late nights in those final months at Dorling & Porter. Really late nights, late enough that there was no one in the office save for maybe a single security guard, who spent ninety percent of his time watching the cameras and sports at the same time.

"I got used to those nights. Got used to being alone with Dillon in his office, sitting across from him at his desk, rifling through his cabinets, writing his notes, all of it. I wasn't afraid of him. Not even a little bit."

She laughed a bitter, aching laugh, and he wrapped his arm more tightly around her shoulders, bracing himself for what he knew was next.

He didn't want to hear it any more than she wanted to say it, but he knew that he had no choice.

Neither of them did. It was too late to turn away from the evil now.

Bristol's only hope now was to cast the secret out into the light, where it could be conquered once and for all.

"I should have seen the red flags," Bristol continued, her words coming quickly now, her voice taking on a new strength the more that she shared. "The way that he complimented my thrift-store outfits, the way he asked if I had a boyfriend, the way that I thought I heard him talking about me with a couple of the less pleasant young attorneys.

"But I didn't want to believe it. I respected him. I actually enjoyed working with him, at least most of the time. He taught me a lot. I liked Dillon, and I don't expect you to believe that. I can hardly believe it myself, but it's the truth."

She glanced up at him, her features contorted with disgust.

"It's not only believable, but totally understandable," he said, his voice as sure and firm as he could make it. "It's not always the slimy creep who is the predator. Sometimes it's the last person you'd expect who is the most dangerous of all. The person who knows how to blend into the crowd, concealing their true nature until it's too late."

She allowed her eyes to meet his for just a

moment before tearing them away again, leaning into his chest, her face hidden.

"Well, he had me fooled. All of my talk about female independence, all of my New York street smarts, even the pepper spray I carried with me in my purse every day. All of it was worthless."

He braced himself again as she drew a shuddering breath.

"It had been just like any other one of our many late nights. It was after midnight on a Wednesday. A court date had been moved up unexpectedly to Thursday morning instead of Friday afternoon, and we had a lot to get together before then, down to the wire, the usual story. Just like that whole fiasco with Judge Hammerstein and the alarms on my phone. It happens all the time."

She almost spat the words, and he realized that she was not only in pain and angry, but defensive, as though any of this had been her fault. He wanted to reassure her, but before he could speak, she continued.

"Finally, we were finishing up, and he asked me if I wanted to stay a little longer. It was clear by the way he said it and by the hungry look in his eyes what he meant. I was shocked and offended, I guess, but I don't remember being scared. I can't even remember my exact words. I think I told him that I respected him as a boss and I saw him as a friend, but I didn't have time to pursue any more than that."

"He laughed at me, Cam," she said, her voice lowering to something just above a whisper, the anger gone out of it in an instant, replaced only with grief. "He actually laughed. And then he told me not to worry about that, because this wouldn't take any time at all. Well, that part was true, I guess. It felt like hours, but it couldn't have been more than a few minutes. I tried to make him stop, and I tried to call for help, but no one could hear me. I never even found out if the security guard was working that night."

Cam pulled her closer to his body, trying to reign in the blind fury that coursed through him.

Bristol still did not look up at him, pausing only long enough to take a breath.

"Anyway, a couple of days afterward, I went to the partners and told them what had happened. They didn't laugh at me, but they probably should have. Dillon Warrington had played me completely. He'd gotten to them first, with his own story about how I tried to seduce him, and about how I offered him 'favors' if he would help me get ahead at the firm.

"It was his word against mine, and they chose to believe him. I know I could have gone to the police, but I couldn't bring myself to do it, especially since any..." she trailed off for a moment, drawing a long breath.. "Any physical evidence was long gone by that point, and I just wanted the situation to go away. Besides, even if he was successfully charged, I would lose in court. Dillon Warrington had the resources of Dorling & Porter behind him. I had nothing. So I quit. It's done."

Cameron swallowed the bile that had risen in his throat, his decision made at once.

"Tell me where he lives. I'll take care of it," he said slowly, his voice escaping in a growl that he hardly recognized.

His mind raced.

He'd have to bring Gabe along. If he went alone, he wasn't sure he'd be able to contain his fury.

As badly as he wanted to tear the man's head off with his bare hands, he couldn't allow himself to do evil, not even to those who deeply deserved it.

"You can't," Bristol said, looking up at him, her green eyes filled with unshed tears.

"He can't get away with what he did to you. You deserve justice. FBS can help you get it. I can help you get it."

Bristol shook her head. "That's not what I mean. You can't go after him. No one can. It's too late. He already killed himself. I just found out recently."

Cameron leaned back against the wall, glancing up at the ceiling tiles overhead.

Of course that piece of human filth had escaped the consequences for his crimes. Now, there would be no justice done in this life, but with what the man had chosen, he wasn't feeling very optimistic about the man's fate when he stood before the Lord.

"I'm so sorry, Bristol," he said, hating the words even as he said them.

They were so inadequate it was almost laughable.

He hated that Bristol had been betrayed so deeply, and that she now carried shame over something that wasn't even her fault.

"I'm sorry I took so long to tell you," she said, hugging her knees to her chest as she shifted her weight. "I actually told Grace already, a little while ago–she's the one who dug up the info on the suicide. I don't know why I've insisted on carrying this darkness around with me for so long when there are good people in my life who have always been willing to listen. Thank you for being one of them, and thank you for believing me."

"I'm sure it took a lot for you to trust me, but I'm glad you did. Not only because you shouldn't need to bear this secret by yourself, but because we now have a partial motive for why someone could be going after you now. It will give us a place to start, at least. And we're going to put an end to all of this. I promise."

He let out a breath. He hated to bring up the current peril that surrounded her, but he couldn't ignore it, either.

Warrington's death complicated things, but still, he had to believe that the crimes were connected somehow. And he was determined to put the pieces of the puzzle together until they fit.

They were both quiet for a long time, staring across the room and out the window, both lost in their own thoughts as the night drew on.

"I think you should get some rest," he said at last, lifting his arm from her shoulder. Though he was sad to no longer be holding her, his muscles were beginning to ache, and he was thankful for a chance to stretch. He glanced down at the glowing face of his smartwatch. "It's getting late."

"I'm totally wiped out," she admitted, pulling herself to her feet and stretching her own arms high over her head. "And I think I'll sleep better now."

She didn't need to explain what she meant. He could see the relief painted clearly on her face. There was still a long way to go toward healing from her assault, he knew, but there was power in taking even a single step forward.

He stood as well, glancing down at the makeshift sleeping area he'd put together on the floor, wishing that he'd had something more comfortable to offer her, but it would have to do for now. "I'm going to sleep in my office tonight. I'll be just down the hall if you need me, and unlike at D&P, our security guys will be patrolling all night. If anything is amiss, I'll be by your side in two minutes."

"That'll help," she said, nodding. "Thank you. Though I hope you'll get a proper rest on an actual bed tomorrow night."

He said nothing, gesturing toward the bag that held the few belongings they'd had a chance to grab.

He had no plans to go back to Silver Grove. Not until she was in a safehouse, at the very least.

"You might want to change into something comfortable," he said. "There's a bathroom two doors over. I'll wait outside for you, if you want."

She agreed, and several minutes later, they returned to the empty office once more. Bristol was dressed in a matching purple pajama set dotted with white teacups, and her hair was piled on top of her head in a messy bun.

He refrained from commenting on how adorable she looked as she climbed into her sleeping bag, resting the side of her cheek against the too-thin pillow he'd found in the storage room.

"Everything good?" he asked, leaning against the doorframe. "I'll keep my phone on. Call me if you need anything at all, even if it's just a glass of water."

She smiled up at him, closing her eyes and letting out a contented sigh. "Strangely enough, I think I'm about to get a better sleep than I've had in ages. I feel safe here."

"Good. And you are," he said firmly, resisting the urge to glance over his shoulder and give the empty hallway yet another spot check. He'd do that once he was out of her sight.

He doubted he'd sleep much, but at least he'd have the energizing power of coffee to lean on come morning.

He flicked the light switch off, bathing the room in shadows, save for the light from the city streets that filtered in through the window. "This okay?"

"Perfect."

It was time to leave, but he found himself stuck where he was, his feet unwilling to carry him away from her. Despite his confidence in her safety while she was sequestered at FBS, she looked so vulnerable now, laying there in the dark. It made his heart ache to leave her.

"Well, goodnight," he said after a moment.

There was a long moment of silence.

No one moved.

"Cam?"

"Yeah?"

He heard her draw a breath, but could no longer see her face amid the shadows.

"Can you stay for a little longer? Just until I get tired," she said, her words coming in a rush. "Which shouldn't be long. I know it's silly, and I'm safe, but–"

"Yes," he said, taking a few short steps toward her and dropping onto the carpeted floor. "Of course I'll stay, as long as you need me to. Just say when."

"Thank you."

The room went quiet again, save for the gentle sound of their breaths.

Despite his less-than-comfortable position sitting in the middle of the floor, and the secret that Bristol had just shared, Cam felt a warm, happy feeling spreading through his chest.

It felt right being here, next to her, her face scrubbed free of any makeup, her hair out of place, her feet bare.

It felt like a glimpse at the future he had prayed for, for so many years, where she was his wife, and she was happy.

"Cam?" she said again.

He smiled to himself.

"Bristol?"

"I'm sorry I've been so closed off."

"Anyone would be. You've been through something traumatic. It's normal."

He heard her sleeping bag rustling beside him, and despite the shadows, he could picture her shaking her head, tendrils of hair escaping the confines of her bun.

"That's not what I meant."

She paused, and he waited, hope swelling within his heart.

"After my dad left, I promised myself that I'd never put myself in the same situation my mother is in. I never wanted to rely on a man like she did, because in my experience, men let women down."

Bristol's father was a scumbag for abandoning his family, sure, but was that enough for her to make the same assumption about every other man in the world?

About him?

"Anyway, I really did–really do–want to be a lawyer. I'm passionate about the law, and I like that it gives me a chance to help people," she continued. "But the way that I left things with you when I decided to go to Columbia wasn't right. I was a jerk, and I should have apologized years ago. I'm sorry."

Cameron was thankful that she couldn't see him wincing at the memory.

After dating Bristol for three years of high school, he thought that finally they had worked things out.

She'd go to school in Texas, they'd stay together, and they'd both get what they wanted.

But in the end, after planning the perfect proposal and getting down on one knee, the girl he loved had told him that she'd changed her mind, and that she didn't want him holding her back while she chased her dreams.

They were done, and everything that he had dreamed of for the future came crashing to the ground in an instant.

"Thank you," he said at last. "I missed you a lot when you went away. It was an adjustment, and I kept praying you'd come home, but you never did."

He tried to keep the lingering pain from showing in his voice. It had been a long time ago. There was no point in making her feel guilty for the decisions that her teenage self had made.

On the other hand, he couldn't pretend that he had forgotten, or that he no longer cared, or that she hadn't broken his heart. Broken trust wasn't easy to mend, but if Bristol was willing to try, so was he.

"I don't pray much these days," Bristol said, her voice lonely in the dark and the quiet. "Usually, it's just when I need something, you know? Once I lost the habit of talking to God, it just got easier and easier to forget about Him completely."

"Do you ever think about coming back?" he asked. "To the Lord, I mean?"

Her voice was a whisper.

"All the time."

He said nothing for a long while. He would have to leave her soon. She needed to sleep, and he needed to make sure she was safe while she did.

Finally, she spoke again.

"Can you pray for me before you go? I feel like talking to Jesus, but I'm rusty, and I hear that the prayers of a righteous man availeth much."

"I'm not sure I'm righteous, but of course I will. I'd be honored."

Butterflies flipped in his stomach as he inched closer to her in the dark, reaching his hand toward her own until they touched.

As his fingers entwined with hers, he felt lightheaded, but he cleared his throat, forcing himself to focus on what mattered so much more than his longing to be near her.

"Lord Jesus, I ask you to bless and to protect Bristol tonight, and over all of the days of her life. I ask that You fulfill Your promises to our fathers, and to grant her a heart of flesh to replace her heart of stone, so that she will hear Your voice and allow You to reveal your love for her as a precious daughter of God. In the name of Jesus, we pray. Amen."

As soon as he'd finished, he felt his cheeks going warm.

He had never liked praying in front of other people, and no matter how much he always tried to speak from the heart, his brain had a way of second-guessing his words the second it was too late to take them back.

Bristol's fingers tightened around his own.

"That was beautiful, Cam," she said gently, tracing the side of his hand with her thumb. "Thank you."

He leaned a little closer, every nerve tingling at her slightest touch.

He wanted desperately to kiss her, but even if she'd been ready, a part of his brain still had enough good sense to know that getting any closer to her here, alone in the dark, would be foolish.

"Goodnight, Bristol," he said, leaning down to plant a peck on her smooth forehead. "I'll see you in the morning."

As he closed the door behind him and walked down the hall, he couldn't contain the smile that spread over his face as he made his way toward his own office.

Chapter 16

Bristol

Bristol opened her eyes and stared up at the ceiling tiles overhead, momentary confusion gripping her before she remembered where she was. Outside the window, the sun had only just begun to rise, bathing the cityscape in shades of soft pink.

Despite the fact that she had gotten only a few hours of sleep, there was a restlessness in her limbs as she climbed out of her sleeping bag, gathered up her clothes and toiletries, and crept down the hall to the bathroom.

As she tried to button the front of her soft pink blouse, she realized that her fingertips were shaking. She felt giddy, like she imagined she would feel after downing five cups of coffee.

She gazed at her smiling reflection in the mirror over the sink, not caring that her cheeks were beginning to ache, and began brushing her teeth.

She had told Cameron about her sexual assault, and he hadn't walked away. He hadn't judged her. He hadn't blamed her.

He'd believed her.

And more than that, it was clear that even after all of these years, and how deeply she'd hurt him, he had never stopped wanting to be with her.

The realization hit her like a physical blow, and she paused where she stood, the motor of her electric toothbrush whirring in the quiet bathroom.

As much as she wanted to let him in, and to keep moving forward, it would take more than a prayer and a kiss on the forehead to quell the fears that arose in her heart.

She gave herself a final glance as she stuffed her toiletries into a cosmetic bag she'd borrowed from her mother the night before.

A little vulnerability, it seemed, had done wonders for her looks. Even though she hadn't even had the chance to shower, she felt well-rested and pretty, ready to face another day.

"Thank you, Jesus," she said softly, her voice lonely in the empty bathroom.

It wasn't much of a prayer, but she hoped He heard her just the same.

Cameron

"Hey, sorry to wake you."

Cameron raised his head from where it lay against his desk, relieved to see that no puddle of drool had settled on any of his paperwork.

"I shouldn't have fallen asleep," he said by way of greeting, glancing up at Bristol, who was resting her fingertips lightly against his shoulder.

Despite sleeping on the floor and, by the looks of it, not realizing that the FBS offices had shower facilities in the gym downstairs, she looked gorgeous and well-rested.

He reached a hand up and gave hers a squeeze, blinking away the last remnants of sleep from his eyes.

"You look stunning."

"I'm not sure about that, but thanks."

"I hope you're ready to get to work."

She glanced down at her watch. "Honestly, it's pretty convenient sleeping here, especially if Jaclyn really needs me to start this early."

He caught her gaze.

"Not exactly what I meant. The team has work to do today, as always, but I requested a morning meeting before we all get started on our usual assignments."

He felt her body tense.

Once again, he was pushing her further than she was prepared for–but he knew that however uncomfortable she was in the moment, it was the right thing to do.

"Look, just to be clear, I'm not asking you to tell everyone the kind of details that you told me," he said quickly. "But if I'm going to stop this maniac, I can't do it by myself. I need my brothers to help."

She gave him a weak smile. "I understand. I can't expect them to go in blind, and I appreciate everyone being here at the crack of dawn to figure this thing out."

"Good," he said, tilting his head back and accepting a kiss on the cheek.

Twenty minutes later, Cameron led her into a conference room, pleased to see that everyone else, including Grace, had arrived on time.

"Hey, Bristol," Gabe said from his place at the head of the table, gesturing toward a chair next to him. "Why don't you come in and take a seat?"

Cameron couldn't help but to feel a flutter of anxiety as Bristol stepped away from him and settled in next to his brother. At last he understood why she always seemed so vulnerable, even when she tried to hide behind a tough shell.

Now, though, her secret was out, and he hoped that their conversation last night had helped to give her the courage she would need in order to fight back.

"As I'm sure Cam has already made clear, you're part of the Forge Brothers Security family now," Gabe continued, giving her a warm smile, "and we take care of our own. No matter what."

Cameron took his own seat across the conference table, a couple of seats down and across the table from Bristol. Reilly and Asher were next to him, and across the table sat Grace, Ben, and Jaclyn.

"Now, before we start, we want you to know that nothing you say will leave this room without your permission, unless it's strictly necessary," Gabe continued. The others nodded in unison, and Cameron watched as Grace reached over and gave Bristol a quick hug around her shoulders.

"And I'll be enforcing that with the full weight of the law, if necessary," Jaclyn said, giving Bristol a wink. "I offered to draw up a no-gossip contract for Grace, but Gabe decided it would be overkill."

"Hey!" Grace protested as Ben began to chuckle.

Cameron couldn't hide his own smile, despite the seriousness of the situation.

He hadn't planned to invite Jaclyn–Bristol was a little bit scared of her, and he needed her to be comfortable if they were going to get everything out in the open–but in the end, he'd realized that they worked together too closely to leave her out of the loop.

In any case, she was also the only lawyer at FBS, and they would likely need her help in dealing with D&P.

"Okay, dorks," Asher chimed in, smirking in Ben's direction as Grace pretended to smack him in the ribs. "I have things to do this morning, so I think we'd better get on with it."

"Me too," Reilly chimed in, glancing up from his phone. "My wife has an ultrasound today, and I'd like to be able to make it for once."

"I'll be here all day," Ben said.

"I wish I could be," Grace said, her gaze lingering on Ben a little too long. "But I have to leave after lunch. I'm going away with my parents to Montana this weekend."

Gabe raised a hand, and the rising chatter in the room went quiet at once.

"If Bristol is ready to talk, I think it's time to listen."

He nodded toward her, and Cameron watched as she pushed her chair back, gripping the armrests tightly as she cleared her throat.

She caught his eye for a long moment, and he stared back, hoping to convey what he was feeling without the use of words.

She could do this.

She was strong.

Her voice wavered as she began to speak, giving the team a quick rundown of her pursuit of the law and her time at Columbia. But by the time she had gotten to the meat of her time at D&P, however, Cameron realized that her fear must have begun to fade away.

She relaxed her white-knuckled grip on her chair, and her voice was confident as she met the eyes of the others at the table. Her mouth was set firm as she discussed Dillon Warrington, and the way that he had fooled her into thinking he was her friend.

Righteous anger seemed to be driving her now, and Cameron listened intently as she went over that fateful encounter once again, so different from the frightened woman who had told him the same story the night before.

Finding the courage to bring darkness out into the light for all to see had given her a sense of power that all of his reassurances could never have provided, and by the time she had finished her story, he felt as though his heart would burst with admiration.

It was Jaclyn who spoke first.

"I'm not really surprised that D&P is involved," she said softly, tucking her blonde hair behind her ears. "They've gotten so huge over the last decade or so that it seemed inevitable to me that corruption would follow."

"Power corrupts, and absolute power corrupts absolutely," Ben recited, his face set in a scowl. He looked like he wanted to tear Dillon Warrington limb from limb nearly as badly as Cam did.

Despite his computer-nerd persona, he suspected that the mere sight of the huge, bulky redhead would have been enough to send the coward running.

Shame he had taken the easy way out before they got the chance.

Jaclyn nodded. "There are definitely some things I can do on the legal side to rattle their cage, so long as I have the financial backing of FBS if things go south."

"Like I said, we protect our own," Gabe said. "Let them threaten us. Our coffers are healthy. I'm not scared of them."

Bristol shook her head. "Wait, wait, wait."

"Bristol, we–" Cameron started, but she ignored him.

"I never said I wanted to rattle cages. I just want

the terror to stop, and going after D&P seems a lot like poking the bear."

"Poking the bear is what we need to do," Cameron said. "They need to know that you're not afraid of them."

There was a chorus of agreement from the rest of the table.

Bristol gave a humorless laugh. "But I am afraid of them. I worked for these people for two years. I know what they're capable of."

"And I know what this company is capable of," Gabe said calmly. "They're not just harassing you. They're poking a bear of their own."

As always, Cameron was amazed and a little jealous at the way his oldest brother could command a room, without needing to so much as raise his voice.

"Look, if the actual scumbag who hurt you is dead, then there must be a reason that someone is still harassing you," Asher said. "We need to find out what that reason is. Starting with looking into Warrington's former employer, especially considering how they treated you after the attack. We know what we're doing. You don't need to be worried."

Reilly and Grace nodded in agreement, and Cameron watched as Bristol leaned back in her chair, her brown hair fanning out behind her.

"You guys are the experts," she conceded. "If you think this is the way to go, I suppose I should have the good sense to listen."

"Cam has given this a lot of thought already," Gabe said. "And now that I have more of a picture of what we're dealing with, I agree with him. We need to begin with a direct approach. In a case like this, and dealing with potential suspects like this, there's no point in being coy."

Cameron smiled over at her, wishing that he was still at her side, able to reach out and give her hand a comforting squeeze.

He'd spent most of the night before–at least, when he wasn't obsessively checking security cameras–figuring out exactly how they were going to start investigating D&P. Even with hardly any sleep, he felt wired and ready to get going.

"I'm planning to head to their office this morning to have a nice talk, and then I have to meet with another client on my way back," he said.

"I already told them what their favorite junior associate did, and no one believed me," Bristol reminded him. "I'm not sure what you can say that's going to get anything out of them, aside from a bunch of PR-speak."

"It's going to be different coming from your personal security muscle," Grace said with a grin.

"And even more intimidating when it's backed up by threatening letters from your legal counsel," Jaclyn said, nodding to Cameron. "I'll have them signed and ready before he leaves."

Bristol looked pale. "I don't know. If they are behind this, and we push them too hard, I'm the one that's going to face their wrath. I have a feeling they won't just stop at scaring me. I could wind up–"

"Do you trust me?" Cameron cut in.

Bristol's eyes narrowed, but after a moment, he saw her relax.

"Yes," she said, her cheeks going ever so slightly pink. "I do."

"Then trust me when I say that nothing is going to happen to you," he said firmly, glancing toward his brothers, who all nodded in agreement. "We're all here to keep you safe. Just stay in the office until I get back."

"All right," Gabe said, giving his hands a loud clap. "Let's get moving. If you get time to do any investigating of your own today, go for it. We'll regroup after Cameron talks to D&P."

Cameron stayed in his seat as the others filed out of the conference room, and Bristol did the same.

He waited for their chatter to die down in the hall, and then got to his feet and hurried over to her, pulling her up from her chair and giving her a tight hug.

The thrill of being close to her hadn't faded, but despite the fact that she seemed to welcome his touch, there was an uneasiness in her eyes that hadn't been there the night before.

"Is everything okay?" he asked, forcing himself to release her.

"I'm fine," she said. "I just want you to be careful. Don't underestimate them. They're dangerous."

"I promise I'll watch my back," he said, his mouth quirking in a half-smile. "But I doubt they'll let me bring my gun into their office."

"Ha-ha," Bristol scolded. "Seriously. You know what I mean."

"I do," he said, leaning over and planting a gentle kiss on her cheek. "Be careful. I'll see you soon."

He opened the door for her and walked her to the elevator. With a final goodbye, she was gone, the silver doors sliding closed between them.

Despite her touch, and her smile, he couldn't shake the fact that something nearly imperceptible had shifted between them since the night before, but he couldn't worry about it now.

They would have time to talk more later about whatever was bothering her.

For the time being, he had a lion's den to visit.

Chapter 17

Bristol

"Hey, Melanie, I didn't know you'd be in today," Bristol said as she entered the legal department, balancing a cup of tea along with an armful of files.

"I wasn't supposed to be, but Jaclyn asked that I put in a few hours," she replied, smiling over at Bristol, her tight brown curls bouncing as she plucked away at her keyboard. "You know how she is. As soon as she assures us things are going to ease up after the latest big-deal case, she finds another one to panic over."

Bristol suppressed a grin, giving the clerk a final wave as she strode toward her own office and shut the door behind her.

She liked Melanie, but after the night and morning she'd just had, she could use some time alone—even if she had to spend it buried in paperwork.

It had felt so good to be close to Cameron the night before, but now, in the light of day, there was an undercurrent of worry that she couldn't seem to shake.

The meeting with the rest of the team had only made her more confused.

She was glad that her secret was out in the open, despite the shame that clung to her, but now, the stalker situation was out of her hands.

Cameron had taken control, just as he always had.

In some ways, it was a trait that she appreciated. She couldn't deny that he made her feel safe whenever he was around.

In other ways, though, his assertiveness bothered her.

Was this what it would be like if she entered into a relationship with him again?

Him taking the lead, and her trailing behind him, like she was nothing more than a shadow?

Before she could ponder the matter further, however, she heard a knock.

She tried her best not to sigh out loud.

"Come in."

Jaclyn entered the room, dropping three massive file folders onto Bristol's already-overflowing desk.

"Sorry," the blonde lawyer said, making a face as she fiddled with a book that she had nearly knocked onto the floor. "Those are heavy, and I wasn't sure I'd make it any longer without dropping them."

"It's fine," Bristol said, glad that she'd put her green tea safely out of reach on top of one of her filing cabinets.

"I was hoping to give you a light day after that meeting," Jaclyn said, lowering her voice to a whisper for the final words, as though Melanie might somehow hear them from her desk. "But I have a last-minute client meeting near Silver Grove, and I really need these to be dealt with before I get back, which will probably be after lunch. I had Melanie come in to help out, so maybe give her the Woodhouse revision so that you can focus on these. Again, my apologies."

"It's totally fine," she said again, giving Jaclyn a pinched smile.

The work didn't bother her. She expected that.

If anything, it was the fact that Jaclyn was being so pleasant–relatable, even–about it that set her teeth on edge.

She'd told everyone what had been done to her, and now they wouldn't ever look at her quite the same way again.

* * *

For the next two hours, Bristol focused on the task at hand, trying as hard as she could to banish her anxieties from her mind.

Every time that her fears bubbled to the surface, she pushed them down again, reminding herself that the best thing she could do right now was to show everyone—including Cameron—that she was a competent professional.

She couldn't let them see just how much her own shame threatened to throw her off balance. She refused to give anyone a reason to think that she was weak.

Besides, though tedious, her work on the Woodhouse case was important. It could be the deciding factor in whether or not justice was served in a complex fraud case, and she owed it to the client to take the endless stacks of paper seriously.

She glanced down at her watch for the fifth time in the last ten minutes.

Cameron wouldn't be back from Dorling & Porter for a while, which was a good thing, because she had no idea what she was going to say to him.

Finally, after several more minutes trying to read the dense legalese, her computer pinged with the welcome distraction of a new email.

It was Grace, asking if she was ready for a lunch break. Apparently, there was a new place a few doors over that she wanted to try before she headed off for her trip to Montana.

Bristol sat back in her seat, playing with a strand of her hair as she considered it.

Cameron had told her to stay at the office, but despite the attack the night before, she wasn't feeling super worried about taking a five minute walk during lunch hour in the middle of downtown San Antonio.

The other incidents had always happened when she was vulnerable. Whoever this predator was, he was clearly a coward, and she was confident that he wouldn't pick today to radically change his risk-averse approach to terrorizing her.

She felt her jaw going tight. She didn't have to answer to Cameron Forge, or to anybody else. She was an adult, and she could make her own decisions.

She clicked the 'reply' button and let her fingers fly over the keys, telling Grace to meet her near the back entrance in ten minutes.

She gathered up most of the papers covering her desk as quickly as she could and piled them in the top drawer of her filing cabinet, which she always kept empty and ready for use.

Jaclyn insisted that open files be locked away whenever she left the legal department for anything longer than a bathroom break, and though she found the policy a little paranoid, it was hardly the most ridiculous request she'd heard from a lawyer.

She located the key to the cabinet and clipped it to her lanyard so she could take it with her–another security requirement–and rooted through a few of the lingering stapled papers that were spilling over onto her computer keyboard.

One of the documents caught her eye, and she drew it closer, trying to think why she had noticed it at all. A bright red logo was printed at the top of the first page, nothing more than a stylized version of the company name, Grapas.

For some reason, it looked familiar, though she had no idea where she might have seen it before.

She stood there for a moment, leaning against her desk, and skimmed the document. It was just a few pages long, and it seemed to be nothing more than some sort of office supply delivery contract between this Grapas entity and FBS, followed by several old inventory and order sheets.

She wondered why Jaclyn had it instead of Grace, but it hardly mattered.

There was nothing suspicious about it, save perhaps Ben's joke order for 'one office manager who actually knows what a blotter is' scribbled in pen at the bottom of the last page.

Shaking her head, she stuck it on top of the pile of files, locked the door, and headed downstairs.

Cameron

"Thank you," Cameron said, accepting a second cup of coffee.

"Let me know if you need anything," the immaculately groomed receptionist said, smiling with all of her perfect white teeth.

He forced himself to smile back, not wanting to vent his annoyance to an innocent underling, and sat back in his chair as the woman clacked across the marble toward her desk on several-inch-high heels.

He had been waiting for more than half an hour already, and as delicious as the coffee and croissants on offer were, he hadn't come to Dorling & Porter in search of breakfast.

He sipped at the steaming, dark liquid, images of Bristol filling his head every second that he tried to relax.

He could imagine the expression on her face after this morning's meeting, and the guarded look that her pretty green eyes had once again begun to hold.

She said she trusted him, but he could tell that part of her was still holding back, and it was frustrating.

He knew what he was doing, and so did the rest of FBS, but that, it seemed, was not enough in her eyes.

Neither were the gentle touches of their fingertips the night before, their hands entwined in the dark as he kissed her forehead.

Those moments had been so perfect, so beautiful, like traveling back in time to another life that he thought he'd lost forever.

The possibility that he had messed everything up somehow was almost too much to bear.

And yet, he couldn't shake the fear that that was exactly what had happened.

He could almost see the walls going up around her heart once again, and it required all of his self control to sit here and wait instead of running back to FBS.

All he wanted was to be alone with her again, somewhere they could talk, where he could find out where he stood, but he knew that pressing Bristol would only make things worse.

In a way, he supposed, God was looking out for him by keeping him from acting rashly.

Instead of being in a position to say or do something stupid, he was trapped right here in the lobby of D&P, his imprisonment complete with complimentary baked goods.

"Cameron Forge?"

He snapped his head up, his coffee wobbling dangerously close to the edge of the glass mug before he set it on the table.

Standing in front of him was a tall black woman in a gray suit, her neck, ears, and several of her fingers accented with gold jewelry. So far, it seemed that the firm had quite the dress code. He wondered if Bristol had been given a clothing allowance, or if she'd been expected to spend half of her pay on passably designer suits instead of saving more money for law school.

"Hello," he said, getting up from his seat and extending a hand toward the woman, who shook it firmly. "You must be Georgia Porter."

She gave him a warm smile. "Actually, I'm Takara Keith. I'm a junior associate, but I'm happy to assist you with whatever you need."

"I think there's been a misunderstanding," Cameron said. "As I explained at the front desk, this is a very sensitive matter, and I need to speak to one of the senior partners."

"You'll need an appointment, I'm afraid," she said. "They're currently booking about three weeks out, but it might be possible to get you in a little sooner–"

Cameron didn't wait for her to finish before

taking the folder he'd been carrying under his arm and laying it open on the coffee table.

He forced his voice to remain friendly as he pointed to the documents that Jaclyn had drawn up.

"I'm not waiting three weeks, Ms. Keith. I'm speaking to a senior partner *today*."

Bristol

Bristol pushed open the nondescript side door of Forge Brothers Security and stepped out onto the sidewalk, a brisk breeze lifting her hair and fluttering against her skin.

"It feels so good to have the sun on my face," she said, turning to Grace beside her. "I've spent way too much time shut up indoors."

"I'm enjoying it while I can," Grace said, closing her eyes and letting the sun fall across her already-bronzed skin. "It's going to be freezing in Montana. This Texas girl usually prefers to head further south in the winter, but my parents weren't having it."

She opened her eyes again, gesturing to the right, and the two women headed off down the street, passing several other smartly-dressed men and women on their own lunch breaks.

"Are you and your parents staying away for long?" Bristol asked, glancing over her shoulder.

"No, only a few days," Grace said, making a face. "As much as I hate snow, I wish we would have made it to Cobalt River Ranch in time for Christmas. I'm sure it was beautiful."

"Handsome cowboys and prancing horses sound pretty lovely to me, even in February," Bristol said.

She had spent Christmas with her mother, at home in Silver Grove, and the rest of the year would be the same. Vacations hadn't been a part of their lives since her dad had walked out.

"I'm sure you're right," Grace said, "though cowboys aren't really my type."

Bristol gave her an exaggerated eye roll. She couldn't exactly picture Ben roping cattle.

A few minutes later they had settled in at the neighborhood's newest lunch haunt, and were working their way through a platter of mini sandwiches.

Bristol had already forgotten the name of the place by the time she had gotten through half of her tea. It was nice enough, and the food was tasty, but it lacked the memorable old-school charm of the Screaming Peach.

She tried to focus on her conversation with Grace, thankful for the chance to keep things light for the first time in what felt like days, but she couldn't help but to give her surroundings a once-over every couple of minutes.

Though she saw nothing and no one that worried her, Cameron's warning to stay in the office echoed in her ears.

She'd noticed Grace watching, too, her eyes roving over the entrance every time someone new walked in. Despite her office manager role, Bristol was sure she'd learned a thing or two in her time at FBS, and she was thankful that her new friend was taking things seriously.

Even though she'd been willing to take the small risk of going out for a bite to eat, she had no doubt as to what her pursuer might be capable of. Last night's break-in had proved as much.

Just as Bristol had swallowed the final bites of her cheese and cucumber on rye, Grace's phone rang, the ringtone sudden and loud in the calm of the restaurant.

"Jerusalem crickets!" she said, fumbling to answer the call.

Bristol grinned into the top of her drink. She'd forgotten how much she missed what passed for swearing in Texas.

"Sorry, mom, I lost track of time," Grace was saying into the phone, tapping on the glittery pink case with a long acrylic nail. "We're still at that new place. I don't remember! It's the one with the green stripe-y awning, across from the yarn store. No, not by the Joann's! Downtown, mum. He'll figure it out. Yes. Okay, love you too."

She hung up, opening the gaping maw of her Louis Vuitton tote bag and tossing the phone inside.

"Sorry about that. I was going to get picked up at FBS. Anyway, the driver will be here in a second, and we'll drop you off on the way."

Bristol shook her head. "It's in the opposite direction of the airport," she said, glancing down at her own watch. "And didn't you say your flight was at two?"

"I hope that's not what I said," Grace said with a grimace, reaching back into her bag and digging around until she pulled out her wallet. "But probably. Are you sure you can get back okay?"

Bristol wrapped her fingers around her mug as a familiar ripple of anxiety traced down her spine.

She was tired of living in fear. FBS was just around the corner. If she kept her eyes open, she'd be fine.

"I'm fine," she said firmly.

"I can get you an Uber," Grace suggested, pulling out several bills from her wallet and placing them on the table.

"You're already buying me lunch, apparently," Bristol said. "Don't be silly. I'd feel ridiculous asking an Uber driver to take me a few hundred feet away."

"They'd probably just think you're a celebrity or something."

Bristol glanced down at her basic knee-length skirt, pink blouse, and logo-free work tote.

"I don't think so."

"Fine," Grace said with an exaggerated sigh. "But if anything happens to you, Cameron will kill me. So be careful."

Bristol followed her from the table and out the front door.

Barely a minute later, a sleek black Lincoln town car with tinted windows rolled to a stop in front of them. She had a feeling that her friend had been mistaken for a celebrity more than once.

"Make sure to text me some photos while you're there," Bristol said, leaning over and wrapping Grace in a tight hug. "I demand horses, and I won't say no to cowboys. Or food! Don't forget to show me the food."

"Yes, ma'am," Grace said, tipping an invisible ten-gallon hat in her direction before climbing into the back seat.

The town car headed off down the street, swept up into the San Antonio traffic in an instant, and Bristol found herself completely alone.

She started down the sidewalk in the direction of the office, and with every step that she took, a little bit of the fear faded away.

There was something about the chilly winter air, the friendly smiles of the people she passed, and even the occasional carelessly thrown empty coffee cup that made her remember what she loved about the city.

It felt vibrant. It felt alive, especially today, and she felt alive right along with it.

She drew in a breath, the cool air filling her lungs as the winter sun continued to warm her skin.

As she turned the corner onto the back street that led toward the FBS garage and side entrance, she surveyed the street for anyone out of place, finding it deserted save for a few nice-looking cars parked further up the block.

The assault had taken so much from her.

It had clouded every waking moment of her life, a constant darkness that followed her everywhere.

And today, for just a moment, she'd been able to forget about it.

To walk down the street like she used to do, back when the world seemed a whole lot brighter, back when–

She felt a tight grip closing around her upper arm, her stream of thoughts rushing to a halt.

She tried to turn, but she couldn't.

Whoever held her was strong.

It was a man. That was all she knew. She tried to squirm away, hoping for even a brief glance at him, but his fingers were like a vice around her bicep. He didn't even seem to be struggling.

Panic welled in her chest, her heart racing, thumping again and again.

She was stuck. Helpless. Weak. Just like she had been that night.

No.

It was different. This time, there were people around, people who would step in.

She opened her mouth to scream, but she never got the chance.

"Scream and you're dead," came a voice, dangerously quiet.

She felt a hard object being jammed into the small of her back.

She swallowed the bile that had risen into the back of her throat.

It was a gun. It had to be.

He shoved her forward, suspending her weight effortlessly as she tripped over an uneven piece of sidewalk paving.

"Move," the man said, his voice a whisper in her ear. "Now. And look natural."

She had no choice but to comply, forcing her feet to move one after the other.

As she walked, she tried to take in her surroundings, desperate for anyone or anything that might help her to break free.

There was a white van she didn't recognize parked a few doors up from the unmarked side entrance.

She had little doubt it was where he was going to take her.

She turned to the office, praying she'd see one of her colleagues in one of the few smaller windows at this side of the building.

It was lunch. Most of the staff would be out, or in the cafeteria, which was on the other side of the first floor.

Still, there would be a couple of security guys nearby. There had to be, and surely the man breathing down the back of her neck knew it, too.

He just didn't care, and that terrified her almost as much as the gun pressed into her spine.

Chapter 18

Cameron

Cameron sat at a red light, ignoring the two teenage girls who were pointing and staring at the company-owned Maserati he was currently driving. He'd wanted to show D&P that he meant business, but now that the meeting had finally ended, he was eager to trade the ostentatious vehicle for his familiar green Jeep.

He tapped his fingers on the steering wheel as a stream of cars continued to pass in front of him. He'd already had to cancel the client meeting he'd intended to attend, which meant an even busier day tomorrow.

Despite his efforts, the whole thing had been nothing but a waste of time.

After some convincing, he'd managed to get in to see Albert Dorling himself, but the old man had been even more slippery than he'd expected.

He'd made it sound as though D&P had taken the assault seriously, and that Bristol had overreacted, even bringing out a file confirming that Dillon Warrington had been terminated mere weeks after the attack.

The senior partner had claimed that Bristol demanded he be fired immediately, and didn't want to wait for an internal investigation to be done, which had led to immediate tension in the office. Even then, according to Dorling, they'd never tried to force her out.

She'd simply quit on her own, unhappy that he and the other partners had not simply taken her word at face value and fired one of their most promising associates.

Cameron shook his head to himself as the light finally turned green, and he eased the sleek car forward into yet another tangle of seemingly endless traffic.

Jaclyn's printed legal threats taunted him from where they lay on the passenger seat.

The whole thing was ridiculous.

Dorling had given him no real explanation as to why he and the other partners hadn't gone to the police. He'd insisted that in order to protect their clients from media blowback, it was their policy to conduct rigorous internal investigations as a first step, especially when the credibility of an accusation was in doubt.

Of course, when Cameron had asked the man what he was trying to say about Bristol's credibility, he refused to answer.

It was infuriating.

He believed Bristol's story completely, but he also knew that D&P had had plenty of time to get their own story planned out. The paper trail would be impeccable.

As he pressed gently on the gas, inching forward as far as he could before red tail lights lit up ahead of him again, he tried to look on the bright side.

There was one faint glimmer of hope that he'd managed to uncover.

When he'd asked Albert Dorling about Warrington's suicide, the man had put on an impressive display of surprise, but Cam wasn't fooled. Despite the partner's insistence that the man had simply been fired, Cam was certain that he knew about his untimely death. And for some reason, he didn't want Cam to know that he knew.

He reached over into the console and took hold of his phone, using voice control to dial Allie Parker, their police liaison. She didn't answer, so he left a brief voicemail asking her if she could give him some more intel on a recent suicide case.

Ben could find the records by other means, if necessary, but he tried to keep FBS within the law–and within the good graces of the San Antonio Police Department–whenever he could.

Finally, after several more minutes in bumper-to-bumper traffic, he pulled onto the quiet side street that led toward the FBS garage.

As soon as the familiar building came into view, however, something strange caught his eye.

There was a white van parked along the sidewalk, near the side entrance rather than the ramp that led into the garage.

He slowed the car, squinting at the logo on the back of the van, but the majority of it had been scratched off, the peeling paint revealing streaks of rust.

Definitely strange.

It was a wealthy neighborhood full of upscale businesses and homes, and there was minimal street parking. Usually, any car he saw parked here was at least as decent as his Jeep.

He saw movement out of the corner of his eye, and forced himself to turn slowly, pressing gently on the brake without coming to a complete stop.

He felt as though his heart had stopped beating.

It was Bristol, rounding the corner, with a tall man in a neat navy-blue suit walking directly behind her.

His fingers were clamped around her upper arm,

and it was clear by the expression on her face that she was not being led willingly.

He accelerated slightly and reached for his phone again, not daring to stop or to do anything else that would set the guy off.

Not yet.

They were headed for the van, he was sure of it, and he only had moments before they reached it.

Fingers shaking, he hit Gabe's number in the recent call list, praying that he would answer. As soon as he did, he spoke, not bothering to wait for a greeting.

"Gabe, it's an emergency," he said under his breath. "Don't talk. We need the police to block off Costa Street and Cherry Road, and I need immediate, armed backup at the side entrance and the garage. Hurry."

He hung up, confident that Gabe would handle his requests in mere minutes, but minutes would be too long if he wanted to save Bristol before she was shoved into that van.

His knuckles white against the leather of the steering wheel, he eased the Maserati into a parallel space a few cars up from the van, not daring to look over his shoulder to check on Bristol.

He took a deep breath, grabbed his pistol from the glove box, and slid out through the passenger door.

Bristol

Bristol walked as slowly as possible, desperate to buy herself every second of time that she could.

She tried to ignore the feeling of the gun against her back, but all she could imagine was it going off, and the pain blinding her as the bullet lodged into her spine.

She closed her eyes for several long seconds, letting the man guide her closer to the van, struggling to fill her lungs with air.

She never thought she'd feel as helpless as she had that night in Dillon Warrington's office.

She was wrong.

She opened her eyes, a surge of anger rising within her.

"What do you want?" she demanded, figuring if he wanted to kill her, he was going to do it anyway, whether she angered him or not.

He didn't answer, and ignoring her terror, she turned her head as far as she could while still walking, trying to get a look at his face.

She felt a fresh jolt of pain searing down her tailbone as the man jabbed her again, hard.

"Nice try," he said, chuckling. "Face forward, act natural. Just a sexy girl on a date with her handsome boyfriend."

Before she could decide whether to push the man further, she noticed Cameron cruising past them, facing straight ahead, driving some kind of black sports car she didn't recognize.

She did as the man had told her to, facing straight ahead even as she heard Cameron pulling the car to a stop somewhere up ahead.

The man behind her didn't seem to have recognized him. He probably thought he was one of the usual wealthy civilians who frequented the area, looking for a decent parking space while he shopped or ate nearby.

She wanted to scream at him to get away, to go around to the front and to call the police.

This man wanted her alive, at least for the next few minutes, but she had no reason to think he'd have any qualms with gunning Cam down in broad daylight.

It was all her fault.

If she'd listened to him, neither of them would be in danger now. Instead, she'd chosen her own pride, and she couldn't bear the idea of Cameron paying the price.

As the van drew nearer, she heard the sound of a phone ringing behind her.

The man paused, pulling her to a stop while he answered. She could still feel the gun touching her back, but he'd eased up some, mumbling something into the phone that she couldn't make out.

Clearly, the man was distracted, but she'd never make it to the side door or the garage gate if he decided to open fire as she ran. Her sanctuary was so close, but at the moment, it may as well have been on the moon.

"Okay, okay, I hear you," the man was saying, his voice rough and loud against her ears. He made no effort to lower his volume.

Not that anyone else save Cameron was around.

She couldn't make out any other words on the other end, but she could hear yelling.

"Calm down, boss–"

There was another angry shout, and then the phone went silent.

Her captor shifted his body forward until he was standing beside her, but the insistent press of the barrel of the gun kept her looking at her feet rather than up at his face.

She saw him raise the phone in the direction of the van, but she couldn't see if anyone else was there.

She saw only the pavement beneath her feet, rushing past altogether too quickly.

Any second now, they'd reach the white van.

Her prison.

She risked a tilt of her head, her breaths quickening as she felt the snare closing around her, desperate for anything or anyone that could help her to break free.

She saw Cam, crouching between two parked cars. He caught her eye and placed a finger to his lips. She couldn't even nod.

She could only stare as the sun glinted off of the sleek black gun in his hand.

Cameron

Cameron felt the familiar weight of the Beretta as he rested against the front fender of a parked car, trying to catch his breath and to think of any way he could approach the man in the suit without getting Bristol shot.

For the first time in his private security career, he wished that one of his brothers was in his place, preferably Gabe. He wouldn't be panicking, not after his years in war-torn, unpredictable Afghanistan. His own background in the family agriculture business just wasn't cutting it.

Gabe would have had a plan by now. He would have *acted* by now.

As Bristol came briefly into view, he gestured for her to remain quiet and calm, willing her to understand.

The haunted look in her eyes made his palms sweat, but he couldn't let her see how terrified he was. No. Help was on the way. In the meantime, he'd just have–

Everything happened at once.

He heard the driver's side door of the van slamming shut before he saw it, watching as a man fled across the street, toward an alleyway two buildings over from FBS.

The man holding Bristol shoved her toward the ground without warning, taking off after his friend at a run.

Cameron watched as her body crumpled against the solid concrete, adrenaline coursing through his veins as he got to his feet, gun raised.

He raced out from between the cars, fumbling for his phone with his free hand as he covered the distance, voice dialing Gabe for a second time.

"Gabe, they're on foot. Two guys, white or possibly hispanic, cutting through the alleyway beside Hoffman Jewelry. They left their van."

By the time he reached Bristol's side, she was already getting to her feet. Relief flooded through him as he helped her up.

"I'm fine," she insisted as he took her elbow, leading her gently toward the side door. Her legs were shaking beneath her, but she didn't appear to be hurt.

He glanced off toward the alleyway, every nerve on high alert. All he wanted to do was to stay with her, but he couldn't bear the thought of letting them get away.

He couldn't afford to be indecisive.

"Go inside and get upstairs," he commanded, releasing her and gesturing toward the door as he gave a final glance up the now-empty street. "I'll be right back."

She nodded, her eyes filling with tears as she took off at a run.

By the time her fingers took hold of the door handle, he was already running, his muscles pumping as he ducked into the shadowy space between the two buildings.

He dodged trash bags and piles of cardboard, willing himself not to trip, until finally he emerged on the busy street in front of FBS.

His breath burned in his lungs as he came to a stop, shoving his gun into the back of his jeans, his eyes scanning the busy road for anything out of place. He hadn't even asked for a roadblock here, and now he was kicking himself for it.

Leaning against the front of the building, he closed his eyes, pressing his fingertips against his temples as he tried to gather his memories of the men before their faces began to mingle with everyone else he saw.

He'd gotten a decent enough look at the man who had taken Bristol.

He was of average height and build, with tan skin, dark hair, and dark eyes. Normal nose, normal ears, normal mouth. There was very little to differentiate him from half of the other men he saw on any given day, aside from perhaps how well he was dressed. Even his race was ambiguous.

He swore under his breath, ignoring the stares as people walked by him, no doubt noticing that his face was slick with sweat.

Pulling out his phone, he sent Gabe another text, letting him know that their potential break in the case had just disappeared into the crowds of downtown San Antonio.

Chapter 19

Bristol

Bristol sat back in her chair, trying to stop her fingers from shaking as Jaclyn looked over at her, her eyes brimming with concern.

The two of them sat in the upstairs lounge, and despite the fact that the lawyer had brought her coffee instead of tea, the familiar room was comforting.

Still, she struggled to let herself relax. Despite the logical fact that she was safe here, her body insisted on remaining in fight or flight mode.

"Bristol, I'm so sorry," she heard Cam say, his muscled form taking up a good portion of the doorway as he rushed into the room.

Before she could say anything, he was next to her, leaning over and crushing her in a desperate embrace.

He lingered there for several long seconds, and she could feel the racing of his heart through the sweat-soaked dress shirt and jacket that he had worn to his meeting with D&P.

She forced her breaths to follow his own, and to her surprise, the closeness helped.

At last, she felt a little of the tension in her own muscles melting away.

However confused and muddled her feelings were, her body didn't lie.

When he was near her, her heart rate slowed, her hands stopped shaking, and her lungs remembered how to breathe.

She was safe.

She was safe because even when it was her own stupidity that got her into trouble, he was willing to put his own life on the line to protect her.

"I'm sorry," she said, pulling away, a fresh wave of guilt replacing the peace she'd felt just seconds before.

"Can we have a moment, Jaclyn?" Cameron said, glancing over at the lawyer, who got up from her own seat in an instant. "Of course, sorry," she said, giving a jerky little laugh as she strode toward the door on her practical two-inch heels. "If you need anything at all, Bristol, I'll be back in my office."

Bristol thanked her, and listened until her footsteps had disappeared down the hall before turning back to meet Cameron's eyes.

"I know I should have stayed at FBS," she said. "I messed up. I'm so sorry. I should have listened."

Cameron shook his head, anger flashing in his blue eyes. "I thought I'd lost you. I had no plan, and backup wasn't going to make it before you reached the van. I don't know if I would have made it to you in time, not without you getting shot."

She watched the muscles in forearms tighten as he rested his elbows on the table in front of them, her untouched mug of coffee sending plumes of steam into the air.

"I didn't get shot," she said. "I'm not hurt, just shaken up. I promise."

"You didn't get shot because those lowlifes decided to abandon their plan!"

His voice was so loud that for a moment, she sat back, stunned.

Cameron Forge never raised his voice. Certainly not in front of her.

She said nothing, glancing down at her lap, feeling guiltier than before.

He was right.

She had walked directly into danger, and so far as she could tell, only Providence had prevented the situation ending with her tied up in the back of a van, or worse.

"I stood there paralyzed while the woman that I–" Cameron started to yell again, but as he glimpsed the look on her face, he lowered his voice. "I almost let someone I care about get hurt because I couldn't think of a plan. It was like my mind went blank. I panicked back there, and in this business, that's not something I can afford to do."

She nodded numbly, feeling even worse than she had a few moments before.

Whatever he'd been about to let slip, it proved her fears true.

Why did he have to care about her so much?

All she'd ever done was hurt him, and make him feel like he'd never be good enough.

Was that how he felt now?

She watched as he blinked away what might have been tears, resting his forehead in his hands.

If he honestly thought that this was his fault, nothing she could say would change anything.

The adrenaline had faded away now, and all at once she realized that all she could feel was the ache in her spine where the thug had repeatedly jabbed her with his gun.

Cameron

"Why did they let me go?" Bristol asked after several long seconds, releasing a shaky breath as she spoke.

"I have no clue. None of it makes any sense," Cam said.

He looked over at her, his heart shattering anew as he watched her brush at her eyes with the pink sleeve of her now-ruined shirt.

How much trauma could one person be expected to endure, even someone as tough as Bristol?

He doubted that God would give him an answer, and the thought filled him with bitterness that made him feel even more ashamed than he did already.

"I saw the guy who grabbed you take a phone call before he bolted," he said. "Did you hear anything?"

She shook her head, her brow furrowed in concentration. "Not a whole lot. But I know that he called whoever was on the other end 'boss', and I could hear said 'boss' yelling. I just couldn't make out the words on his end."

"So it was a male voice? Could you tell how old? Any accent?"

"I'm certain it was a man. But I couldn't make out anything else."

Cameron picked at a hangnail on his thumb, trying to think of something she might have overlooked.

Even if she had been able to guess at the man's age or ethnicity, he doubted her judgment in regard to either would have been accurate, anyway. Eyewitnesses were notorious for getting the details wrong, especially in moments of extreme stress, and in any case, he was a security operative, not a trained police interviewer.

Still, it was worth trying to get as clear of a picture as he could of what had taken place.

"Okay," he said, letting out a breath. "Can you tell me what happened, from the beginning?"

Bristol recounted how she had gone to lunch with Grace, and how their friend had left for her trip directly from the restaurant instead of from FBS as she'd planned.

Cameron was frustrated with Hinton's role in the whole mess, but decided to hold his tongue. When news of the day's excitement reached her in Montana, she'd be angry enough at herself already. There was no point in placing blame.

What was done was done, Bristol had made it back in one piece in the end, and all that he could do was make sure that there was no next time.

"So after Grace left, you didn't see anyone suspicious on the sidewalk out front, correct?" he prompted.

"I was looking over my shoulder constantly, and no, I saw no one. Not out front and not on the connecting street. I turned the corner and that street was quiet, too. Someone grabbed me from behind. I never got a good look at him, just at his back as he took off. It's possible he blended in so well that I didn't take note of him as I walked back to FBS."

The thought made the hairs on the back of Cameron's neck stand up.

After what Bristol had survived at the hands of Dillon Warrington, she was almost certainly even more vigilant than the average women, and women's instincts were generally excellent when it came to their safety. And yet, this man had likely been able to sneak up behind her after following her in broad daylight.

This left open two possibilities.

Either this man was a cunning psychopath of the highest order, able to hide completely among the general public as he pursued his prey, or, more likely, he was nothing more than a hired goon who didn't set off Bristol's alarm bells because he saw her as nothing more than a package to pick up and deliver.

"Anyway, after he grabbed me, he had a gun to my back, so I didn't want to look around too much and get hurt," she continued. "But just before he ran, I saw him raise his phone toward the van."

Cameron nodded, pushing aside his criminal psychology theories for the time being.

"It was probably just what it looked like–a signal to the driver that it was time to bail."

"I tried to get a look at the driver, too, but I didn't even really see his back. I was distracted and confused when he shoved me down. I wasn't expecting it."

Cameron noticed her eyes moving toward her scraped knee and dirt-encrusted skirt, and he felt fury rising within him again at the thought of how these men had hurt her.

"From what little I could see as they took off," he said, forcing himself to stay calm for Bristol's sake, "I would guess that both guys were in their late thirties, white or hispanic, and totally unremarkable."

"That sounds right. Do you know if the van is still down there?"

Cameron nodded.

"Probably will be for a while. Gabe would have called SAPD by now, and they'll probably bring in the bomb squad to secure the area just in case, though I'm pretty sure they won't find much. I think it was exactly what it looked like, just a simple getaway vehicle, at least until their plans changed at the last minute."

Bristol shivered and picked up one of the mugs of coffee sitting on the table, curling her hands around it as though it might displace the chill of fear that she felt.

"I guess God has been looking out for me," she said after a brief pause, giving him a tight smile.

He smiled back.

Despite the chaos that continued to surround them, all he wanted right then was to bring her to church on Sunday and hold her hand in the pew. But that fantasy would have to wait.

As it was, Bristol looked shaken. Now that he was no longer holding her, she seemed to be pulling away from him, keeping her distance.

It wasn't the time to push, however badly he wanted to hug her again and tell her everything would be okay.

"Do you have any idea what's going on with all of this?" she asked, her voice small in the quiet of the lounge. "Any hunches, any brilliant insight as to why Dillon Warrington's evil twin, or whoever else, is after me?"

He felt the muscles in his jaw tighten.

He wanted so badly to tell her something better, but for the moment, all he had was the truth.

"I have no idea, Bristol. If I'm being honest, I'm even more confused about why you're being targeted now than I was before."

Bristol

The emotional magnitude of the day's events seemed to hit Bristol all at once.

Not even Cameron had any idea what was going on, and she certainly didn't.

Suddenly dizzy, she put her head in her hands, not bothering to quell the tears that had begun to flow in force.

She heard Cameron pushing his chair back and getting up, closing the distance between them in moments.

Before he could reach her, however, she got to her feet, bumping the table and making the ceramic mug rattle against the wooden surface.

She felt like she was going to suffocate.

This, all of this, was way too much.

She thought that by coming here, she'd be able to start over, to escape the damage that

Warrington had caused, but there was no way out. Certainly not here.

"I'm sorry," she stammered, refusing to meet his eyes as she started to walk toward the door. He followed, his footsteps heavy against the floor, but he didn't come close enough to touch her. "I'm sorry for coming here and for putting you, your brothers, and everyone else at FBS at risk."

"This isn't your fault," Cameron said, his voice firm. "No. We're not afraid of these people. We're all committed to putting an end to this terror and keeping you safe. You belong here."

She stopped walking, pressing her eyes shut for a long moment.

He sounded so sincere, so willing to put up with any level of danger, just because–for whatever delusional reason–he wanted her close to him.

Her heart was racing again, willing her to turn around, to wrap her arms around his neck, to let his breathing guide her own.

But she couldn't do it.

She'd already gotten too close, and today had

made it clear that it was too dangerous. She had to get away, for all of their sakes.

She swallowed, turning to face him at last, not wanting to utter the words that she knew she had to say.

"Bristol, you need to stop," he said huskily, raising his hand as though he was about to reach out and touch her before letting it fall to his side once more. "We want you here. *I* want you here."

She drew a long breath, sending up a silent prayer and begging for forgiveness for the hurt she was about to cause.

"Maybe that's part of the problem, Cameron," she said, forcing herself to meet his eyes. "You want me as this woman who wants to follow your lead, who knows how to trust you more than I trust myself. And I'm just not that girl."

He crossed his arms over his chest, waiting for her to finish.

The fact that he hadn't interrupted her made it even worse.

"I wasn't that girl back then, either, which is why I had to reject your proposal–"

"It's why you ran away, you mean," Cameron said flatly.

"I thought that maybe things were different now. Since you came back into my life, I thought maybe I'd changed. But I haven't. I keep falling back into old patterns and making the same mistakes, and I don't know how to stop."

"You don't have to be perfect," Cam said, shaking his head. "You just need to try. That's all I could hope to ask of you. Don't be like this."

The hurt in his eyes was too much to bear.

She looked down at the ground, cheeks burning with shame, but she couldn't stop now.

She wouldn't. Not when he could have died today trying to save her.

Not when he was so determined to love her, even when all she knew how to do was to offer pain in return.

"I can't. Trying isn't good enough. Not when the stakes are this high," she said, unable to conceal the way her voice was shaking. "I can't do this. I'm sorry."

Chapter 20

Cameron

Cameron waited for Bristol to finish, each sentence washing over him like freezing water.

At last, she had said what she wanted.

She didn't move any closer to the door, and he willed himself to remain where he stood, not wanting to give her the satisfaction of listening to him beg.

He'd tried so many times, but in the end, perhaps he really was just pathetic.

She'd been telling him the truth from the start.

She didn't want him. Maybe she didn't want love at all.

Coming here was about nothing more than collecting a paycheck, and he'd been too naive to realize it.

Or maybe he'd just pushed her too hard, trying to force her to be vulnerable, even after knowing what that filth Warrington had done to her.

He'd been so focused on his picture-perfect idea of mending what was broken, when Bristol Chaplin had made it clear over and over again that she didn't want to be fixed.

It was his fault, he knew, but still he couldn't shake the anger that kept him rooted in place, facing off with a woman who had every reason to keep walking out of the lounge, out of the office, and out of his life.

Several more seconds passed.

Still, she didn't leave.

He let out a sigh, his indignation melting away into defeat.

He lifted his hands in the air, as though he was surrendering.

Maybe that was exactly what he was doing.

"I understand what you're saying," he said. "I do. And I promise, I am not going to try and change your mind. If you want me to leave you alone, I'll leave you alone. Message received, loud and clear. I should have figured it out before now."

She crossed her arms over her chest, raising her eyes to meet his own for just a moment before her gaze fell to the floor once more.

"But," he continued, trying to suppress the bitterness that had seeped into his words, "today has made it very clear just how much danger you're in. Now. Present tense."

"I'll figure out a way to stay safe," Bristol said. "I'll get out of San Antonio, maybe even Texas. I can go back to New York if I really have to."

He tightened his fists, his fingernails biting into his palm.

"Whoever is after you has almost succeeded twice now. All while you were under the protection of the best private security firm in the state. Not to offend your independent woman sensibilities or anything, Bristol, but you don't stand a chance against these people on your own."

He waited for her biting retort, but to his surprise, it didn't come.

"I can't stay here. I'm putting everyone at risk."

"Everyone here has signed up for risk. It's part of the job, even for non-operatives. This is the best place for us to keep you safe. Let me do my job."

He paused, their eyes meeting as she considered his words.

Risking his life to protect his clients was something he'd gotten used to.

But risking his heart?

Maybe that was more than he'd bargained for.

Bristol

As she searched Cameron's eyes, she felt her resolve beginning to slip.

He wasn't so easy to push away, even if she knew she had to, even just to keep him safe.

The man was infuriating.

"I appreciate everything that you, your brothers, and your staff have done for me," she said, knotting her fingers together behind her back so that her hands couldn't shake. "But I have to go. I can't just hide away here."

"So running off to hide in New York is better? Have you already forgotten last time, or do you need to make the same mistake again, just to be sure?"

Cameron's words stung.

He was right, and they both knew it.

She'd run off to university to find her freedom, but it had never worked out like she'd hoped.

She wondered how much gossip Cameron had heard about her time in Manhattan. The expense and the stress of Columbia had been a burden, sure, but in the end it was the loneliness that had been too much to bear.

Despite the thousands of people she passed every day, she'd never felt more invisible—just as Cameron had warned her, all those years ago.

God had been the only one left who cared, but she'd pushed Him away, too.

Before she could think of anything she could say in her own defense, Cameron took a half step toward her, his tone softening as he spoke again.

"What are you going to do about your mom?" he asked. "Her house isn't safe, clearly, and I wouldn't be surprised if whoever is after you knows everything about her as well. Whatever you choose, I hope she'll accept our help. The offer is open, whatever you decide."

She felt a flicker of anxiety dancing in the pit of her stomach.

She couldn't put her mother at risk.

"I appreciate that, and I am sure she'd be willing to take you up on any protection you can offer, but this person has made it pretty clear they're after me. If I go away, I suspect they will, too."

"Not to sound like a jerk again," Cameron said, giving her a humorless smile, "but it might not be all about you, Bristol. It seems pretty clear to me that there's more going on than we can see right now, especially with D&P.

"When I talked to them today, it seemed pretty clear that Albert Dorling knew about Dillon

Warrington's apparent suicide, but he tried to sound surprised."

Bristol frowned. "That's odd. Why would he know about it, and if he found out in some innocuous way, why lie?"

"Exactly," Cam said, nodding. "It's weird, and FBS is going to look into it. Look, whatever you want to do, something's going on, and I'm not going to call off the digging until we find a bone."

She glanced up at him, her gaze tracing the chiseled line of his jaw and the firm line of his mouth. He meant every word.

Another crack in her armor.

Another reason not to run.

Why did he always have to do the right thing?

He closed the distance between them in a couple of long strides, resting a hand gently on the top of her shoulder.

"Even if you don't want anything more than friendship with me—heck, even if you don't want anything to do with me at all—you should keep working here at FBS," he said.

His blue eyes were filled with hurt, she could tell, but only because she'd known him all her life.

Anyone else would see only his loyalty, and his determination to protect the innocent, no matter what.

"Let those jerks at D&P know that you're not backing down. Give me and the team time to figure out who's doing this. Please."

The seconds passed, but he did not let his hand fall away.

She could feel the warmth and strength emanating from him.

Just touching her shoulder, apparently, was enough to make her question every word she'd said.

If he leaned in and kissed her, she knew she'd never find the strength to push him away. But he wouldn't try, wouldn't press her into anything she didn't want.

He'd keep his word: she'd stay on as paralegal, and he and the other Forge boys would hunt down her stalker before she once again became his prey.

"You're right," she said at last. "I'll stay here until you guys catch the baddies, but after that, I have to find something else. Deal?"

He finally broke the connection between them, running his hand through his dark hair, contemplating.

"Fine."

"Good," she said, giving him a brisk nod.

"Are you willing to keep sleeping here in the office for now? I'll be able to find you a more comfortable bed before a safehouse opens up, I promise."

His tone was casual, but she could read the underlying concern, and her heart began to ache anew.

"For now, I would rather be here than at home, bringing this chaos straight to mom's doorstep," she admitted. "Though if we could find a better arrangement for her, at least until we know that no one is going to go after her, I'd appreciate it."

Cameron nodded. "I'll figure something out."

"Thank you," Bristol said, giving him a final glance before turning toward the door.

"Where are you going?" he asked. "Are you sure you're okay? You should rest for the rest of the afternoon."

She shook her head, pausing against the doorframe.

"I have to catch up with Jaclyn. Attempted kidnapping or no attempted kidnapping, there's a lot to do today. And after that, I have my own research to do on Dorling & Porter, Attorneys at Law."

Chapter 21

Bristol

"Hey, I have the records you asked for," Cameron said, lingering at the threshold of her office.

"Great," Bristol said, smiling a little too brightly as she got up from behind her desk. "Jaclyn did say something about the El Paso job, though, so I might need to email you about those records, too."

"No problem," he replied easily, reaching out to hand her the stack of papers.

His fingertips brushed hers for less than a

second, but it was enough to make her heart flutter.

With an awkward wave, Cameron headed out of the office, said goodbye to Melanie as he passed her desk, and strode off down the hall.

She let out a puff of breath, sinking back into her chair and adding the new paperwork to the pile that had accumulated on her desk over the course of the morning.

More than two weeks had passed since she'd told him she was pulling away from him, and no one had made much progress on figuring out who was after her.

Fortunately, there had been no further incidents, but seeing as an open safehouse had yet to materialize–apparently, winter was a busy time of year for personal protection services–she'd spent most of her life trapped within the four walls of Forge Brothers Security.

She'd used the time to focus on her work as intensely as she could, and it seemed to be paying off in her working relationship with Jaclyn. She'd finally begun to really feel as though she had a handle on how things worked in criminal law, and it pained her to think that soon enough she'd have to leave.

Despite how much easier it would make things, it was impossible to avoid Cameron entirely, and whenever he was around, awkwardness and longing mingled in equal measure.

No matter how hard she tried to avoid so much as meeting his eyes, her sweaty palms and racing heart would not let her deny the emotions that still ran strong.

No, she had to leave FBS, and that meant that there would need to be a break in the case. But only God knew when that stroke of good fortune would come.

"Hello? Hey, Bristol, are you alive?"

Bristol's attention snapped to the door, realizing that she had not even noticed that Grace Hinton had made her way into the legal department.

Her friend stood there looking as stunning as ever, with her hair flowing in loose waves at her shoulders and her eyeliner applied in the sort of perfect cat-eye wing that Bristol had never once managed to achieve.

"Hey, yes, sorry," she said, recovering, as Grace tapped the side of her black riding boot against the doorframe. "I was, uh, making sure I'd locked everything sensitive up before lunch."

She had long since finished doing so, but she could hardly admit to the real topic that had sent her brain off into outer space.

Grace raised a single eyebrow, staring at the disaster that was Bristol's desk.

"I'd hate to have seen it before you started putting things away. Anyway, since you're apparently actually eating lunch today, would you care to join me? It's been a minute."

Bristol smiled, unable to avoid feeling a pang of guilt.

She hadn't spent much time with Grace since she'd gotten back from her trip to Cobalt River Ranch. Despite her general absence in favor of overtime and working lunches, her friend hadn't given up on trying to include her–even if it meant being forced to stay within the safety of the office instead of exploring the downtown restaurant scene with her bank-of-dad credit card that never seemed to hit its limit.

Today, Bristol decided, it was time to set the work–and her endless anxieties–aside.

"Cafeteria?" she suggested.

Grace shook her head, lowering her voice to a conspiratorial whisper. "I'd prefer the lounge. I'm avoiding Dolly today."

Dolly was one of the oldest employees at FBS, who also happened to be one of the toughest.

Despite looking like a grandmother, she was the de facto head of the daytime security team, and Bristol was pretty sure that even Gabe was a little bit scared of her.

Bristol shrugged her shoulders and stepped out from behind her desk, grabbing her bag and following Grace out into the hall. As usual, the section of the fourth floor that housed the legal department was deserted.

"What happened?"

Grace examined her fingernails as they waited for the elevator.

"Oh, you know. I accidentally corrupted three days worth of security footage for the upper floors."

Bristol stifled a laugh, though she supposed it would have been less amusing had the mistake happened a couple of weeks prior.

"Do I want to know?"

"Probably not. Anyway, needless to say, Dolly looks ready to throw me in the oven with her next apple pie."

"Can't Ben help you fix the footage?" Bristol asked with exaggerated innocence, blinking her eyelashes in Grace's direction.

"I'm sure he can, but I'm not sure it's the best time to ask him," she said, swatting Bristol with the leopard-print lanyard that held her keycard. "No one has told me much, but it sounds like there's some big job coming up. Cartel stuff. Most of the guys are working on it, I think."

Bristol nodded. "That makes sense, considering the reports Cameron just handed me a little while ago. Not that anyone ever tells me what's going on. I've been hiding out in legal land."

"Exactly why I needed to drag you out of your cave," Grace said, pulling open the door of the lounge and following Bristol inside.

After a few moments to grab their drinks of choice and some caesar salads from the minifridge, Grace dove straight into gossip mode.

Bristol listened, nodding her head and trying not to think about the mountain of work that awaited her that afternoon.

She'd learned right away that trying to stop her friend from gossiping was a lost cause, and in any case, it was never of the malicious variety. Grace Isabella Hinton didn't have a mean hair on her head.

"Speaking of El Paso," Grace said suddenly, though no one had in fact mentioned El Paso for the last twenty minutes. "I wonder if that has anything to do with what's going on with Reilly."

Bristol sipped at her tea, refusing to take the bait, but Grace would not be deterred.

"Word at the water cooler is that Reilly asked Gabe if he could start his paternity leave early. Supposedly, he wants to help Lauren get ready for the birth of the twins, but I heard from Asher that he's been struggling lately. Even though it's already been over a year, what happened the last time FBS crossed the cartel really has him messed up with guilt."

Bristol felt a heavy weight settling over her.

She'd heard about that case.

It was how Reilly had first met Lauren, but unfortunately, it had also ended in tragedy when he'd accidentally shot a twenty year old kid. The wound had been fatal.

"That's awful," Bristol said. "It wasn't his fault, though. He did what he thought was right at the time. He obviously didn't realize who was in his line of fire, or he might have chosen to act differently."

"Of course. But sometimes what we have to do still hurts," Grace said, giving Bristol a pointed look. "And sometimes we do things that we think we have to do, but we end up being wrong. Sometimes we place expectations on ourselves that we don't really need to live up to. We just convince ourselves that we do."

Bristol froze, her tea raised to her mouth mid-sip.

Clearly, Grace wasn't here just to chat. Clearly, what had happened between her and Cameron wasn't a secret around the office. Then again, when it came to the investigative gossip powers of Grace Hinton, few things were.

"Are you trying to tell me something?" she said, stabbing at the last piece of lettuce with her plastic fork until it was thoroughly demolished.

Grace nodded. "I mean, yeah. I think you're making a mistake by pushing Cameron away just as you guys were starting to get somewhere."

Bristol pushed her chair back and stretched her arms over her head.

Grace stayed where she was, her arms crossed sternly over her chest.

"Seriously, Bristol. Cam didn't put me up to this or anything, if that's what you're wondering. I hope you're not mad. I'm just worried about you, that's all. And I really am glad we got a chance to have lunch for the first time in fifty years."

Bristol kept her back turned for a few extra seconds as she tossed her leftovers into the trash bin, trying to decide whether she was angry or not.

Sure, Grace could be a little blunt and more than a little intrusive, but at least she cared enough to give her honest opinion, even at the risk of ticking Bristol off. She could respect that.

"I'm not mad, okay?" she said, giving Grace what she hoped was a genuine-looking smile. "I'll think about what you said, but that's the best that I can do. In the meantime, I really do have to get back to work. I can't avoid Jaclyn like you can avoid Dolly, and if I don't get these assignments done this afternoon, she'll want to put me in her oven, too."

Grace broke into a dimpled grin. "I can't picture Jaclyn Mercier making a pie."

"Me either," Bristol said, chuckling. "She'd skip the extra steps and go straight for the knife."

"If she owns any. I kind of picture her as one of those people who lives in a condo that doesn't have an oven at all," Grace said, getting up from her own chair. "Then again, she might also live in some giant house in Alamo Heights. Or maybe not. I don't think she makes *that* much money, and I don't think she has a rich husband. Actually, is she even married?"

Bristol shook her head, rolling her eyes good-naturedly as they made their way out of the lounge. Despite her ulterior motives and the excess of gossip, it was nice to spend time with a friend again.

As they parted ways on the fourth floor, however, Bristol's thoughts returned to what Grace had said.

Doing what she had to do definitely hurt.

But unlike Reilly's drug bust gone wrong, she'd at least had a choice in the first place.

And every time she thought of Cameron's intense blue eyes, she couldn't help but to wonder if the choice she'd made had been wrong.

Bristol headed down the hall toward her office, trying to gather her thoughts. She was in for a busy afternoon, and she couldn't afford to lose focus.

As she reached the legal department, however, she couldn't help but to overhear Jaclyn's voice from behind the closed door of her interior office. Melanie wasn't in, and she doubted Jaclyn realized she'd returned early from lunch.

She shook her head, trying to ignore her boss's loud, private conversation, and strode toward her own office door.

Before she could make it across the room, however, something Jaclyn said caught her attention.

"I don't know, Albert," Jaclyn was saying, irritation in her voice. "Are you sure everything is actually set up properly this time? No plans to go rogue?"

Albert?

She felt her heart beginning to pick up speed, but she knew that the response was illogical. There were a lot of Alberts aside from Albert Dorling in San Antonio. If she hadn't been so keyed up, she never would have noticed the name at all.

Still, she wondered what Jaclyn could possibly be talking about.

She sidled up beside the copier at Melanie's desk, pretending to fiddle with the paper tray, though she doubted anyone would walk by and see her.

"No," Jaclyn snapped. "I'm not waiting any longer. He's going on early paternity leave next week!"

Bristol gripped the edge of the machine, her head spinning. She was talking about Reilly, of all people–but why?

She waited, wishing desperately that she could hear anything from the other side of the conversation, but she didn't dare get any closer to the lawyer's door.

"Just look at what almost happened with Bristol! No more carelessness, Albert. I mean it. Okay. Yes, I'll be good to go on my end for Friday."

She heard Jaclyn give an exasperated sigh.

"I know, but as I keep trying to tell everyone, it's a waste of time. She doesn't know anything about it. Fine. Fine. Just make sure Grapas does what they're supposed to."

Bristol frowned.

Grapas.

The name stuck out, but for the moment, she was too distracted to give any thought to where she'd seen or heard it.

Jaclyn said nothing for several long seconds, and then Bristol heard what she could only assume was the click of the phone being placed back in its cradle.

She could have made it to her office, but instead, she crossed the legal department in three steps, heading back out toward the hall.

She still had fifteen minutes of lunch left, and even though there had to be a logical explanation for everything she'd heard, the conversation had sent up red flags that she didn't feel she could safely ignore.

She had to talk to Cam.

Chapter 22

Cameron

Cameron leaned back in his chair and closed his eyes, drawing several long breaths before he opened them again.

He had allotted his lunch hour to organizing his office, but if his current progress was any indication, there was absolutely no way that he'd be getting it done today. If anything, he'd be lucky to finish it in a week.

He gathered up the wrappers of the two takeout burgers he'd had delivered and tossed them across the room into the trash, imagining Gabe's smug 'I told you so' if he dared complain about how messy the place had gotten.

The cleaning service did their best, but he supposed it was pretty difficult to work around the mountains of clutter that filled the place.

He peered down at his smartwatch and frowned. He still had enough time to get more done, and he figured that he may as well try before the calls started coming in and colleagues started showing up at his door.

He reached for a drawer near the bottom of his desk at random. It looked more like a second recycling bin than anything, with papers stacked and rolled haphazardly until they almost prevented the drawer from closing fully.

Taking hold of one, he squinted at it, wondering how it was possible that he had zero memory of what it was or why he had it.

The Forge & Sons logo stared back at him, the little blue tractor puttering along over a hill of bright yellow corn. He flipped the page and found the same thing on the next one, and then the next.

He groaned, dragging the rest of them out and stacking them on his desk, trying to straighten the bent corners as he remembered what they were. He had promised to bring these files to his father's office at least a month ago, if not before that, and he doubted that Gabriel Forge Sr. was going to be amused when he finally received them.

To make matters worse, he wouldn't be able to put off the conversation for long.

According to Reilly, his dad had already heard through the usual Silver Grove gossip mill that Bristol was back in town, and he'd told Reilly to invite her and her mother over for Sunday dinner. And Reilly had told Cam that she'd agreed.

He'd argued against the idea, of course, citing security concerns that convinced no one. His father's home was nearly as fortress-like as FBS, and Reilly was more than capable of keeping watch over Bristol without his help.

No, deep down, he was just upset that it wasn't him bringing her home for dinner, preferably as his girlfriend.

Not to mention the fact that his own father hadn't bothered to invite Cameron at all.

A pang of guilt flooded his belly as he dug out the last pile of half-crushed files from the bottom of the drawer, wondering if he could make copies of the worst few to conceal their mangled edges.

Maybe if he hadn't missed so many Sunday dinners, he would have been asked.

Reilly had been more of a son than he or the rest of his brothers lately, despite being, technically, his father's nephew.

Whatever was going on with work, with Bristol, or with anything else, he really did need to make more of an effort when it came to the family he had left.

As he sat in front of his computer debating how to start an email about the forgotten invoices, there was a knock at his door.

He minimized the email program, not in the mood for one of Gabe's lectures–not that he'd be able to conceal the Forge & Sons logo plastered all over about two hundred sheets of paper scattered all over his desk.

"Come in," he said.

He couldn't decide if he was relieved or not when he realized it was Bristol, but as soon as he took in the expression on her face, worry immediately drove out any other possible emotion.

"Hey," he said, getting up from his seat for a moment and removing a box from one of the chairs in front of his desk. "What can I do for you?"

Bristol tucked a strand of hair behind her ear as she sat, looking suddenly nervous.

"Are you okay? Did something else happen?"

She shook her head.

"Sorry, I'm fine. Just confused."

"Well, I'm glad you're okay," he said, letting out a slow breath. After two weeks of peace, he was still on edge. Danger seemed to follow Bristol constantly. "So what's up?"

"I came back from lunch a little early, and I overheard Jaclyn on the phone in her office. I didn't mean to eavesdrop, obviously, but then..."

Bristol's words trailed off, and she stopped meeting his eyes.

"Look, if she was talking loud enough to be heard from the main area of the legal department, it barely even counts as spying. Grace would call you an amateur," he joked, trying to keep things light despite the storm that was quickly brewing behind Bristol's green eyes.

"She mentioned someone named Albert, and I know there's probably a thousand other ones, but I couldn't help but to keep listening after that," Bristol said quickly.

Cameron nodded, trying to keep his expression neutral.

She was right. The name Albert was hardly suspicious. Then again, there had to be more. It wasn't like she'd come down to his office just for that.

"Anyway," she continued, "I can't remember the exact words or anything, obviously, but she asked him if everything was set up, and if anyone planned to 'go rogue'. She told this Albert person that she was set up on her end for Friday. She said something about how 'she' doesn't know anything. It wasn't clear who she meant."

She paused for a moment, her brows furrowing as she tried to think.

"But she mentioned what almost happened to me, and she didn't sound happy about it."

"Well, that's a good sign, I guess," Cameron said, giving Bristol a quick smile.

"Oh, and she mentioned Reilly," Bristol added. "Right. That was the strangest thing. She talked about him going on paternity leave next week."

Cameron frowned.

It was a weird conversation, to be sure, but hardly something that set off immediate alarm bells. For all he knew, Jaclyn could've been talking about an upcoming court case that required Reilly's involvement before he left.

"Anyway, I know there's nothing too nefarious, and that there's probably a totally innocent explanation," Bristol said.

He gave her what he hoped was an encouraging smile, and he tried to choose his next words as carefully as he could.

"Jaclyn hasn't been here very long, but she's never given me, or any of my brothers, or any of the senior staff a reason not to trust her."

"I agree. She still intimidates me, and she's definitely not someone who suffers fools lightly, but everything I've ever seen from her has been totally above-board," Bristol admitted.

"Has she been behaving professionally toward you? Any concerning interactions I should know about?"

Cameron cringed at his own words, hating the HR-speak, but it was worth asking. After all that Bristol had put up with at D&P, her perception of what constituted acceptable behavior from a superior had likely become skewed.

"No. She was tougher right when I started here, but she's softened toward me a lot," Bristol said. "Look, I don't want her to feel accused if it's just a simple misunderstanding, but there was a gut feeling that I just couldn't shake."

Her fingernails tapped against the armrest of her chair.

"And gut feelings aren't something that should be easily ignored," Cameron added. "Sometimes our intuition picks up on things that pure logic will miss. I'm glad you came to me."

"Thank you for understanding why I did."

"I'm going to have to talk to her," Cam said.

Bristol shook her head.

"You can't. She's going to know it had to have been me who listened in, seeing as our clerk wasn't even in today. And even if someone else could have come into the office, she's still going to know it was me because I talked to you."

Cameron gave her a questioning look, and Bristol rolled her eyes.

"She's not blind, Cam. She along with everyone else figured out pretty quickly that I don't treat you the same way as Gabe or anyone else here. I'm not exactly the best at hiding my feelings, and you're even worse."

He couldn't decide whether he should feel hopeful or not.

"Anyway, considering that, maybe you can ask Gabe to talk to her. He's the big boss, and maybe if it's coming from him, Jaclyn will believe that it was someone else who overheard her."

Cameron doubted it, but there was no need to tell Bristol as much.

"Good idea," he said. "Gabe won't care. He's used to handling most of the tough conversations around here."

"Good," Bristol said, though she looked about as convinced as he felt.

"I'll talk to him today and try and get this figured out as soon as I can. Like you said, I'm sure there will be nothing to tell."

An awkward silence descended, and as usual, Cameron longed for things to go back to how they'd been just weeks ago.

He watched Bristol sitting there, fiddling with the ends of her sleek brown hair as the seconds ticked past.

Clearly, she wasn't getting up to leave, but she didn't look eager to speak, either.

He caught a glimpse of her eyes as she stared down at her lap, lost in thought.

In the soft light of the room they looked especially almost gray instead of green, reminding him of a northern sea in winter.

Every time she came near him, he was reminded just how difficult it was to keep his distance–especially when she couldn't seem to decide whether she wanted to trust him, or to keep pushing him away.

Bristol

Bristol wanted to run, but her limbs refused to move, as though some larger force held her in place.

Instead, she sat still, waiting for an invitation that Cameron wouldn't dare to extend, not after the way she'd reacted to him so many times before.

She dared a quick glance up at him, unsurprised to see that he was looking over the desk at her, his eyes filled with confusion.

She wished that he could understand how difficult it had been to open up to him, even a little, and even about something that wasn't directly personal. But she also wanted to tell him how much it meant to her that he had taken her concerns so seriously, like she was actually part of the team, and not just some airhead client that he was obligated to shield from the danger that surrounded her.

She drew in a quick breath, offering a silent prayer in her heart for courage.

She couldn't just keep sitting here, letting him wonder what he'd done wrong, and she couldn't run away, either, no matter how badly she wanted to.

She cleared her throat and looked up at him, leaning in closer, until only a few stacks of messy papers separated them across the desk. His eyes caught hers, filled with a swirling tempest of emotion that she couldn't hope to read.

"I talked to Grace today," she said, unable to think of a better opening line.

"Oh?"

"She said something that made me think. About the last couple of weeks, and about how things have been."

Cameron nodded, his expression revealing nothing as he relaxed in his chair.

Bristol forced her hands to remain still against the desk.

If she wasn't brave now, she would never be able to forgive herself.

She had to at least try.

"I wanted to leave FBS because I wanted to keep you and everyone else safe," she started. "And I wanted to step back from you because I knew you'd only end up getting hurt. That was true–that *is* true–but it isn't the whole truth."

She paused again, wishing that Cameron would say whatever it was he was thinking, but he only waited, his arms crossed over his muscled chest.

"I–I guess I've had to think about the fact that my fears aren't really about you as much as they are about me."

"Ah," Cameron said, a smile teasing at the corner of his lips. "So you came to tell me that it's not you, it's me?"

She shook her head. "That's not what I mean. I was right about what I said, before–I haven't changed since coming back to Silver Grove. I haven't become the person that I told myself I needed to be."

Cam ran a hand through his hair.

"But?"

"But maybe that person–that girl I've been trying to become for as long as I can remember–maybe that's not who I really am."

She let out a nervous laugh, hating the way she stumbled over the words.

"I know that doesn't even make sense. I'm sorry. Maybe I should just–"

"Bristol," Cameron said, shaking his head. "It makes perfect sense. And I'm glad you're talking to me about how you're feeling instead of holding it in."

She paused as her eyes met his, drawing several breaths as she waited for the knots in her stomach to subside.

She was safe with him.

She could talk to him. Even after everything that had happened, he had promised to listen, and he was.

"I think I was afraid to marry you back then because it would make me into this person that I didn't want to be. But the person I was? I never really gave myself a chance to figure that out. I just...chose. I chose not to be my mother, abandoned and alone and powerless. I chose to be strong. I chose to succeed."

The words were coming quickly now, and her voice no longer shook.

The bandage had been torn free, and now, all she wanted was to release every last bit of poison that was trapped within her heart.

"I chose to not need love, because love makes you vulnerable. Love opens you up to the possibility of getting hurt. I believed I would be better off without it. And for a long time, I was able to convince myself that it was true.

"But what Dillon Warrington did to me changed all of that. I was forcibly reminded that no matter how much I tried to guard myself against pain, we live in a fallen world. Evil and the suffering it brings are inevitable. All we can do is decide if we are going to try and choose our own crosses, or let God choose them for us."

Cameron smiled. "Your mom used to say that all the time."

Bristol smiled back.

Though Cameron's office had no windows, she could have sworn that a ray of warm sunshine had just fallen upon them, warming her from the inside out.

"She still does. I'm pretty sure she has it on a fridge magnet somewhere," she said. "I've been choosing crosses for a really long time, and I'm getting tired. I guess I just came here to tell you that I'm ready to start trusting God a lot more than I have been, and hoping that He will make it clear in time who He wants me to be."

Cameron's eyes were filled with unspoken questions, but instead, he only smiled across the desk at her, sending the butterflies in her stomach fluttering anew.

"In the meantime, if you can handle the mess, I'm not exactly opposed to trying again," she said quickly, her cheeks going hot. "I mean, if you can get past how cold I've been lately. I'm sorry about that, by the way, but I can't promise it won't happen again, I can't promise anything, really. Every time you've come near me, I've been falling apart inside, honestly, and–"

Before she had realized what was happening, he had gotten out of his chair, stepped around the desk, and pulled her to her feet.

She felt clumsy, but his grip was sure and strong, and she allowed her body to collapse into his, trusting that he wouldn't let her stumble.

He paused for a moment, searching her face, waiting.

Waiting to be sure that she was ready, even now.

Bristol gave him a single nod, not wanting to ruin the moment with what were sure to be imperfect words.

When his lips finally met hers, she felt certain that her heart was going to explode in her chest.

There was no fear, no reluctance, not even when his fingers found her jawline and tangled in her hair, drawing her closer for several perfect seconds. She felt warm all over, the feeling of connection and security pouring through her from her head to her toes.

When he finally pulled away, she braced her hand against the desk, afraid she might fall over.

His eyes held hers, fierce and longing.

"You don't have to have it all figured out, sweetheart," he said, tracing a finger over her lips. "All I want is for you to try. That's all I'm asking for."

She nodded, certain that he must be able to see that her legs were shaking beneath her.

"Now," he said, leaning down and planting a final kiss on her forehead. "You get back to work, and I'll talk to Gabe and make sure he schedules a meeting with Jaclyn today. We'll figure this all out from there."

Bristol stood there for a long moment, unsure how he expected her to just go back to work, as though everything hadn't just changed forever.

In a way, she supposed, maybe it hadn't.

After so many years, and so much confusion, maybe things between her and Cameron were finally just shifting into place.

Chapter 23

Cameron

Cameron set his fork down against his metal tray, listening to the clattering sound reverberating through the hollow, empty room. He frowned, glancing up at the clock on the wall. It was only eight o'clock, but the sun had long since set, and the cafeteria always felt rather eerie after dark. Everyone had gone home at least a couple of hours before, with the exception of the night security guards and Bristol, who had already retired to her slightly-improved makeshift bedroom on the third floor.

He pressed a finger to his lips, remembering the feel of the kiss they had shared in his office, and the much more innocent goodnight peck he had bestowed after that.

He had only had a moment with her–Jaclyn had run her around most of the afternoon and after she finished around six, he insisted that she rest–but even the small interaction played on repeat in his mind.

There would be time for more kisses, real and deep. More time to pick up where they left off, and, Lord willing, to move forward.

There was a sudden clanking sound beside him, loud enough to echo.

He shot up from his chair, his palm already resting against the holstered Beretta at his belt before he realized it was only Gabe dumping his tray down on the table beside him.

"You okay, bro?" Gabe said, raising his hands and giving him a funny look. "Little jumpy, are we?"

"I'm fine," Cam said, his heart still hammering away as he watched his oldest brother casually stab a piece of grilled chicken with his fork. "You just startled me, that's all. I assumed you'd gone home hours ago."

Gabe shook his head, pausing for a moment as he chewed his chicken. Somehow, half of it was already eaten, though he'd been sitting down for only about a minute.

"That was the plan, but Jaclyn couldn't meet me until well after six, and I thought you'd want an update ASAP."

Cameron nodded, glad at once that Gabe had stopped by. "What did she say?"

"It's what I suspected, Cam," Gabe said, pausing as he started in on his brown rice. "Just a misunderstanding. Nothing too crazy."

Cam wanted to feel relieved, but relief didn't come. Bristol had been so sure that something was off, and he had told her to trust her instincts. But she was also a survivor of sexual violence, and a whole lot more as of late. It was certainly possible that paranoia was creeping in. Even the most level-headed people were not immune to it when faced with trauma.

"Jaclyn was really understanding when I asked her about it. She told me that she was talking to one of the courthouse clerks. Albert. Apparently, she's gotten to know him pretty well, hence the fact that they're on a first name basis," Gabe continued. "It was about the Senera Pharmaceuticals case. Reilly was the secondary operative on that job, following Asher, and as it stands now, she's almost certain she'll need him to testify in court. Problem is, the hearing has been delayed for months now, mostly by Senera's lawyers, and Jaclyn doesn't want to have to pull Reilly from leave if she needs him."

Gabe paused, tucking in to the remainder of his rice, and Cam leaned back in his chair, trying to puzzle out anything that he might be missing.

"If it was months ago, Bristol might not have worked on the case at all," Cameron admitted. "She probably wouldn't have picked up on the details, anyway. But what about–"

Gabe raised his fork.

"Correct, Bristol hasn't touched the whole Senera fiasco. And if you're going to ask if an Albert actually works as a clerk at the courthouse, I already checked. One Albert Ziggoni, age thirty-nine. I made an executive decision that calling him up to inquire about his relationship with Jaclyn was probably not necessary."

"Of course not," Cam said, letting out a sigh. "But there's one more detail I wanted to look at. Jaclyn said something about how 'she' doesn't know anything, and mentioned the name Grapas."

"I know how to conduct an interrogation," Gabe said, his blue eyes darkening slightly as he frowned. "I asked about everything you mentioned, and that comment had an explanation, too. This Albert character asked Jaclyn if her new paralegal would be helping on the case, probably because, and I quote, 'he seems like the type who likes to see pretty girls around the courthouse'. Jaclyn told him that Bristol wasn't going to be getting involved just yet, because she was still getting up to speed on their current files, let alone such a complex case from over a year ago."

Cameron rubbed his fingertips against his temples. Everything was lining up so far. It was good news, but he wasn't convinced that Bristol was going to see it that way.

"I asked about Grapas, too," Gabe said, getting out of his seat and piling the scraps of his dinner in a neat pile on his tray. "Jaclyn said she can't remember exactly why she mentioned them, but she figured she was probably just complaining about having to waste time messing in the legal department's supply order again after it was supposed to be finished weeks ago."

Cameron put his head in his hands, a sigh of frustration escaping him.

"Which would make sense," Gabe went on, "considering that Grapas is our office supplier, and that Grace did in fact lose several department inventories. It might have been a little rude for Jaclyn to bring it up to someone outside of the company, I guess, but it's hardly suspicious."

"Okay. I'll tell Bristol that she has nothing to worry about," Cam said. "Thanks for staying late and putting my mind at ease, man. I appreciate it."

Gabe clapped him on the shoulder and headed toward the exit nearest to their table, yawning as he went.

Cameron got up from his chair, picking up the remains of his microwaved lasagna as well as Gabe's tray, yawning himself as he threw the food into the trash.

He'd let Bristol sleep tonight, and make sure the night guards did a few extra patrols.

He was heading home for some much needed rest.

Telling Bristol that she'd been wrong would just have to wait until morning.

Bristol

While Bristol had headed down to the office gym early the next morning to shower, dress, and put on a little makeup, breakfast from the Screaming Peach had appeared in her makeshift bedroom.

She smiled as she looked over the morning's offering of green tea, pancakes, and fresh fruit, thinking to herself that she could get used to this just as Cam himself appeared at her door.

"Morning, gorgeous," he said as he strode up beside her. She gave him a peck on the cheek, grinning up at him.

"I was significantly less gorgeous about thirty minutes ago," she joked. "Good timing."

"Impossible," he said, shaking his head as he popped a strawberry from her breakfast into his mouth. "You're always perfect. Shower optional."

She wrinkled her nose at him. "Gross."

As she took her first sip of still-hot tea, she couldn't help but to imagine waking up next to him in their own home, his face being the first thing she saw every morning. The thought didn't make her feel anxious, even considering that he'd be forced to endure her snoring and morning breath.

It was a life she could have had already, had she made different choices. She could have already been Bristol Forge for years by now.

She reached over to the plastic container that held her pancakes, prying off the lid and tearing off a corner of one of the fluffy creations before stuffing it into her mouth.

There was no use in dwelling on what might have been. All she could do was what she'd told Cameron already. She could try to open her heart to figuring out the future she really wanted, and maybe, if it was God's plan, it would include pancake-filled domestic bliss.

"Okay, I'm glad I got the double stack, 'cuz I'm totally having some of those," Cam said, reaching for the packets of syrup and butter that Iris had packed in the brown takeout bag.

"Please do," Bristol said, rolling a second chair over to the empty desk so that both of them could sit side by side.

As Cameron covered the pancakes in copious amounts of fat and liquid sugar, Bristol leaned over and nuzzled her face into his shoulder, soaking in the smell of his shower gel and whatever delicious cologne he always seemed to be wearing.

The breakfast was good, but this was even better.

They ate in comfortable silence for a few minutes, each tearing through two of the large pancakes and most of the fruit, until finally, Cameron set his fork down and looked over at her.

"So," he said, giving her a quick smile, "I talked to Gabe last night."

Bristol swallowed her tea too fast, coughing for a moment before she recovered.

"That was quick," she said. "I didn't think he'd get a chance to talk to her yesterday. I barely saw her. She had me running back and forth between file rooms all afternoon."

"He stayed late," Cameron said. "But I'm glad he did, because it was good news. Very good, actually."

"Oh?"

Bristol listened patiently as Cameron recounted what Gabe and Jaclyn had discussed, chewing on bits of the remaining pancake to keep herself from fidgeting as he spoke.

Gabe knew what he was doing. By the sounds of it, he had looked for an answer for every concern she'd had, even going so far as to find out the identity of the second Albert.

"I should feel relieved," she said at last as he finished, pushing aside the last few bites of the third pancake that she immediately regretted eating.

"But?"

Cameron's voice was gentle, but she couldn't help but to wonder if there was an undercurrent of exasperation running through it.

Still, she'd promised to attempt to be vulnerable, and that meant being honest about how she felt, even if she was worried that he'd find it foolish.

"I can't get the alarm bells to stop ringing," she confessed. "Something tells me that that call wasn't what Jaclyn says it was. My instinct, my gut, whatever you want to call it."

She picked up her tea and sipped at it, glad to be able to hide her reddening face as the words hung in the air, waiting for his response.

"Like I said, it's good to listen to our instincts," Cameron said, reaching over and placing a hand on her forearm. "But there's also nothing wrong with trusting an outside source, especially if there might be something else skewing our perception."

She felt a prickle of uncertainty tingling against the back of her neck.

"What do you mean? I heard what I heard. Jaclyn hasn't driven me to the 'hearing voices' stage of insanity yet."

Her joke came out without humor, and she gripped the cardboard cup tight, suddenly wishing that Cameron would pull his hand away and stop touching her.

"I have zero doubts about what you heard," Cameron said carefully, a muscle twitching along the edge of his jaw. "That's not what I meant. I'm talking about other things. Other things that have happened lately. Things that might be causing you to feel more anxious than normal. Paranoid, even."

Bristol froze.

"Like the rape, right? Or was it the vandalism? Or when someone broke into my mother's house?"

"Bristol, that's not–"

She couldn't help herself from continuing, the words bitter on her tongue as her voice continued to raise. "Oh, I'm sorry, were you referring to the time that a stranger grabbed me in broad daylight, shoved a gun into my back, and came this close to chucking me into the back of a kidnapper van?"

Cameron tried to reach for her hand, but she yanked herself away from him, the rolling chair scraping loudly against the leg of the desk.

"Bristol, I worded that poorly," Cameron said, his voice sounding especially calm after her own anger. "Please don't be like this."

She crossed her arms over her chest, forcing air into her lungs, but she could find no calm of her own. If anything, his patient attitude had succeeded only at ticking her off.

"I'm not some crazy, irrational victim," she said, the rage in her voice cooling into ice. "I started looking over my shoulder long before I came to FBS. I know what it's like to feel like someone is lurking behind every hedge. I know how to tell that paranoid anxiety voice to shut up. This is something else."

"Gabe is certain that Jaclyn is okay," he replied, gripping the edges of his own chair and staying seated. "Not only did he look into every claim that she made—as I said, it all checks out, right down to the two Alberts and the timing with Reilly and Senera—he went home last night, grabbed more coffee, and took another deep dive into her personnel file."

Bristol pursed her lips. Gabriel staying up late to make sure he was being thorough was admirable, but she still felt uneasy, as though Cameron was attempting to convince her to ignore her instincts.

"We do extensive checks into every single person we hire, including the maintenance staff and interns. Needless to say, we were exceptionally thorough when it came to hiring the person who was going to be our emissary to the legal system.

"Jaclyn has almost as high of a security clearance as me and my brothers. We didn't make the decision to hire her lightly, and Gabe took the time to confirm every bit of documentation again, just because he trusted me and wanted to take my concerns seriously. And my concerns were based purely on the fact that I trust you, including your instincts."

Bristol felt as though she'd been slapped.

"So, you trust me, until your big brother says the word. After that, I go back to being the paranoid, crazy rape victim," she said, her voice sounding hollow to her own ears..

She should never have come to him with any of this. She should have found something more concrete on her own, something impossible to dismiss.

Even Gabe could miss something, and this time, he must have. She was sure of it.

"Please, try and understand this from my perspective," Cameron said, his face filled with hurt. "I still trust you. Present tense. I'm just trying to be fair to Jaclyn as well as to you. I can still have someone check into Albert Ziggoni–"

"It's not about him," she said, her voice soft. She had run out of the energy that snapping at him would have required. "It's not about Gabe, either, and it's not about Jaclyn."

The familiar sick feeling in her throat bubbled up again, tears threatening to pour over.

She was so tired of crying over him.

"It's about us, Cameron," she continued. "It's about the fact that before you came in here this morning, I was thinking about what my life would have been like had I agreed to marry you all those years ago."

Cameron winced as though she had slapped him.

"I thought about what it would have been like to wake up next to you every day. I thought about you bringing me breakfast, and making me laugh. I wasn't expecting for you to turn around and treat me like I've lost my mind. But maybe I should have."

"I've never said anything like that," Cameron said, his voice dangerously low. "But I'm sorry you took it that way."

Bristol felt herself clenching her hands into fists against her lap.

Some apology.

Who she was, who she wanted to be, what did that matter?

No one believed her anyway. Thanks to Dillon Warrington, not only her body had been tainted, but her mind, as well.

She'd hoped that he was different, and that he could see her more clearly, could see that her word was still trustworthy.

But she was wrong.

"Look," Cam said, his voice pleading now as he tried to catch her gaze. "I don't want to fight like this. We both knew when we talked last night that this was never going to be a simple situation. It doesn't mean we throw away what I know we have.

"I know I'm not perfect," he continued, swallowing hard as he leaned ever so slightly toward her. "I know you warned me that you were going to mess up again, and I should have been clear that the same is true for me. I've changed a lot since I was that cocky nineteen year old kid with a diamond ring in his pocket, but I know I still have a long way to go. I'm trying. I just need you to let me."

As she looked at him, she felt her resolve beginning to falter once again.

His blue eyes, his charm, his promises.

They were the right words, but that was the part Cam was good at, and always had been.

He had always known how to make her stay, which is why she'd flown across the country to put him and their relationship behind her.

"Maybe you think that you've changed," she said, refusing to shrink away from the fire in his eyes as he stared at her. "And in some ways, I'm sure you have. Good for you. But when it comes to you and me? I have my answer. I know exactly what my life would have been like if I'd stayed, and I think eighteen year old Bristol was a lot smarter than I've given her credit for."

Cameron

Cameron shrank back in his chair, letting Bristol's words fall over him like flaming brimstone.

He took a few breaths before finally looking up at her, expecting to see guilt in her expression, or perhaps regret, but there was none.

All he could see was fury in her eyes. Even the pain that she'd so often hidden within their green depths had been pushed aside as she continued to glare at him.

Something inside of him snapped.

All this time, he'd been groveling. He'd been apologizing. He'd been doing everything he possibly could to fix things with her, and in the end, she was worse off than when she'd first darkened the door of Forge Brothers Security.

"Maybe you're right about me, Bristol. You've got me all figured out, just like you've figured out everything else," he said, not bothering to hide the bitter anger in his voice. "I want to be with someone who respects me, and who extends me the slightest benefit of the doubt when she's not sure where I stand. Guilty as charged, Your Honor."

Bristol stiffened, opening her mouth to speak, but he kept going, unable to close the floodgates of anger now that they had opened.

"Maybe that means I'm going to end up alone in the end, but at least I'll have my family and my God to lean on. Despite staying in boring old Silver Grove and going to church every Sunday, I've still managed to make my life my own. I joined this company instead of working in agriculture for the rest of my life. I broke the mold, too, Bristol. And I did it without shoving aside the people who care about me the most."

"Good for you," Bristol spat, sliding her chair back and getting to her feet.

He followed her as she made her way toward the door, not caring who heard their argument. What did it matter now?

"You keep saying that you're going to trust, and to let God work on you, but when it actually comes down to it, you put the same old walls up," he said to her retreating back, her shoes making more noise than necessary as she stomped across the room. "You're right. You don't know who Bristol Chaplin really is, but I'm starting to feel like maybe I do. And I feel really, really bad for her."

Bristol whipped around, catching him in a deadly glare.

He half expected her to walk up and slap him.

Instead, she lowered her voice until it was just above a whisper, shaking with every word.

"I'll be out of your office and out of your life just

as soon as I find another job, assuming you don't feel the need to fire me here and now."

Cameron crossed his arms over his chest. "I'm not firing you."

Bristol gave him a brisk nod.

"Great. Glad that's settled."

A moment later, she was gone, slamming the door behind her.

Bristol

Bristol splashed the cold water against her face again and again, hoping that it would somehow hide the evidence of her tear-stained face.

She'd already passed Ben on her way up to the fourth floor, and though he didn't say anything, she could tell by his expression that she looked like an absolute wreck.

In any case, he and the rest of the office had probably heard about their fight by now, and anyone who hadn't would soon.

She turned off the tap and leaned against the sink, closing her eyes for a long time, glad that the fourth floor bathroom was almost as isolated as the legal department itself.

Being here at FBS reminded her so much of growing up in Silver Grove.

She'd found the same tight-knit community, friendships, and sense of belonging–and she'd also realized that as soon as she stepped out of line, everyone would turn their backs on her in a heartbeat.

Just as she thought she'd gathered enough courage to head back to her office, however, the one person she least wanted to see–save Cameron himself–stepped into the bathroom.

She forced a smile onto her face as Grace sidled up beside her, setting her makeup bag on the edge of a sink and beginning to pull out what looked to be about twenty different products.

"Hey," Grace said, sounding cheerful as she reached for a tube of foundation. "I look like trash. I was running late, and I decided to just get ready here to save time, but the lighting in the gym is *horrible*."

Bristol nodded, noticing that Grace looked incredible without doing anything to get ready at all. She stole a quick glance at her watch. It was still early. Maybe Grace had miraculously made it all the way up here without hearing about her and Cameron's screaming match.

Still, she was glad that she was more focused on applying dabs of concealer cream to her own face rather than looking over at Bristol's bloodshot eyes.

"And your first choice of alternative makeup application station was here in the upper dungeon?" she joked, cringing at the hollowness in her voice.

She had to get a grip. No matter how furious she was at Cameron, walking out without a job and burning bridges in her wake was not something she could afford to do.

She leaned on her mother enough as it was. Becoming unemployed without another job lined up was out of the question. She just had to stay out of Cam's way until she figured out her next move.

"Actually, today I'm hiding from Gabe," she said matter-of-factly. "He made me promise to organize the reception desk before the morning clients start rolling in. Apparently, and I quote, he 'hired the part-time front desk staff to work at a security firm, not a waste-disposal-depot-slash-Sephora-clearance-aisle'. The absolute nerve!"

Despite her mood, Bristol couldn't help but to laugh.

On her first day at FBS, she'd assumed that the front desk must have been as sleek and aesthetically pleasing as the rest of the reception area, but that illusion was shattered the first time she stepped behind it to chat with Grace.

There were body sprays, makeup items, and knick-knacks everywhere, not to mention an endless supply of empty takeout cups and food wrappers. She hadn't glimpsed Grace's computer setup, but she had a feeling that she probably had about two hundred icons cluttering the desktop.

"I feel like you're hiding from someone at least once a week."

"I can't help it. It's not my fault that no one else understands my systems," Grace said, opening her mouth wide as she combed mascara onto her long lashes. "Just because Gabe can't understand my setup doesn't mean that I don't have one that works."

Bristol shook her head as she gestured toward one of Grace's powder compacts. "Can I borrow this?"

Without a word, Grace handed her a makeup brush, and she got to work attempting to conceal some of the redness. The powder was too dark, but she doubted it could look much worse than she already did.

She felt a flicker of guilt for comparing FBS to her hometown. Despite her penchant for gossip, it was clear that Grace Hinton had been a real friend to her since day one. And while she obviously couldn't keep working here, she owed it to everyone else to try and find out what was going on before she left, including with Jaclyn. If the danger didn't leave with her and someone else got hurt, she'd never be able to forgive herself.

"Anyway, I told Gabe that I was going to clean it, and that I was just waiting for some cute organizing stuff I ordered to get here in the mail, but he wasn't sympathetic."

"Yeah, somehow I can imagine that."

Grace swiped a coat of lipgloss on and began tossing the products she'd used back into her still half-full bag. "Oh, speaking of procrastination, I also need to simultaneously finalize the Grapas order in the next hour so I can get everything on the Friday truck, since I have to be at this boring course in Austin for most of the day."

"You need a clone. Or to be in two places at once."

As soon as the words escaped her mouth, Bristol froze.

A memory came flooding back in an instant, pushing out everything else that had been crowding her brain that morning. She felt as though she'd walked out into a sunny day after being lost in shadow, blinded by clarity.

The impossible nightmare of a puzzle she'd been dealing with for the past few months began to click into place.

"I know I was supposed to be done, like, two weeks ago. But I lost some stuff, and then there was a glitch, and I had to redo some of it. So, if you could ask your people in legal if they had any final things they need, that would be super helpful," Grace was saying, reaching into her purse and drawing out a curling iron and a huge can of hairspray.

Bristol nodded, struggling to comprehend the words.

"Right, yeah," she said, swallowing hard. "I'll do it first thing. I have to get back over there now, actually."

She made a show of staring down at her watch, the numbers not even registering in her brain.

"Sounds good," Grace said, humming to herself as she began wrapping a thick strand of blonde hair around the barrel of the iron.

"I'll see you later," Bristol said, her black flats squeaking on the tile floor as she rushed out of the bathroom.

She knew now why the name Grapas had stuck out to her each time that it came up.

She'd seen their company name and logo at least six months ago.

It had been plastered on a bunch of the suspicious restricted files that she'd accidentally stumbled upon while working at Dorling & Porter.

Chapter 24

Bristol

Bristol's heart pounded as she turned the corner and headed down the long hallway toward the legal department. She forced her breaths to slow. She wanted to look calm and casual, but if Jaclyn noticed that she was acting strangely, she'd confess that she and Cameron had an argument.

It would be embarrassing, but better than raising the lawyer's suspicions.

As she walked, she mentally replayed the conversation she'd overheard. Though the exact words used had long since escaped her memory, she knew that Jaclyn had mentioned being ready on her end for Friday, and told Albert to be sure that Grapas did what they were supposed to do.

Jaclyn's explanations to Gabriel had been nothing but an attempt to obscure the truth.

She was smooth, but Bristol wasn't fooled.

And now, even if no one else would listen, she had to find out exactly what was going on before it was too late.

Come Friday, a Grapas truck would be entering the secure garage of Forge Brothers Security and heading straight into the loading bay, and she was terrified it could contain something much more dangerous than a bulk carton of thumbtacks.

The file she'd seen back at D&P was certainly not a standard supply delivery contract.

The firm had defended a man who had been accused of plotting a bombing at the mayor's office. The plan was thwarted, and in the end the charges were dropped, but none of that mattered now.

What mattered was the fact that the man had

been working at the Grapas warehouse when the plot had been uncovered.

Bristol hesitated as she spotted the half-open door to the legal department up ahead.

She could still turn around and head to Cam's office to tell him what she knew.

With the information she'd remembered, it was likely he'd take her concerns about the phone call a lot more seriously.

But after a few seconds of consideration, she shook her head, dismissing the idea.

She couldn't bear the weight of his doubt again. She would let him and his brothers handle the situation in the end, but first, she needed proof.

Grace had said the truck was coming Friday. If she could prove that the threat was legitimate, they would still have several days to prepare for it.

She drew a final breath and headed into the office before she could change her mind.

"Good morning," Melanie said, looking up from her computer and smiling over at her. "Jaclyn stepped out of the office for an early meeting, but she told me to ask you to proof the Dorfman file before you get to your other stuff."

Bristol only barely stopped herself from looking up at the ceiling and thanking God out loud for His miraculous timing.

She had to find those contract files that she'd seen before, in case there was some sort of clue. Hopefully, they would still be somewhere in Jaclyn's office, and if they were, she doubted they would be very well-guarded, at least not from those within the department. After all, the lawyer hadn't seemed to be too worried about her seeing them the first time.

Which probably meant there was nothing useful.

Still, she had to try, now that she knew what she was looking for.

At least for this sort of work, she didn't need Cam or anybody else.

She knew how to slog through legalese with the best of them, and with any luck, she'd be able to prevent any potential danger long before it happened.

"Thanks, Mel," she said, leaning against her desk, hoping that she looked casual despite the adrenaline coursing through her.

Now to get rid of the clerk.

"I was wondering if you could do me a favor, actually."

"Of course."

"Grace needs any last minute supply orders before she leaves for the day," she said, struggling to speak at a normal pace. She could see Jaclyn's office door out of the corner of her eye, beckoning to her. "Jaclyn was handling it, but I don't want to interrupt her meeting. It would be really helpful if you could take a look at her list and cross reference it in the system to make sure nothing's missing before we send it off."

Mel nodded. "You bet. I know where she left it."

"Awesome," Bristol said. "Make sure to ask someone in admin downstairs if you need help."

The intern looked relieved. "I will. I find some of the software they use super confusing."

"That makes two of us," Bristol said, forcing a smile as she waited for the young woman to gather up her files and head out the door.

At last, she was alone, and fortunately, she had a key to Jaclyn's office.

Cameron

Getting any work done was impossible.

After an hour of staring at his computer screen, reading emails without taking in anything they said, and shuffling papers around on his desk, Cameron decided that he needed to find another way to get his fight with Bristol off of his mind.

A few minutes later, he'd made his way to the first floor and found a quiet corner in the gym. For once, it was empty, and he was thankful to have at least a few minutes to start lifting weights before someone else showed up.

He had an important meeting with a client that afternoon, and before that, he'd have to supervise the annual firearm and ammunition inventory count.

None of it felt important at the moment, but he knew that it was all part of the non-exciting, behind-the-scenes side of his work protecting others. He owed it to his company and especially to his clients to have his head in the game.

Whatever had happened with Bristol couldn't get in the way of doing his job. He was a protector. It was who he was.

"Maybe that's why she sees me this way," he said out loud, using a free weight to do a few bicep curls. "Even as a security operative, she knows that deep down, I'm just this safe, boring guy who will only hold her back."

"What are you on about, bro?" came a voice from the locker room door, making him jump.

His free weight fell toward the ground, a tremendous crash echoing through the silent gym.

He stifled a curse. "Reilly. You scared me, man."

He bent down to scoop up the weight, cringing at the words he'd allowed his cousin to hear. That's what he got for talking to himself like a crazy person.

"I heard there's some drama around the office today," Reilly said, climbing onto a leg press machine a couple of feet away and adjusting the weight. "What happened?"

Cameron rolled his eyes. FBS was generally a friendly, supportive environment, which meant that what little juicy gossip there was usually made the rounds almost immediately.

So much for coming down here to clear his head.

Instead, he figured he may as well set the record straight.

Reilly listened patiently as he went over the painful argument, omitting the part where he'd more or less told Bristol she was a bad person and that he felt bad for her.

For a moment after he'd finished, Reilly said nothing. All he could hear was the gentle thunk of the leg press machine as he finished out his reps.

"Well," Reilly said at last, "she sounds like she's being a bit of a jerk. But what did you say?"

He picked up another free weight, refusing to meet his compassionate brown eyes.

Reilly knew him far too well to let him get away with coming off as the innocent party. Though they were technically cousins, he was just as much a Forge brother as the rest of them, and as difficult as it could be at times, Cameron was thankful that he had men in his life who kept him honest.

"A lot of stuff I shouldn't have," he said, letting out a sigh. It was true. Now that most of the anger had faded away, he felt disgusted with himself and the harshness of his words. "Some of it was true, of course, but a lot of it was my own pride talking. At that moment, I wasn't trying to let iron sharpen iron. I just wanted to lash out and to hurt her like she hurt me."

To his credit, Reilly didn't ask for the grisly details.

He leaned back against the machine, giving Cameron a grim smile.

"You know you can't leave things like this. Even if the whole Jaclyn phone call thing is nonsense, Bristol's still in danger, and if she leaves now, you're not going to be able to guarantee her protection. None of us will."

Cameron nodded. He was right. No matter how angry he was with her, the thought of her getting hurt was unbearable. While they knew how to guard clients outside of their own walls, Bristol was especially stubborn. The smart thing to do was to make sure she stuck around until this whole thing was finished.

"Even if you ruined your chances at getting back together with her, and she ruined her chances at getting back together with you," Reilly continued, raising an eyebrow, "you need to apologize, and you need to get her to see enough sense to let us protect her a little longer. It doesn't matter if she was wrong to treat you the way she did. You need to be the bigger person here."

"Great," Cameron said flatly.

He didn't bother to rebuke Reilly's claim that he still wanted to be with her.

Despite everything he'd said, and all the fury he'd felt, it was true.

Everything had been easier in the seven years that Bristol had been out of his life, but he wanted something more than a life that was easy and comfortable.

Somehow, despite all they'd been through, there was still a flicker of hope hidden away in his heart. Foolish as it was, he still believed that even the most broken things could be mended.

"I'm kidding, brother," Reilly said, shaking his head. "You've forgiven her for worse, and I suspect you would do it again. If she can't do the same for you, well, she isn't the girl God has planned. But either way, we need to keep her safe."

Cameron got to his feet, reaching for a towel and wiping the remaining beads of sweat from his brow.

"Thanks, Reilly," he said, surprised at the emotion in his voice. His family drove him crazy at least half of the time, but whenever things got tough, one of them always knew just what to say. "I'm gonna find a peace offering and head upstairs."

Reilly got up from his own machine and pulled him into a sweaty embrace, clapping him hard on the back. "Love you, man. You got this."

Cameron started to make his way across the gym, leaving Reilly to finish his workout, but as soon as he'd reached the door that led to the locker room, he turned around.

"One more question," he said, waiting as Reilly finished a few more reps.

"Shoot."

"Is my dream of having a wife and a family worth it? Because the process of getting there really and truly stinks."

Reilly paused.

"For my relationship with Lauren, and for our girls, I'd walk through any fire God could throw at me, as many times as it took," he said, giving Cameron a soft smile. "That's one thing I know to be true: real love is worth all of the suffering and sacrifice that it demands of us."

Bristol

The next hour passed far too quickly.

Bristol had begun by going through the files she wasn't familiar with one by one, trying to take a systematic approach, but as the minutes began to tick away, she'd realized that she had to move faster.

Jaclyn could come back any time, and even though she would have an easy enough time coming up with an excuse as to why she was rooting through her files, she'd hardly be able to explain the untouched pile of work on her own desk. The lawyer would be suspicious, and if Bristol's intuitions were correct, she couldn't afford to underestimate what the woman might do if she realized how much she knew.

She was moving more quickly now, shuffling through what felt like endless drawers, cabinets, and cardboard boxes, praying that God would lead her to whatever it was she needed to see.

Just as she'd plopped down unceremoniously onto the floor to go through the two bottom drawers of Jaclyn's desk, she heard the sound of Melanie's heels as she clicked her way back into the office.

For a moment, she froze, before remembering that the intern wasn't going to think anything of Bristol being in her boss's office, even if she was sitting on the floor surrounded by a sea of paper.

Still, she could hardly believe it when Mel knocked at the edge of Jaclyn's door and asked Bristol if she minded her taking her half-day today instead of Thursday as usual. Bristol listened politely as she explained that her boyfriend had been cut early from his shift and was driving in from Dallas to see her.

"That sounds nice of him," she said, smiling up at her. "So long as there's nothing urgent on your desk, go for it. I'll let Jaclyn know when she gets back."

Melanie beamed, rushing back to her own desk and flinging several personal items into her bag before calling out a final goodbye and heading for the door.

Once again, Bristol was alone, but the mess before her was still overwhelming.

She began to pick up some of the potentially sketchy documents that she found, piling them up on the corner of Jaclyn's desk. She'd just have to hide them and read them all later that night. Hopefully, she wouldn't accidentally take anything that Jaclyn would be looking for.

Risky as it was, if she couldn't find what she needed now, she would have no choice but to drag out her charade a little longer.

As she picked up the rest of the files off of the floor, she heard voices coming from somewhere down the hall. Though she doubted anyone would make their way into the secluded area that housed the legal department, she was beginning to feel panic rising.

She had to find those files. She was running out of time.

At last, after rifling through three more drawers and adding a handful of potentially useful folders to her stack, she got to her feet and made her way quietly over to the door of the main office.

Seeing no one in either direction, she ducked back inside, rushing toward the potted plant that Jaclyn kept on her desk and rooting around until she found the small golden key her boss kept hidden beneath a thin layer of soil.

Her heart pounded as she moved toward Jaclyn's most secure cabinet. She'd seen Jaclyn hiding the key once, and she'd remembered its location, figuring that it might prove useful one day. She'd hoped that she wouldn't have to use it, but with Mel gone, she could take the risk.

There were only a few files in the drawer, and none of them were the contract she'd been hoping to find. Most of it was stuff about the Senera Pharmaceuticals case. Though she wanted to take a look at it as well, there was no time to worry about anything that didn't directly relate to Grapas. And if she took these files to read later, Jaclyn would surely notice their absence.

She pushed the drawer shut and turned the key in the lock before striding back over to the plant and burying it once more.

Nothing.

If the info she needed wasn't in the files she was planning to delve into later, she'd officially hit a dead end.

It was time to get out of here.

She found an empty cardstock folder and began gathering up the stack on Jaclyn's desk, trying to move as quickly as she could without leaving behind any evidence of her mess.

Within minutes, she was lost in her work, watching as the surface of the desk gradually came into view. There were just a few more to put back, and she'd be–

"Oh, very good," Jaclyn said loudly from somewhere over Bristol's shoulder, her voice oozing with fake cheerfulness. "Albert was right after all. You're way smarter than you look, Chaplin."

Bristol froze, the last of the files still in hand.

No.

How could she have been so careless?

She felt dizzy as she listened to the door of the office closing and locking with a click.

She set the folder on the desk, forcing herself to take a few slow breaths, not wanting to face Jaclyn even a second before she had to.

Her heart hammered in her chest as she stalled, but no plan came to mind.

The office had a single door, and Jaclyn was in front of it.

She was trapped.

She turned around.

Jaclyn stood straight, her eyes filled with ice.

Grasped in her hands was a gun, pointed straight at Bristol.

"Put the files back, close the drawer, and don't talk."

Chapter 25

Bristol

Bristol did as she was told, biting her lip as she tried to lay the thick folder neatly in the top drawer of the desk. It kept getting stuck on the screws that held the handle, and at last she shoved it in, not caring if the paper tore.

It made no difference now, and in any case, Jaclyn didn't seem to have noticed.

As Bristol turned to face her once more, she forced herself to look the woman in the eye, not wanting to reveal just how terrified she was, though she doubted that she could conceal her shaking hands.

Jaclyn's own fingers were completely steady, and one was resting calmly beside the trigger of the pistol she held.

She looked colder and more frightening than Bristol had ever seen her.

It was clear by the set of her jaw and the shark-like stare of her pale eyes that any decency or kindness that Bristol thought she'd seen in her was nothing but an illusion.

An illusion that the entire Forge Brothers Security staff had fallen for.

Neither woman spoke as Jaclyn let one hand fall away from the gun, reaching into her purse and drawing out her phone. Her eyes–and the barrel of the gun–remained trained firmly on Bristol.

"W-what are you doing?" Bristol asked as Jaclyn began typing something, pecking away with her index finger as she balanced the phone in one hand.

"Just letting my guys know that there's been a change of schedule," she said, sounding as if she was discussing something no more interesting than a sudden forecast for rain. "We'd planned for Friday, but it shouldn't be a big problem for

Grapas to make our special delivery a little early."

Bristol tried to think of something to say.

"Oh," Jaclyn added, her mouth opening in feigned surprise, "I forgot. I had to text Reilly and tell him to stay in his office for the next little while. I told him I'll be dropping off some extremely sensitive case files for his eyes only. He'll stay put, I'm sure. He really takes his job so seriously, don't you think?"

Bristol nodded numbly, her mind racing as she tried to assimilate the new information. She still had no idea why Jaclyn had become wrapped up in such a plot, let alone how Reilly fit into it. Surely, if Jaclyn and Reilly had known each other somehow prior to her coming to work at FBS, she would have known about it by now.

And even if she didn't, Gabriel certainly would have.

All she could think of was the excuse Jaclyn had given about the phone call, that she'd needed Reilly to testify on the Senera case before he went on paternity leave.

If only she'd had a chance to look at those files more closely. Perhaps there had been a clue there, after all.

Or, perhaps, it was something else entirely.

Either way, it was too late now.

A knock sounded at the office door, and it took every ounce of self-control that Bristol possessed to stop herself from bolting toward it.

Jaclyn swore under her breath, but the gun remained just as steady in her hands as it had been a moment before. Bristol watched as the lawyer made her way over to the small window that looked out into the main legal department office, and when she turned back, some of the tension had faded from her expression.

"Act natural, or I'll shoot you," Jaclyn said, her tone almost casual.

Bristol had no doubt that she'd do it. In fact, as much as it terrified her to admit it to herself, she could see no reason that Jaclyn would keep her alive for long in the first place.

For the moment, she assumed she was serving as a convenient insurance policy, but the cold calm in the lawyer's eyes made it clear to her that she had to get out of this, and fast.

Jaclyn ushered Bristol to sit in front of the desk, and went to stand beside the door, so that Bristol would be in full view but most of her own body–and the gun–would be hidden when she opened the door.

Bristol once again considered making a run for it, but she put aside the idea as soon as she saw who the unexpected guest was.

Ron Rollins had been making deliveries for the Screaming Peach for most of Bristol's life. Thanks to his developmental disabilities, his employment options were limited, but he was an incredibly sweet man who seemed to enjoy working for Iris.

"Hi, Ron," she said weakly as he waved to her, hoping that the man wouldn't pick up on the grimace hiding beneath her forced smile.

"Special delivery," he said cheerfully, holding up a large paper bag with the cafe's logo plastered on the front. "Already all paid up."

"How nice," Jaclyn said sweetly, leaning over and taking the bag before Bristol could move.

"Forgive me, sir, if you don't mind, we do have some rather urgent things to finish up here."

Ron turned toward Jaclyn, who slid the gun further behind the door and out of sight.

It was a perfect chance to run, and there was no way that Bristol could take it. Not if it meant that this innocent man might be caught in the crossfire.

"I'm sorry, ma'am," Ron said, shaking his head. "I hate to interrupt, I'm sure work here in the security world is real important. But they told me to bring it right to Bristol, and when she wasn't at her desk, I had to bring it in here, since your office was the only one that had someone in it."

He chuckled nervously, and Bristol watched in disgust as Jaclyn stared at him as though he was nothing more than a bug on the bottom of her Italian leather shoes.

At last, she gave him a final fake smile and began to close the door, and without another word, he was gone.

Bristol let out a breath as Jaclyn locked the door again. She was glad that Ron was safe, but she may have just passed up her best chance at getting away.

Jaclyn waited several seconds before she spoke.

"I figured there's no point in arousing suspicion prematurely," she explained, sounding almost apologetic, as though the man had interrupted some important task she'd asked Bristol to complete. "Besides, we might be holed up for a few hours yet. Kind of nice of the universe to provide us with something to eat."

Bristol nodded, unsure how to respond to someone who revealed so little emotion. She was like a robot, and it made the situation all the more terrifying.

She was growing more certain by the minute that the delivery truck really did contain a bomb, just like in the case she'd read about at D&P. This time, however, she feared that their wicked operation would be successful.

She was the only one who knew what was coming, and she had no way to alert anyone else. The phone sat mere inches away on the desk, but if she so much as reached for the receiver, she was as good as dead.

She watched in silence as Jaclyn pulled out several plastic forks and knives as well as a small stack of napkins from the takeout bag.

"It's really in there," the woman muttered to herself, trying to get the last, large item free of the too-small bag. Bristol said nothing.

At last, Jaclyn drew forth a square box and laid it on her desk. She opened the lid, plastic knife in hand, revealing one of Iris's favorite peach pies, which happened to be Bristol's favorite.

On top of it were the words 'I'M SORRY', written out in coffee beans.

Bristol felt a swell of tears in her throat and struggled to swallow them back.

Jaclyn closed the lid a little too fast, sending several of the brown beans falling over the edge of the pie.

"Lunch would have been nice, but it's all calories, I suppose," she said, but Bristol barely heard her. Even the constant terror of the gun that was pointed at her had begun to fade into the background.

All she could feel was regret.

Had she gone to Cam right away, had she given him the benefit of the doubt, she wouldn't be here now, held hostage by a madwoman. She wouldn't be waiting helplessly as the good people of FBS were put in mortal danger, including the man who deserved so much better than what she'd offered to him.

She'd relied on herself, and in the end, she'd let everyone down.

It was all her fault.

Cameron

After his pep talk with Reilly, the morning had passed by in a rush.

Most of the time had been taken up by the firearm audit, and by the time lunch rolled around, Cam realized that he'd scarcely managed to put even a dent in the rest of his endless piles of work.

Instead of heading for the cafeteria like he usually did, he'd asked one of the security trainees–a nice young guy called Braden–to bring him something from downstairs. He was still at his desk now, typing up reports between bites of cold-cut sandwich.

He'd tried to stop thinking about Bristol long enough to get some work done, but thoughts of her face still managed to distract him every few paragraphs.

All he could do was hope that Iris's famous pie might smooth things over enough that she'd at least tolerate his presence for a few minutes.

Whether or not she would ever want to take another chance on being with him was irrelevant. What mattered most was that she forgave him enough that she'd allow FBS to keep on protecting her.

He set the report he'd just finished typing aside and picked up another one, making it a paragraph and a half and two bites of sandwich in before he paused again.

It was all too tempting to imagine her sitting up in her office, indulging in a second slice of pie and thinking about how much she wanted to patch things up with him.

Reality, he knew, wouldn't be so simple.

Bristol was stubborn to a fault, but if groveling was what it took, groveling he would do, baked goods and all.

Before he could think about it further, however, he heard the insistent beeping of his phone as it vibrated across his desk. When he picked it up, he was surprised to find a message from the garage duty guard.

Grapas order pushed up. They're here now, requesting gate access for Bay 8.

Cameron paused, his fingers hovering over the screen as he read the message over once again.

Something about it set off alarm bells.

He knew, logically, that it was almost certainly nothing–after all, Grapas had sent dozens of deliveries to FBS, often using that exact loading bay–but Grace had been running around all morning in search of any last minute updates, since she'd messed the order up the first time.

In fact...

He swiped away from the messenger app, pulling up his email inbox.

He was right.

That very morning, Grace had copied him on a reminder email she'd sent to everyone in every department at FBS, stating that she'd be sending Grapas the final supply list that morning, before she left for a training course for the rest of the day.

At the time, he'd thought nothing of the message.

Despite her competence as office manager and uncanny ability to work logistical miracles, it wasn't the first time she'd made use of the 'send to directory' function of their network when she got behind on her own deadlines. Most of her alerts didn't apply to him at all, so he tended to mostly ignore them.

But now, reading it again as yet another text from the garage duty guard lit up his phone, he knew that something wasn't right.

There was no way that truck contained their order, not if she hadn't even submitted it until that morning. Nor would Grace schedule a delivery for a time when she wasn't here to sort out the inevitable chaos herself.

Most importantly, Jaclyn had mentioned Grapas on the phone call Bristol had overheard. It was the one part of the conversation that she'd offered no real explanation for when Gabe had asked about it.

Bristol was right, even if he didn't know exactly how or why.

He could feel it.

Something was up, and it wasn't good.

His thumbs felt clumsy as he tapped at the phone's screen.

Stand by until I contact you. Tell them that there's a gate malfunction and they'll have to hang tight.

At last, he hit send, cringing at the lie, though at the moment no better option was coming to mind. He pocketed the phone and got to his feet, confident that the guard would do as he was asked. Bobby Ramos had been with FBS for a long time, and he was a pro–but whoever was in the Grapas truck would only wait so long.

He had to figure out what was going on, and fast.

Cam made his way out into the hall, pulling his office door shut behind him. It was time to talk to Gabe.

Chapter 26

Bristol

Bristol glanced up at the clock on the wall, watching as the second hand ticked slowly across its face.

It had been well over an hour since Jaclyn had taken her hostage, but somehow, the passing of time had ceased to make sense. Bristol had let her mind race, trying to think of any way that she might escape, any way that she might distract Jaclyn, but so far she could see only risk. Even if she could somehow slip out of Jaclyn's office without being shot, there was no way she was going to make it to safety.

Compared to most of the departments at FBS, legal was largely autonomous. Apart from Grace, Gabe, and very occasionally Cameron and the other brothers, few employees ever had need to come into the outer office, let alone to knock on Jaclyn's closed door.

She met with clients in a meeting room off of the lobby downstairs. As far as Bristol knew, with Melanie gone for the day, there was no reason to assume that they'd see another soul before the night guard came on shift and started making his rounds.

Her only hope now was that Cameron would show up to apologize in person, but for the moment, it didn't seem likely. She knew that he had an important client meeting in the afternoon, outside of the office, and that he might be gone for hours. It was even possible that he'd go straight home without returning to the office after all, especially when he never heard anything from her in response to the dessert he'd sent.

Bristol glanced over at the pie box sitting on the desk, trying to stop herself from showing any emotion. Jaclyn had already eaten a slice and offered Bristol some, but she had no appetite. Her boss's cold indifference as she held her captive was made even more terrifying as she brought forkfuls of flaky pie crust to her mouth, as though nothing was wrong in the world at all.

Bristol felt her breath catch in her chest as she heard a loud ping from Jaclyn's phone.

The lawyer reached over and picked it up, brow furrowing as she glanced down at the screen before her face broke into a wide smile.

Bristol eyed the gun that Jaclyn had laid across the desk, inches away from her fingertips in case her hostage tried anything.

She couldn't stand the silence any longer. She figured it was worth the risk to at least try and get some answers. At this point, she didn't have much to lose.

"Since you clearly have no intention of letting me go, you may as well tell me what's going on," Bristol said, willing her voice not to shake.

Jaclyn paused for a moment, glancing up from her phone and offering Bristol a flat smile.

"I suppose that's fair enough," she said. "What do you want to know?"

"Everything," Bristol admitted, keeping her eyes locked on Jaclyn's own. "But you could start with why that text has you looking so perky."

"Well, my contacts at Grapas came through, just as I'd hoped," Jaclyn said, giving a little laugh. "The wait is nearly over. The truck I called for is at the back gate now, waiting for security to clear them. Sounds like there's been some kind of delay, but at least they're here."

Bristol felt a coldness tracing its way down her spine.

Everything was unfolding exactly how she'd feared, and there was nothing whatsoever that she could do about it.

"The truck contains a bomb, of course," Jaclyn continued, not waiting for Bristol to ask any clarifying questions. "My main guy at Grapas is a bit of an expert with them, though law enforcement got in the way last time before the artist could properly unveil his masterpiece. To think that history almost repeated itself, all because I misplaced some files and underestimated a paralegal who grew up in a trailer park."

Bristol felt her fingernails biting into her palms.

Jaclyn had indeed underestimated her, but what did it matter now?

Even with the advance warning she had, she'd failed to thwart Jaclyn and Grapas in the end, all thanks to her insistence on doing everything herself.

Jaclyn paused for a long time, glancing across the office toward the large windows that looked out on the building opposite FBS.

Bristol had briefly considered trying to break one of the windows and alert those working across the street to her predicament, but she'd dismissed the idea quickly. The windows were almost certainly far too strong for her to shatter, and even if she did, there was nowhere to go.

Even on the fourth floor, the ground was a long way down.

Finally, Bristol dared to ask another question.

"How are you tied to Dorling & Porter, Jaclyn?

Why are you doing this? I just want to understand."

Jaclyn smiled, turning until her pale blue gaze fell upon Bristol once more.

"It'll all make sense soon enough," she said calmly. "Assuming you live to hear about it, anyway."

Bristol's heart hammered against her ribcage, but she forced her breathing to remain steady. The woman held all of the power as it was.

Bristol didn't need to give her anything else, including the satisfaction of witnessing her fear.

Jaclyn let out a long sigh, rubbing at one of her temples.

"It's a rather large bomb, and we'd like to destroy as much of FBS as we can, but this particular area is quite far from the garage. You and I might survive just fine. Of course, in the original plan, I wasn't going to be inside the office when the truck blew."

"You were booked for court all day on Friday," Bristol said, remembering, her voice hardly above a whisper.

"Exactly," Jaclyn said, nodding. "But thanks to you, the original plan didn't quite work out. Now that I'm here, though, I find that I'm thankful."

She must have seen the confusion on Bristol's face, because she continued, "I'm kind of looking forward to dying. At least, if it happens, I'm ready for it. I don't think it'll be so bad, though I suppose it might not be the most pleasant if it isn't quick."

Her cold gaze made Bristol feel like a ghost.

Jaclyn stared straight at her, but it was as though her eyes had pierced right through the layers of her flesh and bone, seeing something else that lay behind her.

Bristol wanted to tell her that what was coming after death would be horrible, considering where she'd be spending eternity, but she decided to keep her mouth shut.

It was becoming more clear with each passing minute that the intelligent, competent lawyer might not be exactly sane. And if she'd learned anything from her own time in court, it was that insane people were never predictable.

"I just want to see him again," Jaclyn said, her eyes settling on something invisible over their heads.

Bristol bit her lip before she could ask who she was talking about.

She had a horrible feeling that whatever happened with this bomb, Jaclyn wouldn't be leaving the room alive.

And Bristol feared that she wouldn't be, either.

Cameron

Cam rushed toward the stairwell, his phone pressed to the side of his face as he took the steps two at a time.

Grace wasn't answering.

She'd be able to confirm with certainty if there'd been a change of schedule with Grapas, but someone had had the brilliant idea to send her off to database training all day. She probably didn't even have her ringer on.

He swore under his breath as he heaved open the heavy stairwell door that led out into the top floor of FBS.

It had been all he could do to keep going when he passed the fourth floor exit. Bristol was probably there, unless she'd been angry enough at him to leave early, and he couldn't shake the feeling that she might be in trouble.

Still, common sense had won out. If something really was wrong, he'd do no good by rushing in on his own. He'd need backup, and the sooner he could get Gabe on board, the better.

He might only have minutes left before the truck downstairs made it into the basement of the building.

"I need to talk to you," he said as he burst his way into Gabe's corner office, not bothering to knock. "Now."

"Hey, Paul, can I call you back? Something urgent came up," Gabe said into the phone he was holding as he turned to glare at Cameron.

"This better be good."

As quickly as he could, Cameron outlined the situation, and told him that security had already been stalling downstairs for at least the past ten minutes.

When he'd finished, Gabe sat back in his chair, raising his eyebrows.

"Cam, this doesn't make any sense. We've worked with Grapas for years. I fail to see how an unexpected delivery warrants this level of suspicion."

Cam opened his mouth to argue, but Gabe didn't give him the chance.

"Please tell me you at least talked to Grace about this. Did it not occur to you that maybe they thought they had all of the order ready to go, considering that the actual deadline for us to order has already long passed?"

Cameron shook his head.

"I couldn't get ahold of her," he admitted. "She's at that database thing in Austin, remember?"

Gabe let out a puff of breath and rested his forehead in his hands for several long seconds.

Cameron twisted his fingers into the hem of his t-shirt, trying to resist the urge to raise his voice. They were wasting precious time, and arguing with Gabe was only going to waste more of it.

"You need to get a grip, bro," Gabe said finally. "Send another guard down there to talk to them and peek at the van, if it makes you feel better. I think that's taking more than enough caution."

"No. It could put the guard in danger," Cam said firmly.

"What are you thinking is in this truck," Gabe said, letting out a chuckle. "A bomb?"

"I have no idea," he snapped. "But it feels off, and I trust my instincts. We're a private security company with plenty of enemies. We're used to crazy things happening. Is a possible bomb threat at our back door really so far-fetched?"

"It's far-fetched because the only reason you're acting like this is thanks to Bristol's paranoia," Gabe said. "I get that she really is being targeted, and I don't blame her for being scared, but suspecting Jaclyn and now our office supplier without evidence is totally out of line."

"That phone call she overheard was weird," Cameron said, trying to keep his voice level. "Maybe we shouldn't have been so quick to dismiss–"

Gabriel smacked the palm of his hand against his desk, startling him into silence.

"If you want to let this girl stomp all over your heart again, that's your business. But we're not losing a great lawyer and risking our partnership with a long-term vendor because of Bristol's traumatized imagination. Tell the guards downstairs to check the truck, and then let them in if it's clear. I've had enough of this."

Cameron sucked in a breath as he got to his feet. His hands were shaking as he leaned on the desk, his face barely a foot away from Gabe's own.

"No. We're not letting them in here. Not without the SAPD bomb squad checking them out."

Gabe pulled back as though he'd been slapped, and in that moment, Cam was struck by just how much he reminded him of their father, in both good ways and bad.

"Cameron," Gabe said, his voice dangerously low. "I don't say this often, but I'm the boss, and this is my decision. Call Bobby now, or I will."

Cam stared at his brother and set his jaw, taking only a moment to make up his mind.

When Gabe was in stubborn mode like this, any chance of him cooperating was already long gone.

"Please," he begged, "give me another thirty minutes to look into things. If I don't find more evidence, I'll call them. I promise."

Gabe glanced at his watch.

"You get fifteen."

Without another word, Cam rushed out of the office, breaking into a run as he reached the long expanse of hallways that crisscrossed the fifth floor.

He passed several people in their offices, ignoring their stares. There was no time to explain.

Gabe was right. There wasn't a lot of evidence.

But his intuition had rarely led him astray, and right now, every signal he'd honed over the years in this business was blaring at full volume.

If only he'd trusted Bristol's intuition as much as his own, he would have had a lot more than fifteen minutes to figure this puzzle out.

Chapter 27

Cameron

Cameron made his way into the stairwell once again, glad that he was in good shape.

Waiting for the elevator was out of the question.

With shaking fingers, he dialed Bristol's cell phone, and after several rings it went right to voicemail.

He tried to get her at her desk next, but there was no answer there, either.

Not good.

A few moments later, he reached her floor. There were a few occupied offices here near the stairs, but he ignored the questioning glances of his employees, racing through the seemingly endless maze until at last he reached the secluded corner that housed the tiny legal department.

He slowed to a walk, leaning against a wall for a few seconds as he forced air in and out of his lungs. All he wanted to do was to close the rest of the distance and race inside, but he knew it would be foolish.

If Bristol wasn't in danger and he rushed in, she'd be even more angry at him than she already was.

And that was by far the best case scenario.

More likely, if his intuition was to be believed, she was in danger. And if he wasn't careful, if he acted without thinking, the results could be catastrophic.

Once a few more moments had passed, he crept forward toward the door of the department, leaning against the wall and tilting his head just enough to be able to see through the edge of the window.

The main area seemed to be deserted. He could see no sign of the young student who worked as an intern, and though Bristol's office door was wide open. The screen of her computer monitor was black, and there was no mug of tea, suggesting that it had stayed empty for a good while now.

Jaclyn's door, however, was shut tight.

He looked up at the ceiling, closing his eyes and trying to ask the Lord for guidance despite the panic twisting in his gut. He considered calling Jaclyn, but decided against it.

Gabe was right. There was nothing on paper that made him suspect her, but that didn't matter. If there was any possibility that Jaclyn was involved in whatever was going on, and if Bristol was somehow in there with her, the last thing he wanted to do was to alert the lawyer of his presence.

Ducking back out into the safety of the hall, he pulled out his phone and began typing the long password that would get him into the FBS security cameras.

He sent up a silent prayer of thanks as he found the right footage. Though there were no cameras inside of Bristol's office or Jaclyn's, he could see the rest of the open legal department area–and thanks to a lucky angle, he could just see the back of Bristol's head through the small window in Jaclyn's office door.

His heart picked up its pace once more as Bristol lifted a hand and tucked a strand of brown hair behind an ear at the edge of the frame.

If everything was fine, why hadn't she picked up her desk phone when he'd called? Surely she would have been able to hear it easily from where she sat.

He squinted at the screen, wishing that he could see her face in the small area of coverage that the camera provided through the window.

Somewhere down the hall, he heard the sound of two people talking, followed by a burst of cheerful laughter. It was surreal to think that all over the office, FBS was getting on with business as usual, all while there might be a bomb beneath their feet.

As he waited impatiently for something useful to happen on the screen, he considered pulling the fire alarm and evacuating the building. Gabe would be furious, of course, but it would be worth it to ensure his staff was safe.

However, if he did that, he didn't know what it could mean for Bristol.

It was a possible course of action, but first, he had to find out more–and he was running out of time.

Just then, he noticed a larger movement on the screen as Bristol sat back in her chair.

His breath caught in his chest as he realized Jaclyn was indeed there, sitting on the other side of the desk.

In front of her, gleaming against the smooth maple, was a gun.

He fumbled to take a screen grab of the security footage, his mind racing as his thumbs found the correct arrangement of buttons to capture the image and to text it to Gabe.

Jaclyn, who had never so much as stepped foot in the company's private shooting range, even when Asher had offered to teach her to shoot, had a gun.

And she also had Bristol.

He allowed himself a few more seconds to watch the screen, not wanting to miss it if something was about to go down, but the two women stayed where they were.

All he wanted to do was bust down the door and drag Bristol to safety, but he couldn't take the chance, not with that gun resting on the desk in front of her.

Jaclyn seemed stable enough for the moment, but he'd handled enough hostage situations to know that things could change in a heartbeat.

He needed backup, and then he needed a plan— even if it meant leaving Bristol alone with a possible killer.

As he turned away and headed back down the hall, he felt as though his heart would shatter before he made it to the stairs. Bristol had already been through so much, and now, a new nightmare had come to haunt her waking hours.

"Hey, boss," someone said as she passed him near the stairwell, her face pinched in confusion. Some part of his brain registered that she worked in accounting, but that was all.

He forced himself to wave back as he jogged past, but he could offer no other explanation.

Causing a panic wasn't an option.

He glanced down at the glowing screen of his phone as he pushed his way through the heavy staircase door. Somehow, he still had just a little under five minutes before Gabe would call down to security to let the truck through–not that it mattered.

He had the proof he needed, but there was no sense of triumph.

The phone rang a moment later, and he answered it, pressing it to the side of his sweaty face.

"What is going on with this footage?" Gabe demanded.

Cameron's shoes pounded against the metal stairs as he hurried down toward the second floor, but he could hear his brother's raised voice loud and clear.

"Jaclyn is holding Bristol hostage in her office," he said matter-of-factly. There would be time for I-told-you-so's later–for the moment, he needed Gabe to help him get ahold of the situation before it spun totally out of control. "She's armed. I need you to get the cops here, but make sure they come in quietly. Jaclyn can see the front of the building through her windows, so keep that in mind."

"Noted."

"I'm going to see what Ben can dig up on Jaclyn. Obviously, we missed something. After that, I'm going in to extract Bristol, and I could use some help."

To Cam's relief, Gabe didn't argue or ask any needless questions. He was in security professional mode, and it showed in every word he spoke.

"I'll tell the guys what's going on and start

quietly evacuating. It'll have to be through the front, though, even if it tips Jaclyn off."

"I guess calling in the bomb squad doesn't sound so silly anymore," Cam replied, chuckling without mirth.

There was a brief pause.

"Hang in there, bro," Gabe said gently. "She'll be okay. We've got this."

Cameron prayed that he was right.

Bristol

The minutes continued to tick by as the two women sat in silence.

Jaclyn had taken the gun from the table again and was turning it over in her hands, looking out the window every couple of minutes.

She looked calm—relaxed, even—but Bristol had the distinct feeling that she was paying close attention to everything that was going on.

As for herself, she was desperate not to allow the chaos she felt within to show on the surface.

Thinking of her mother or of Cameron was out of the question. If she did, the tears would come, and crying was not something she was willing to do.

Not in front of this sociopath.

Thinking about the delivery van downstairs, however, only brought a fresh wave of fear.

At any moment, it could explode, blowing them all sky-high. Despite Jaclyn's insistence that they might survive the blast, it was hardly a guarantee–and for those who worked in the lower floors of FBS, it was a death sentence.

She glanced up at Jaclyn as she stared out of the window again, her fingertip gently stroking the side of the gun.

Something was off.

Even though her own sense of time felt hopelessly warped, she could still read the clock on the wall, and the delivery van had been sitting down there for a while now.

Had it been coincidentally delayed from entering FBS, or did someone suspect something?

She felt a small spark of hope igniting within her chest, and she did not seek to quash it.

It was better to dwell on hope, however small, than on sadness or fear.

Perhaps Grace had found out about the early delivery before she'd made it to Austin and had alerted security that something was off.

It was possible, but Bristol feared it was more likely that she would have assumed it was nothing more than a mistake, especially considering how disorganized she had been in getting the order together.

Well played, Jaclyn.

A scheduling error was what everyone would assume... unless Cam had decided to go over Gabe's head and investigated further.

Her heart ached.

Had she told him everything she'd remembered about Grapas as soon as the memories had resurfaced, he might have believed her. But with only a suspicious phone call and an unscheduled delivery, she doubted he had any reason to suspect that anything was amiss.

She glanced over at the window.

The street—and her freedom—were so painfully close.

Even now, there were people everywhere, all around her, people that could have helped her.

Instead, as always, she'd chosen to rely on herself, and there was nothing she could do but watch as Jaclyn caressed the gun like a child in her arms.

Cameron

Cameron paced behind Ben's computer chair as his brother's hands flew over the keyboard.

They'd missed things in Jaclyn's records, all right.

The kind of things that could get them all killed.

He reached down and touched the gun at his belt, reassured by the presence of its cool metal. He forced himself to breathe, feeling the weight of the bulletproof vest that Reilly had just strapped over his chest.

On one of Ben's several spare monitors, he could see the security camera feed of the legal department. Just as before, he could see Bristol and Jaclyn through the window in her office door. They were still small and pixelated, but it was a much better view on the larger screen.

Jaclyn had pulled the gun off of the desk, and for a moment, Cameron was certain that he had made a terrible mistake by leaving Bristol there.

Instead of raising it, however, Jaclyn had simply taken the weapon onto her lap.

He could see nothing beneath the edge of her desk, but neither she nor Bristol moved, and their faces looked largely calm.

Still, waiting to act was killing him.

Gabe and Asher were both pacing along with him, near Ben's office door. Each had his phone to his cheek, and Cam could make out snatches of conversation.

It was obvious that Gabe was talking to Allie, their liaison at SAPD, and Asher was coordinating their own guys, including calling in several operatives who were currently off-site.

Cam struggled to focus, unable to sit down, let alone to sit still.

All he could do was think about bursting through that door, running upstairs, and saving Bristol.

Every minute that he managed to keep waiting felt like a hard-won victory.

At last, he watched as his eldest brother hung up the call.

"All right," Gabe said, clapping his hands together. Asher told whoever was on his line that he'd call back, and hung up his phone as well, his attention focused fully on their eldest brother.

"Plainclothes SAPD are already outside in unmarked vehicles as we speak. Bomb squad is en route, but they're gonna be too slow. The van driver is getting antsy, and he still has his cell phone, so let's watch to see if Jaclyn receives any new phone calls."

He paused, glancing over at Ben, who gave him a thumbs up.

"Anyway," Gabe continued, "I suspect that the driver might ditch, and then try to blow the van while still outside of the gate. I don't want to lose him if SAPD's undercover guys drop the ball. Right now, the element of surprise is on our side. I'm going down there to get him myself. Reilly, Asher, if you're up for it, I could use some help."

"I'm in," Reilly said.

"How confident are you that he's not the suicidal type?" Asher asked, his joking tone belied by the grim expression on his face.

"On his last job, he snuck out the back door before the attempted det," Gabe said. "I suspect he's feeling pretty happy with the idea of staying alive."

Cameron clenched his fists as he listened to their back and forth. Every sentence seemed to be taking an eternity.

"I'm not waiting any more, Gabe," he said. "I'm going up there."

"You don't have to wait, but you do need to try and stall if you can once you get to her," Ben cut in, turning around in his chair and stretching his bulky arms high over his head. "Per the blueprints of the building across the street that I just got access to, SAPD snipers will have a clear shot at Jaclyn if you can't de-escalate. I already sent Allie the intel, but I'm not about to tell SAPD how I got it. If you can get someone downstairs to watch the cameras, I'll come and back Cam up."

"Done," Gabe said, nodding. "Let's move. May God be with us all."

Chapter 28

Bristol

Bristol closed her eyes, unable to sit there and watch Jaclyn play with the gun anymore.

She had never felt so powerless in her life.

Even that terrible night in Dillon Warrington's office hadn't come close.

She'd closed her eyes that night, too, trying to pretend that she was somewhere else, but in the end, it had done little to protect her from the trauma that had followed her long after the deed was done.

No.

This time, she decided that she wasn't going to try and bear the pain and the fear all alone.

This time, she knew that she had someone else to turn to, even in the darkest and loneliest places.

Despite how often she'd neglected Him, she knew that He was still there, waiting for her to seek Him.

God was listening, and He cared about her.

If it weren't for God, the bomb would have gone off already, if not the gun.

Her mom had always tried to teach her that the Lord carried the world within His hands, upholding every single part of it in each moment, and finally, she understood exactly what she meant.

Had God not willed it, she wouldn't be breathing right now.

And while she was alive, there was still hope, however dim.

She prayed in silence, feeling her racing heart beginning to slow as an inexplicable sense of peace washed over her.

She sat there for a long time, her eyes closed against the sunlight.

She heard a knock at the office door.

Cameron

With a final nod to Ben, who was standing behind him in the hallway, Cameron walked into the legal department as quietly as he could.

Every footfall sounded heavy to his ears, and all he could think about was the fact that he was wearing a bulletproof vest while Bristol, of course, was not.

He paused near the intern's desk, looking down at his hands, willing them to stop shaking.

He wished that he was holding his gun, but thanks to Ben's advice, he'd decided to stash it in the back of his waistband, out of sight.

There was still a possibility that this situation could be resolved without shots being fired, and he knew that he had to at least try—even if at the moment all he wanted to do was to neutralize the threat against Bristol permanently.

With a final, silent prayer, he covered the last few feet of distance and knocked at Jaclyn's door, peering through the window.

To his surprise, she barely reacted.

He watched as she got up from her desk and strode toward him, the gun hanging loosely from one hand as she turned the lock on the door handle with the other.

As soon as he heard the click, he pushed it open.

"Cameron," she said, her voice light. "Have a seat."

Were it not for the gun that she was now pointing at Bristol's head, it could have been nothing more than an ordinary meeting.

He nodded, taking his place several feet away from Bristol on a firm leather chair. He could feel his own gun pressing against his back, and wished once again that he had his finger on the trigger already.

He dared a glance over at Bristol.

She, too, looked calmer than he'd expected.

For several seconds, their eyes met, and he hoped that somehow, his stare alone could communicate all of the things he wanted so badly to say to her.

He wanted to tell her that his brothers were evacuating everyone from FBS, and that SAPD snipers were assembling right now, anything that could reassure her.

More than that, though, he wanted to say that he was sorry.

Their problems, their arguments, all of it seemed foolish now.

All he knew for sure is that despite it all, whatever she chose, he was willing to die for her if he needed to.

And there was no other word for that but love.

He watched as Bristol gave him an almost imperceptible nod.

Even without words, he knew that, at the very least, she was telling him that she trusted him. She wasn't going to do anything that could ignite the situation.

He needed just a little more time.

If Jaclyn had any inkling that she had lost control of the situation, he feared that she'd shoot Bristol then and there.

It was time to talk.

"Put the gun down, Jaclyn," he said, his tone calm but authoritative.

Jaclyn gave a tinkling laugh, her blonde hair cascading down her back like a waterfall as she threw back her head.

"Does that line ever actually work?" she asked, leaning forward in her chair with the gun still raised. "In your professional experience?"

Cameron gave her a grim smile.

"Not once," he said, gripping the edge of the chair before his hand sought his own gun. "But we always try it anyway."

Bristol

Tears pricked at Bristol's eyes as she watched the scene unfold.

Despite the fact that Jaclyn was still gripping the

gun, and now had it pointed directly at her, she felt more hope than she had in hours.

She'd been wrong about him.

He'd listened to her about the phone call, even though he hadn't acted as she'd hoped at the time.

When it really counted, he'd figured out that something was up–and now he was here to get her out.

But her tears were not only of relief.

On the one hand, she trusted him completely. He'd know what to do. She wasn't going to die, not so long as Cameron Forge was here to protect her.

But on the other hand, it was no longer just her own life she had to worry about, but his, too, as well as the rest of the FBS staff.

She swallowed hard, trying to make sense of the situation as Cameron and Jaclyn lapsed back into tense silence.

How much had he figured out? Did all of FBS know about the bomb, or was Cameron acting alone?

Cameron had come in here without a visible weapon to reason with Jaclyn, that much was clear, which gave her hope that the rest of the boys were nearby as backup.

But she also knew that there was no way the lawyer was going to listen to him.

There was a darkness in Jaclyn that she'd never seen before, not even on the face of Dillon Warrington as he violated her. His was a stupid evil, a weak evil, an evil of opportunity and impulsive lusts.

Jaclyn Mercier was playing for keeps.

"What can I say to make you see that you need to let her go?" Cameron asked Jaclyn. "You're in control here. I'm listening to what you need, Jaclyn. But I hope you can help me, too."

Jaclyn let out a sigh, her finger holding steady along the side of the trigger guard.

"I can't let her go, Cameron," she said. "You must see that."

"Because she's your leverage, right?" Cameron replied, sounding almost sympathetic. "You know that if you hand her over, your time will be up."

Jaclyn nodded.

As Cameron leaned forward in his chair, his hands resting casually on his thighs, Bristol glimpsed his gun, stuck into the back of his jeans.

Her throat felt thick.

She didn't want to imagine him actually using the gun, but she had no doubt that he would if he had to. For the moment, though, it seemed that he wanted to keep her talking.

Maybe she could help.

She drew a breath and thought about everything she'd been trying to avoid for the last several hours, letting the memories, plans, and hopes shift into her mind.

Two faces appeared again and again.

Her mother, and Cameron.

The tears that she'd been fighting to suppress began to fall, and she relished them.

Each salty droplet that touched her lips reminded her of just how much she still had to fight for.

To live for.

"Please, let me go, Jaclyn," she said, leaning closer to the desk and to the gun. "Please. I'm so scared. Whatever you need, I can help you, but I'm begging you, please just stop this now before you do something we all know that you don't want to do."

Jaclyn's eyes went wide for a moment, no doubt surprised by her sudden outburst after hours of stoicism.

Good.

The sobs made her chest ache, and she hated how pathetic she sounded, but it seemed that her shift in demeanor was yanking Jaclyn off balance, just as she'd hoped it would.

"My mother doesn't have anyone else," she continued. "If you shoot me, she'll be all alone. Whatever it is I've done, don't punish her for my mistakes. Please. I want to figure this out."

Cameron glanced between the two of them, waiting.

At last, Jaclyn spoke, touching a finger to her lips as she glanced up at the ceiling.

"I suppose there is one option I'd consider, Forge," she said at last, turning to Cameron.

Bristol's heart skipped a beat.

However cold and heartless Jaclyn was acting, it was clear that she didn't actually want to kill her.

Not directly, anyway.

She was okay with planting a bomb, but when it came to doing the dirty work herself, Bristol had a feeling that she'd prefer to find another way out if she could.

"What can I do to help?" Cameron asked, his face the picture of compassion.

She knew that he wasn't acting either, at least, not any more than she was.

He had always been able to find some of God's love to share, even with the people who deserved it the least.

It was one of the things she'd always loved about him.

"If you bring Reilly in here, unarmed and without a vest, I'll let Bristol go," Jaclyn replied, her tone all business once more.

Bristol sucked in air.

An opportunity was arising now, a risky one, but if it meant being able to alert Cameron and possibly the other Forge brothers to the bomb waiting downstairs, it was a chance she had to take.

She prayed that he would understand.

"Why do you need to shoot Reilly, Jaclyn?" she said quickly, not wanting to give Cameron a chance to interject. "His office is right above the bomb. You planned it that way, I would guess, though I still have no idea why."

She glanced over at Cameron. His jaw was tight, and though he was trying to retain a neutral expression, she could tell that he was surprised. The question was, was he surprised about the bomb's existence, or about the fact that she'd let the information slip?

Jaclyn laughed, but no touch of humor reached her eyes.

"An admirable attempt at a warning," Jaclyn said. "But if the stream of FBS employees pouring onto the street out front is any indication, they already knew a while ago."

Bristol opened her mouth to speak, but Jaclyn cut her off.

"No. The others are concerned about ridding the world of Forge Brothers Security. My personal interests are much more narrow."

Who were these others? How did they fit in?

Bristol felt she was going insane with curiosity, but she said nothing.

Jaclyn's words hung in the air for several long seconds until Cameron broke the silence.

"Why do you want Reilly so badly?" he asked, gently. "You understand that if I'm going to consider a hostage swap, I need to know the reasoning behind it."

Bristol's throat felt dry.

She'd never allow it. Reilly had a wife and two baby girls on the way. Whatever the consequences she had to bear, there was no way that she was going to let him take her place.

Jaclyn swept her fingers through her hair and leaned her head back against them, closing her eyes with a long sigh.

"Well, Bristol, whether you live through this little affair or not, I guess there's no harm in letting you have your answers after all."

Cameron

So far, so good.

Bristol had taken a risk in mentioning the bomb, but he could see why she'd done it–she had no way to know how much he and the team had already figured out.

For better or for worse, Jaclyn was one step ahead of them, anyway. They'd failed to hide the evacuation of their employees, but it was still better than leaving them as sitting ducks with active explosives in their basement.

Still, there was one thing that neither Jaclyn or Bristol knew, and he hoped to keep it that way for the time being.

Cameron glanced down at his smartwatch, the seconds ticking by with excruciating slowness. He trusted that the sniper team was assembling as quickly as they could, but the sooner they could be ready, the better.

At the moment, they had a clear shot.

Bristol was sitting at enough of an angle that her body wasn't overlapped with Jaclyns, but that could change in a heartbeat.

And if it did, they had only a much riskier plan B, unless by some miracle he managed to de-escalate the situation from within the office. The snipers would send Cameron's smartwatch a silent vibration alert, and he'd have to shove Bristol to the ground exactly three seconds later so that they could take their shot.

He tried to make his body language appear relaxed, but beneath the surface he was preparing for the possibility that that alert could come at any moment, forcing him to jump into immediate action.

But both of their potential plans required a little more time to get the snipers in place.

They just had to keep Jaclyn talking for a little while longer–and it seemed that Bristol had found the right topic.

"Maybe start at the beginning," she suggested to Jaclyn, knotting her fingers together on her lap as she spoke.

"Stalling for time. How original," Jaclyn said flatly.

Bristol said nothing, and after a couple of seconds, the lawyer released a heavy sigh and turned to face Cameron.

"Do you remember that El Paso job from last year?"

Before he could answer, she spoke again.

"Nevermind. I'm sure it's long since faded into the rest of your caseload. All in a days' work, right?"

Cameron shook his head.

He remembered that job, all right. It was a major drug deal between the Iron Prophets gang and a major cartel based in Juarez.

Everyone at FBS remembered. Especially his brothers.

Especially Reilly.

"We don't forget cases like that so easily, Jaclyn," he said softly. The regret in his voice was genuine. "Not when people die. Especially people like your son."

Chapter 29

Bristol

Bristol didn't bother to hide her surprise.

It was clear now that Cameron had found out a whole lot more than she knew.

While her own stubbornness hadn't helped matters, she was no longer sure that the situation could have been prevented as easily as she'd first thought. Suddenly, Jaclyn's motives made a whole lot more sense.

"Chase's death wasn't something that any of us wanted," Cameron was saying, offering the same gentle, soothing tone he'd been using since he sat down. "Including Reilly. It was an accident. I want you to know that."

Jaclyn's pale eyes were wide as she stared at Cameron. For a second, Bristol thought that perhaps she believed him, but her hope was short-lived.

The next time she spoke, her voice sounded as hollow as it had before.

"Chase was my life, but that doesn't mean he made things easy for me. But I made things hard for him, too," Jaclyn bit her lip and glanced down at the surface of her desk, her eyes lingering on an empty space next to her monitor for longer than necessary.

Perhaps there had been a photo of her late son there at one time, but it wasn't while she was working here. No one at FBS had ever mentioned that Jaclyn had a son at all, let alone that he'd died and that their own company had somehow been involved.

No. Bristol was sure that the lawyer had omitted that information on purpose.

Whatever Jaclyn was about to say next, she still found the situation incredibly sad.

Dealing with death and loss was always difficult. It had to be a million times worse when the grief was hidden away.

"What do you mean, Jaclyn?" Cameron prompted after a moment.

"Albert and I were young when we met," Jaclyn said, a half-smile rising to her lips for a moment before falling away. "But he was already married. Worse, he was already firmly ensconced in Dorling & Porter's world. It kind of happens that way automatically when your grandfather is one of the firm's founders, and your father is the one who put it on the map."

Bristol's chest felt tight. The Albert on the phone had indeed been one of her former bosses, Albert Dorling, just as she'd thought.

"Anyway, Albert's wife knew her place in the family. She was there to have his children, to host dinner parties, to help him charm clients, all the rest. She was a good match, love had little to do with it, on either end."

"But you and Albert loved each other?" Cameron asked.

"We still do," Jaclyn said, nodding. "But for the last decade and a half or so, it's been a much more secretive kind of affair. I certainly couldn't keep working at D&P, for business reasons as well as personal ones. Needless to say, we've kept my long history there very much out of public view, right along with the fact that I'm in an adulterous relationship with one of the senior partners."

Bristol noticed that as soon as Jaclyn's eyes fell away from Cameron for just a moment, he glanced down at his smartwatch.

He was stalling, but what was it he was waiting for?

"Where does your son fit in?" he asked.

Bristol could see his jaw tightening slightly as he spoke. It was not the safest topic, she knew, but she was glad to finally be getting some answers—even if Jaclyn's gun still rested way too close for her liking.

"I got pregnant with Chase only about a year into our affair. Though Albert's wife had been rather indifferent until then, I guess carrying her husband's bastard was a step over the line," she gave a wry smile. "But I wasn't going to give him up. Albert didn't want to, either. He already had two with his wife, and he was–is–a great father. We adored that boy, but obviously, we couldn't treat him just like one of Albert's other kids. It would have been bad for his image, and more importantly, for the firm's image. So we didn't. In private, he was our son. In public, he was mine."

Bristol's throat felt tight.

Her own father had abandoned her and her mother, and she'd carried the pain with her ever since. But having a father around who pretended you didn't exist seemed somehow even worse.

"Albert supported us financially, but I didn't really need his money. I was a good lawyer. Still am. That much is true," she said, giving a quick laugh.

"I don't doubt it," Cameron said mildly, glancing over at Bristol, who nodded.

"Anyway, I was able to be a part of D&P's inner circle from a distance. I helped them out in various ways while I worked at other firms. It's amazing what a little insider knowledge can do when it comes to how a case pans out in court."

Bristol wanted to tell her that it would be better to be a mediocre but honest lawyer than a lying double-crosser, but she kept her mouth shut.

"When the Iron Prophets deal came around, I made sure I kept up to date on the news. After all, both my firm and D&P had clients linked to the gang, and to the cartel, not to mention the clients that belonged to some of our friends in Mexico. We had interests, you understand."

Cameron nodded. "And when Reilly and FBS helped to thwart that deal with the help of a low-level mule by the name of Lauren Ortega, none of you were happy."

Lauren?

Bristol's mind raced.

Reilly's wife had been a drug smuggler?

She supposed it was hardly the sort of thing that would be brought up with every new employee that walked into FBS, but still, she couldn't think of a more shocking backstory for the soft-spoken hispanic woman she'd met.

Jaclyn laughed aloud. "No, everyone was furious. I wasn't surprised, though. Sure, our clients in both the Iron Prophets gang and the cartel are professionals, but both groups are managed on the ground level by a bunch of junkies. They should have assumed there would be screwups and been more careful, but of course they weren't."

"So why go after FBS?" Cameron asked. "You said it yourself, your clients messed up and got themselves caught."

Jaclyn rolled her eyes.

"Because of money, Forge. I know it's something you and your brothers have never had to think about, but most of us do," she glanced at Bristol, eyebrows raised expectantly.

She nodded, not wanting to argue.

"D&P has plenty of money, I'd say," Cameron said mildly. "Especially for the top-level people who are making the decisions to benefit financially from the activities of gangbangers and drug lords."

Jaclyn raised both hands as though in surrender, and Bristol felt the urge to lunge toward the desk, grab the gun, and turn it on the lawyer.

The moment was gone.

"Oh, I agree with you, Cam," Jaclyn continued, shaking her head. "Greed is all it is. I love Albert, but his appetite for fast cars and diamonds and all the rest of it will be his downfall. D&P got what it deserved when it came to that deal, if you ask me."

"But?"

"As I said," Jaclyn continued, sighing softly. "My interests are more personal. I don't care how the gang screwed up, how the cartel screwed up, or how my friends in the law screwed up. I don't care about Lauren Ortega, either, though I suppose it's a shame for her that she has been caught up in this madness twice now, both times due to her poor choice in men."

Bristol had so many questions, but if she ever wanted the chance to ask Reilly for answers, she'd just have to keep quiet.

"Okay. Your issue is with Reilly. Can you walk me through what happened, from your perspective?" Cameron said.

Jaclyn rested both hands against the edge of the desk and gripped it tightly.

"You know what happened. Enough with the psychobabble."

"There's he said, she said, and then there's the truth," Cam said firmly. "I'd like your side, if you'll indulge me."

Jaclyn peered over at Bristol. "Well, I did say you'd get answers. Fine."

Bristol stared back, unsure how to respond.

Fortunately the moment passed, and Jaclyn continued on.

"Despite his less than fortunate background, at least on paper, Chase was still the son of two top-tier lawyers. From childhood, it was clear he had the aptitude to do great things, and it was no surprise when he became a teenager and decided he wanted to go into law.

"He graduated from both high school and undergrad early, and spent most of his time in those years preparing for the LSATs. We couldn't help him openly, of course, and we didn't need to. On the strength of his application, he ended up as the youngest student at the best law school in Texas."

Jaclyn paused, as though letting the two of them bask in the glow of her son's accomplishments.

For the first time, the lawyer looked genuinely happy.

Despite the fact that she was currently attempting to blow everyone up and threatening to shoot her personally, Bristol couldn't help but to feel a tug of sympathy within her heart. A mother losing her child was always a tragedy.

"Chase sounds like he was an exceptional person," Cameron said carefully.

"He was. But even for the best and brightest, connections help. I had sway with a lot of people in the legal world, of course, but due to the sensitivity of the situation I had to look to lower-level firms. They were less glamorous, with less money for 'the lifestyle'.

"My son was smart, but he was still barely old enough to drink. Certain temptations pulled him in a direction I didn't want him to go. When Albert offered to help him get in with one of the other firms who worked with the cartel–for a lot more money–that was what he chose."

Jaclyn's face had gone pale and hollow once more.

"And yes, despite all of that, I still love Albert very much. He'll regret that decision for the rest of his life. My hatred is unnecessary. His guilt is punishment enough."

Cameron only nodded, his face grim.

"Anyway, he was working as an intern at this firm in El Paso during his second year. They trusted him more than the average law student, thanks to his father's connections, and often allowed him to tag along on client meetings."

Bristol sucked in a breath, and she saw Cameron flinch slightly as the words sunk in.

"Yes," Jaclyn said, nodding. "On the day that FBS was planning to jump into the fray, one of the big dogs in the cartel decided that he wanted to oversee the product delivery for himself and get some contracts looked over a final time. He decided that he didn't trust his lawyers in Juarez or his other lackeys to get the job done. So he dragged his American counsel right to the drop location, and my son was with him."

Jaclyn paused, and for a long time, the room was silent.

Bristol dared to risk a glance out the window, but she could see nothing.

Somewhere on the street below, the employees of FBS would be walking briskly toward safety, leaving them in a soon-to-be empty building with the bomb.

At last, Jaclyn went on.

"You know the details, Cameron, and Bristol doesn't need to know. Reilly tried to shoot El Pez, and one of his bullets hit Chase. He bled out for a while, and then he died."

Bristol already knew the ending, but Jaclyn's words, and the emptiness in her eyes, still made her chest ache. She could only imagine the guilt that Reilly felt.

"I'm sorry about what happened," Cameron said, leaning forward and reaching a hand toward Jaclyn's own, ignoring the gun that rested mere inches away. "Reilly is too. If he'd known who you were, he would have told you as much himself."

Jaclyn let out a bitter laugh.

"I'm a criminal," she said. "I know how you squeaky-clean security types feel about people like me. And people like Chase."

"Just because Chase was involved in something shady doesn't mean he deserved to die," Bristol heard herself saying, hugging herself as she sat back in her chair, away from Jaclyn and the loaded gun. "I'm sorry, too. I truly am."

"It's regrettable that you got dragged into all of this," Jaclyn said. "You have nothing to be sorry for."

Bristol wasn't sure how to respond.

"So why is she here, Jaclyn? And why was she being harassed and attacked in the first place?" Cameron asked the same questions that were racing through her mind.

"Hard as it may be to believe, much of it was a coincidence," Jaclyn said, frowning. "You guys have been messing up D&P's plans–and their bank accounts–for years. The big bust, and the resulting loss of business with one of their most lucrative manufacturing partners, was the final straw. The Iron Prophets and the cartel felt the same way."

"So where do you fit in? And me?" Bristol asked, eyeing the gun.

For the moment, she would take the risk of trying to sate her curiosity. She had to know.

"D&P wanted to play the long game, and that meant they needed intel, especially on the legal end. I was the obvious choice to go undercover. I don't have a record–not a criminal one, anyway–and Albert Dorling himself trusts me entirely."

Bristol caught Cameron glancing down at his wrist again.

Surely, whatever plan he had in place had to have been ready by now, even if it involved gathering police officers and security operatives from across the city.

But perhaps he still hoped that he could resolve the situation using nothing more than words.

As she looked at Jaclyn's drawn, sad face, she couldn't help but to hope that was the case, gun or no gun.

"Anyway," Jaclyn continued, "I was more interested in the cartel's plan, namely the bombing that I assume, by now, has been thwarted. I knew where Reilly's office was, and I made sure they'd send their explosives in right next to it. I knew he wouldn't suffer, not like Chase did, but he would certainly die. An eye for an eye. That was all I wanted."

She saw Cameron's hand curling into a fist, but he said nothing.

"I still don't understand what I have to do with this," Bristol said, ignoring the coldness of her comments about Reilly.

Jaclyn was right. The bomb had almost certainly been dismantled or at least secured by now, and the woman's homicidal fantasies would make no difference.

"Like I said, it was largely a coincidence. When you were working at D&P, you were seen messing around in some restricted files, files relating to allied gang and cartel interests."

"I saw a file about the attempted terror attack at the mayor's office," Bristol admitted. "It mentioned the name Grapas, but I didn't remember until recently."

Jaclyn nodded. "Some of the lawyers were sure that you knew too much. Albert wasn't convinced, but in the end the partners all agreed that keeping you around wasn't worth the risk, even if you were a stellar paralegal. They needed you gone, but they didn't want you going to another firm and potentially spilling what you knew. You had to be pushed out of the field entirely."

Bristol felt hot anger rising in her throat.

Once again, Jaclyn was speaking without a trace of emotion, as though attempting to destroy Bristol's career was as inconsequential as squashing a housefly.

"So you hired Warrington to assault me?" she asked, surprised by just how much her voice shook. She caught Cameron giving her a warning glance, but at the moment, even the sight of the gun wasn't enough to silence her.

"Warrington was already drinking too much and getting sloppy," Jaclyn said, her face contorting with disgust. "He was nothing but a spoiled rich boy who managed to squander every opportunity he was given. He was a liability, just like you were."

"Sort of a killing two birds with one stone situation?" Cameron suggested before Bristol could say anything herself.

"Albert and some of the other partners had heard him make some, shall we say, off-color comments about Bristol. They decided that if they got you two alone together enough times, he wouldn't be able to resist."

"And then they killed him," Bristol said flatly.

The most painful, humiliating experience she'd ever endured had been nothing more than a ploy to keep D&P's cash flowing. Somehow, she felt even more used than before.

Jaclyn winced. "Actually, I don't know anything about that, though I don't think it was a suicide. I assume it must have been the cartel. D&P was ready to pretend it never happened and let everyone move on with their lives, but maybe they found out about Warrington's loose lips and wanted a solution with no potential for loose ends."

Bristol shuddered.

She hoped that none of these people in the gang or the cartel knew she'd seen even a single restricted file, though at the moment, Jaclyn was the far greater threat.

"So, as far as D&P was concerned, it was back to business as usual, at least while they plotted their revenge against FBS," Cameron said. "Until Bristol showed up here. Right in your office, no less."

The side of Jaclyn's mouth lifted in a half-smile.

"I assumed that you were doing the same thing I was, Bristol," she said. "I thought you were here to help FBS pursue D&P, and that you really did know just as much as the most paranoid lawyers at the firm assumed you did."

Bristol wasn't sure whether to laugh at the absurdity of the situation or to cry.

Finally, after so many sleepless nights and days spent looking over her shoulder, the truth was coming out in a way that she never would have expected.

"No wonder they wanted to scare me off," Bristol said, allowing a humorless chuckle to escape. "And when they realized that their harassment wasn't working, they went straight to attempted kidnapping."

"That was a bit of a rogue operation," Jaclyn said. "Those two goons were hired by D&P to get in your face and scare you, not to try and shove you in a van in the riskiest location possible. I told Albert that hiring a couple of gangbangers for a delicate task like this was a bad idea, but as usual, he didn't listen to me."

Jaclyn paused.

She was looking at nothing again, lost in thought, her blonde lashes blinking over striking, spectral eyes.

Bristol felt her muscles tense.

Something was wrong, she could feel it.

Cameron's expression mirrored her own.

The slightest shift, imperceptible, and yet–

"I'm glad I got to make my confession," Jaclyn said, grasping the gun firmly and getting out of her seat. "But nothing changes now. It's too late for that."

Chapter 30

Cameron

Cameron watched as Jaclyn moved toward Bristol, passing him without so much as a glance, as though he wasn't there at all.

He could see the fear in Bristol's eyes as the woman moved around the desk and circled the two chairs, the gun steady in her hand.

She reminded Cameron of a panther eyeing her prey, but unlike an animal, it was something beyond instinct or even logic driving Jaclyn now, something far more sinister.

Bristol's fingers shook as the lawyer drew closer, and he watched the rise and fall of her chest as she tried to keep herself calm.

He was sitting only feet away, but there may as well have been an ocean between them.

Jaclyn grabbed Bristol by the arm and yanked her to her feet, shoving the barrel of the gun against her ribcage.

He wanted to jump in and put a stop to the slow-motion disaster that was unfolding in front of him, but he'd been too slow. The chance to go for the gun had ended as soon as Jaclyn had abruptly gotten tired of talking.

If he pulled out his own firearm now, there was nothing to stop Jaclyn from retaliating.

He'd thought that they had more time, that there was a chance that this broken woman could be stopped without the need for violence.

He'd been naive, and stubborn, and it was the woman he loved who would pay the price.

Bristol stared at him, her eyes pleading, a fawn waiting to be devoured by a dangerous predator.

Jaclyn's expression was completely blank. It seemed that there was nothing behind her eyes anymore, not even pain.

Cameron wondered if she even realized what she was doing, or if the madness that had been growing within her since the death of her son had finally taken hold completely.

Before he could think of a new approach, he felt his smartwatch vibrating on his wrist.

Once, twice, three times.

Somehow, the urgent message broke through his swirling thoughts, red warning bells sounding in his head.

The snipers no longer had a clear shot.

He forced himself into action, his knee slamming against Jaclyn's desk as he rushed toward the two women.

"Bristol, get down!"

It was too late.

Jaclyn had taken hold of her, dragging her to her feet, the cold metal of the gun pressed against her temple.

Bristol's eyes were closed, but he could see tears escaping from them, rolling down her cheeks in twin rivulets as her shaking legs threatened to give out beneath her.

"What's the plan, Forge?" Jaclyn asked. "Ambush from the hallway? Snipers across the street? You security types are so predictable. Seriously, you guys need to learn to innovate if you want to keep up with the criminals in this town."

Cameron reached for his own gun, drawing it out from his waistband, knowing that it was nothing but a hunk of useless metal now.

There was no way to take a shot.

Jaclyn glanced at it, a cruel smile twisting her elfin features. "Very good. Very cinematic. Bringing out the gun at the height of the drama. Obviously, I knew it was there a long while ago."

He gritted his teeth, staring at her, not wanting to take the bait.

She was mocking him. She'd been in control the entire time, and they both knew it.

He had to think, but every time his eye caught

Bristol's terrified face, he felt himself falling into panic.

He had to do something. He had to get her out.

This was his fault. If he had listened to her from the beginning, she might have come to him. He or his brothers could have searched for evidence and gotten ahead of the bombing plot.

He could have protected her, he could have–

The sound of shattering glass filled his ears.

He braced for a gunshot, his hands slick with sweat against his own weapon, but there was none. For a split second there was only quiet and confusion.

He had just enough time to look up and see the surprise on Jaclyn's face before the immense bang that followed.

Blinding light burned against his retinas, forcing his eyes shut as he dove toward the ground, covering his hands with his ears far too late.

The smell of smoke burned in his nostrils, obscuring what little he could see through the splotches of light that lingered in his field of vision.

His head felt like his brain had been shaken loose and left rattling around his skull.

A flashbang.

One of their guys must have snuck into the outer office and tossed it in through the window in Jaclyn's door.

All he wanted to do was lay down and wait for his ears to stop ringing, but he didn't have the luxury.

God had granted him a second or two before Bristol and Jaclyn would recover, and he had to take it.

He crawled a few feet across the floor and found Bristol.

Before Jaclyn could turn and see what he was doing, he'd gotten to his feet and dragged her with him, shoving her body behind his own.

He pointed his gun at Jaclyn as she got to her feet, coughing and rubbing at her ears, her eyes squeezed shut. He couldn't see if she still held the gun, but he no longer cared.

He was wearing a bulletproof vest, and Bristol stood behind him.

She was safe.

All of a sudden he saw Ben's hulking figure marching into view through the haze of smoke, his own gun raised.

Cam couldn't hear the sound of doors opening, or footsteps, but he knew his brothers were there. He hoped that the hearing damage wasn't permanent, but if it was, he'd consider it a small price to pay for his life, and for Bristol's.

Reilly followed, marching right up to Jaclyn.

"We know how to innovate," he said, training his gun on her as she struggled to her feet. "Drop your weapon, Jaclyn. It's over."

Cameron saw the gun then, still gripped in her hand.

But she was now pointing it at herself.

Bristol

Bristol pressed herself against Cameron's back, leaning her weight against his own and trusting that he had more strength than she did to hold her steady.

Everything hurt, and she'd never been so tired in her life.

All she wanted to do was to go upstairs–no, to her own bed at home–and take a long nap.

Her eyes stung, her head was pounding, and she couldn't stop the smoke-choked coughs that escaped from her throat every few seconds. Worst of all, her ears would not stop ringing.

She watched as Ben and Reilly filed into the office, appearing like benevolent ghosts from the dark haze of smoke.

She was safe now, and so was Cam, but the scene before her felt surreal, like she was watching a movie–

Her heart sank, the reality of the scene sinking into stark relief as Jaclyn Mercier pressed the barrel of the gun to the side of her own skull.

No.

She wanted to close her eyes, to hide against Cam's warm back, to shield herself from yet more horror and evil, but she couldn't look away.

Jaclyn was crying now, her chest heaving with sobs as tears poured from her eyes.

"You took my world from me, Reilly Forge," she said. All of her coldness was gone, replaced by mad fury, her voice shaking with each syllable. "He was nothing but some scum criminal to you, but he was my son, and I loved him more than my own life."

Bristol's gut twisted at her choice of words.

She knew little about Chase, but she doubted he would have wanted his mother to kill herself to cope with her grief.

Cameron turned toward Bristol and pulled her against his chest, his free arm encircling her body in a tight embrace as he kissed the top of her head.

He still held his gun with his other hand, but he'd let it fall to his side.

"I'm truly sorry for your loss," Reilly said, his face tight with pain. "It was an accident. I wish it hadn't happened the way it did, but El Pez was about to kill our informant. I had no choice but to try and stop him. What happened next was an accident."

"You always have a choice," Jaclyn spat. Her finger was against the trigger now, and

Bristol could see that her whole hand was shaking.

No. She couldn't do this. This wasn't how it should end.

"You're right," Bristol said, wriggling out of Cameron's warm embrace and taking a few steps toward Jaclyn.

To her relief, Cameron didn't try to stop her.

He didn't need to, not with two other guns still trained on her abductor.

She wasn't in danger anymore, and despite the terror that this woman had put them all through, she realized just how deeply she pitied her.

She would have to pay for all of her crimes, but this wasn't the way.

"You're right that we have always have a choice, Jaclyn," she said, gaining confidence as she felt Cameron, Reilly, and Ben taking a few steps closer to her. "Right now, you have a chance to choose to live. The opportunity to serve your time, and to choose a better path going forward than Chase did."

Jaclyn opened her mouth as though she might argue before closing it again.

Bristol watched her hand, noticing that she had loosened her grip on the gun. It was slight, but it was something. It was enough to give her hope.

She took a step closer, saying a silent prayer that the Forge brothers would stay back, just a little, and give the two women room.

She extended a hand toward Jaclyn, who was still crying, her eyes red and swollen as she stared back at Bristol.

"Killing yourself won't bring him back, Jaclyn," she said. "Please. Put the gun down, and let's end this peacefully."

There was a long pause.

No one moved.

"I'm so tired," Jaclyn said at last. Bristol could only just barely hear her, thanks to the damage the flashbang had done to her ears.

"I know, Jaclyn. It's okay to let go," she said, as gently as she could.

Bristol held her hand out as she waited, ignoring the ache in her tired muscles.

She couldn't see their faces, but she was sure that Cameron, Ben, and Reilly were offering the same prayer in their hearts that she was.

At last, there was a sharp clattering sound as Jaclyn's gun fell to the floor.

She took Bristol's hand in her own and stepped forward, their eyes meeting for a fleeting second before Jaclyn stared down at the floor.

Bristol watched as Ben grabbed a pair of handcuffs from a loop at his belt and snapped them gently onto Jaclyn's wrists before leading her out of the smoky office.

It was over.

Chapter 31

Cameron

It was dark by the time he'd finished giving his statement at the police station, and all that Cameron could think about was getting a chance to talk with Bristol.

Even his longing for some real food could be safely ignored, so long as he could finally catch her alone.

For him and for his brothers, danger was just a part of a normal day's work, but he could scarcely imagine how traumatic the whole day–and the past several months–must have been for Bristol.

On the outside, she seemed to be holding up just fine, but they'd hardly had five minutes to speak all afternoon, and to make matters worse, she'd been interviewed longer and by more cops than anyone else.

He leaned back on the uncomfortable plastic chair that someone had let him place in the hallway, trying to stretch some of the day's kinks out of his neck.

Ben and Reilly had offered to stay with him and wait for her, but he'd told them to go home and get some rest.

Gabriel and Asher had come by to check in several hours before, but they too had headed in for the night, unless Gabe had decided to go back to the office to do yet more work.

For the first time in far too long, he thought of his final brother, Jacob.

He would have been there, too, but Cam figured that asking him to hop on a flight from Niger–or was he in Libya by now?–to come and keep him company at the police station would have been a bit of a big ask.

Then again, considering Jacob's history with the police, perhaps he wouldn't have wanted to darken their door even if he'd only had to drive across town.

Before he could ponder the matter further, he heard the sound of a door opening behind him.

"Thank you for your time, Miss Chaplin," the detective said, ushering her out into the hall. Cameron got to his feet. "If we need anything else, we'll give you a call."

"Any time," Bristol said, shaking the man's hand before he disappeared back down the maze-like hallway.

All he'd wanted the entire day was to have a moment alone with her, but now that that moment had arrived, he felt strangely awkward. He glanced up at the flickering tube lights overhead, his eye catching on a long-neglected cobweb resting in a corner.

So much had happened. He had no idea where to begin.

He cleared his throat, settling on the safest entry point to conversation that he could think of.

"How does fresh air and a very late dinner sound?"

Bristol smiled up at him.

Somehow, despite the day she'd had and the lingering redness that rimmed her eyes, she still managed to look almost painfully gorgeous.

"Everything I've eaten for the last eight hours has come out of a vending machine," she said. "I didn't even get to eat any of that groveling pie. Jaclyn kind of ruined the mood."

Bristol laughed, and Cameron felt the tension of the moment fading away in an instant as they made their way toward the lobby of SAPD headquarters.

"It was a peace offering pie, actually," he joked as they made their way out onto the street.

It was chilly now that the sun had sunk beneath the horizon, and they'd hardly had time earlier to think of grabbing their jackets.

He waited until they were a few steps away from the building before pulling her into his arms, no longer afraid of how she would react.

He had almost lost her today.

It had a way of putting things into perspective.

Still, he felt a tingle of relief as she leaned into his embrace, pressing her face against his chest even as pedestrians continued to pass them on the sidewalk.

"How are you doing?" he asked, his voice thick with emotion as he inhaled the smell of her minty shampoo. So far as he could tell, it was the same kind she'd used when she was a teenager, and it sent a thousand memories crashing through his brain like fireworks.

"I'm okay," she said, her voice muffled by his chest until she pulled away.

 He settled for holding her hand, and the two of them started down the street, the sound of chattering voices around them making it unnecessary to be quiet.

"Why'd they keep you so long?" he asked.

"They wanted to know more about what I saw while I was working at D&P. They helped me to remember things I would never have dragged up on my own," she said.

"I'm sure that we've made our enemies more angry than ever."

"The detectives told me as much. As much as I'd like to put it all behind me, I suspect that everyone at FBS will be watching our backs for a while. D&P will want to lay low while the legal aspect of this case is resolved, but I don't think the gang or the cartel will take the same view."

"Me either."

At the moment, he didn't care if every drug lord on both sides of the border came after Bristol, his brothers, or their employees.

He was prepared now, and he wasn't going to cower in fear.

"Anyway," Bristol said, looking down at her boots as they continued to walk, "I'm sorry you had to wait for me so long. There was a lot to go over. Both about this case and about the last one."

Her voice fell to a whisper.

"You don't have to talk about it anymore, if you don't want to," he said quickly. "I'm sure you've had to rehash a lot–"

"No."

She gripped his hand more firmly, glancing up at him, her green eyes steely with determination.

"I'm sick of letting what happened to me be this shameful, secret thing that I have to hide away. All of the shame belongs to Dillon Warrington. I'm not going to carry it any more."

He leaned over and kissed her cheek.

"Your liaison, Allie, was helpful," Bristol continued. "She assured me that I could say as much or as little as I wanted about Warrington, but if I had more about what happened on the record, it could help me mount a civil case against D&P later if I ever wanted to pursue it. I don't know if I ever will, but I didn't want my discomfort about that night to close any doors in the future."

"That makes sense," he said.

Cameron made a mental note to call Allie Parker the next day and thank her.

At this point, she'd more than proven that she was not just a useful ally but, in a way, a part of the Forge Brothers Security family.

He was glad to know that even though he wasn't able to be there to protect her, someone else he trusted was.

"Allie saw that I was comfortable with her, and insisted on staying by my side the whole time. Obviously, there was no need for physical evidence collection, but the emotional vulnerability wasn't easy, and I'm glad that I wasn't alone."

Bristol let the last several words tumble out in a rush, but she didn't look at her feet.

She was heading down the sidewalk, her hand in his, her chin held high.

"I'm so proud of you, Bristol," he said, not slowing his pace as he leaned over to offer yet another peck on her cold, soft cheek.

They walked in silence for a moment.

"Is there a 'but' that fits in there somewhere?" Bristol joked, jabbing him gently in the arm as she glanced up at him, a smile lighting up her face.

He tried to smile back, but couldn't quite manage it.

"I'm proud of you for giving the police all of the information you had, about both cases," he started carefully. "A lesser person would have kept quiet, not wanting to risk drawing fire, but you chose to stand firm in the truth, and I firmly believe the Lord will protect you in return. Hopefully by using me as His instrument."

Bristol nodded, letting their clasped hands swing between them as they continued to walk.

"But D&P are playing in the big leagues. Their tracks will be covered well, and they'll be more than happy to let Jaclyn and Grapas take the fall."

"Unfortunately, I agree," Bristol said. "Jaclyn's grief caused her to slip up, but I suspect she's the exception. I figure that even Albert Dorling will find a way to slither out of trouble in the end."

Cam nodded.

"Just know that if and when you decide to pursue further legal action–and when we can hire a new in-house lawyer–FBS will be representing you. And paying every last cent of whatever it costs you to do it."

Bristol said nothing.

As the seconds stretched on, Cameron began to feel anxious, despite the comforting weight of her small hand clutched in his own.

Had he upset her again? Was he being too controlling, too bossy, too–

Before he realized what was happening, Bristol had stopped short, still clinging tight to his hand.

She looked up at him, her eyes filled with the same longing that he had been feeling himself ever since she walked back into his life.

She stretched out a hand to touch him, her fingertips soft against the stubble of his jaw, and his own fingers found the back of her neck and entwined in her hair.

He closed his eyes as his lips found hers, the warmth of her body against his own sending electricity through him as he pulled her in closer.

He'd let her go once, and he had no plans to do it again.

Bristol

As they kissed, Bristol forgot everything else.

She hardly noticed the good citizens of San Antonio weaving past them as they embraced in the middle of the sidewalk, or the chill of the wind biting at her neck as the night grew colder.

After everything she'd survived, she was finally ready to start living.

She was ready to let go of what she thought she wanted, and hold on to something better, no matter the risk to her heart.

Too soon, Cameron pulled back from the kiss, letting his hands fall until they rested gently on her waist.

"What was that for?" he asked, his smile filled with warmth. "You surprised me."

She smiled up at him, remembering just how much she enjoyed the difference in height between them as she considered her answer.

"For knowing when you need to change, and when you need to stay just as you are," she said at last.

"I'd say that's something you're learning yourself, too," he said gently. "I hope we can both keep learning to be the people God wants us to be."

Bristol swallowed hard.

Despite the joy that filled her heart when they kissed, she knew that there were a few more words she still had left to say before they could keep moving forward.

"I'm sorry for all of the times that I refused to rely on you," she said carefully. "Both back when we were kids and now. I was so scared of making a bad choice and ending up like my mom that I let myself lose the most important kind of vulnerability. I guess God knew that it would just take a near death experience or three for me to realize it."

A gust of wind whipped down the street, making her shudder as it bit at her exposed neck.

Cameron's fingers tightened slightly on her waist, pulling her closer until her head was resting against his chest again.

"What kind of vulnerability do you mean?"

She let a sigh escape, glad to be able to hide her face against his shirt and to listen to the steady thrumming of his heartbeat.

"No matter which path we choose in life, pain is always a possibility. We risk failure. We risk heartbreak. We risk death."

She paused, thinking of Jaclyn's grief-stricken eyes.

"And the more people we choose to love, the more we have to lose."

Cameron stroked her back gently as he listened, and at that moment, she felt brave. She felt safe.

And it wasn't because of her. It was because of him.

"But God doesn't want us to live in fear," she continued, smiling an unseen smile against the firm muscles of his chest. "He wants us to trust him with this fragile life, because ultimately, it's in His hands. Every minute. Every breath. And when it comes to my life, and my path, it's become pretty clear where I should place my earthly trust."

She pulled back a little, letting his blue eyes meet her green ones as she tilted her chin up to look at him.

"I love you, Cameron Forge. I don't think I ever stopped. I was just scared. I hope you can forgive me."

The words escaped with a finality, her hopes and dreams suspended in time as he continued to look down at her for several long seconds.

"I love you too, Bristol," he said, his handsome face breaking into a smile. "I can think of no greater honor than being the man who gets to provide for you, to protect you, and to pray for you. Preferably for the rest of our lives, if you'll let me."

She closed her eyes and let him kiss her, the world falling away once more, the future stretching out before them.

She had no one else to be, nowhere else to go.

She was done running.

She was home.

Epilogue

Ben

Three Weeks Later

It was way too early for this.

"Ben, hi! I'm so glad you picked up. I'm sorry about the time, but clearly I didn't wake you up, so I guess I'm not actually that sorry," Grace was saying, her voice pouring loudly from the speakers of his car as he attempted to adjust the volume dial. "Anyway, can you just swing by my house quickly on your way? Please? My car is in the shop. And no, before you say it, I didn't crash it into anything."

Ben rubbed at his temple with one hand, leaving the other gripped firmly against the wheel of his sedan as he considered it.

The Hinton family mansion was closer to Silver Grove than to San Antonio, hardly within the distance that would allow for 'swinging by'. Fortunately, there was little traffic this early, aside from the occasional work truck, and he knew they could make it if they hurried.

He didn't want Grace to miss the special occasion, even if, as usual, she was late thanks to her own lack of time management skills.

"Fine," he said, suppressing a yawn as he took an eastbound turn. "I'll see you in ten."

"Ten?" Grace exclaimed. "Benjamin Forge, don't you dare kill yourself speeding."

"Yes, mom," Ben grumbled. "Fine. We'll be there in fifteen minutes."

His twin brother Asher raised an eyebrow from the passenger seat as Ben hung up the call before Grace could say anything else.

"What?" Ben asked.

"Nothing," Asher said, still smirking. "Just funny how she always chooses you to call, that's all."

"We live near her," Ben said quickly, refusing to meet his brother's eyes. Instead, he focused on the rising sun up ahead, which had bathed their suburban neighborhood on the outskirts of San Antonio in a soft orange glow. Spring was coming fast, and the hot weather wouldn't be far behind, but for the moment it was a mild, gorgeous morning.

"Uh, in case you forgot, Cameron and Bristol actually live *in* Silver Grove," Asher said. "Not to mention dad. I'm pretty sure she just wanted to hear your voice."

Ben drove in silence, ignoring him and his obnoxious sing-song tone.

He wouldn't take the bait this time.

Everyone at Forge Brothers Security seemed totally convinced that Grace had a thing for him, but he wasn't so sure. And even if he was, he would see to it that nothing ever came of it. Grace was their office manager, and if things got complicated, which he was certain they would, there was a not-zero chance that half of their operation would fall apart.

Not to mention the small fact that she was a total pain in the butt, and drove him crazy on a daily basis.

Or that he'd already sworn off love for the foreseeable future.

Nope. No way.

He was steering clear of Grace Isabella Hinton, no matter how much his brothers pestered him. If she really did have a crush on him, it would pass, and he had no intention of hurting her in the meantime.

A few minutes later, he pulled up to an imposing iron gate.

He considered just texting Grace to let her know that they were here, but thought better of it, instead unrolling his window and hitting the talk button on the nearby security speaker.

"Ben and Asher Forge, here to pick up Grace," he said.

"She's waiting in the foyer. Pull through," came a clipped voice on the other end that he didn't recognize. Despite its rural location, Grace's parents' mansion had almost as much security as the FBS office did.

"Thanks," Asher called out from the passenger seat just before Ben rolled up the window and started up the long, tree-lined lane, trying not to let his face reveal any reaction to the opulence of the Hinton family home as they approached the horseshoe driveway out front.

By the time Grace was settled in the passenger seat–Asher had insisted that a lady shouldn't have to sit in the back–the sun had already risen well over the horizon.

"I give us ten minutes before Gabe calls and yells at us for being late," Ben said, pulling out onto the road once again.

"I'll take that bet," Asher chimed in from the backseat. "Grace?"

Grace crossed her arms over her chest and shook her head, attempting to look stern. "Oh, be nice. He just wants to keep the family together. I know first-hand how hard it is to get all of you Forge boys in one place at the same time."

"Like herding cats?" Asher joked.

Grace leaned back against the passenger seat and laughed, her curly blonde hair ringing her face like a halo.

She was pretty. He could admit that much.

Ben focused on the road ahead as his two passengers continued to chat. Usually, Grace tried to pull him into whatever conversation she found herself in, but this time, she left him alone with his thoughts until they reached Trinity Medical Center several minutes later.

"You owe me five bucks," Asher said as he pulled into a parking space and killed the engine.

"No way," Ben said, unable to conceal the smile that tugged at his lips. "It's been seven and a half minutes, I checked."

"But we're at the hospital already and he never called!"

"Doesn't matter, it still counts," Ben said with a chuckle. "You lose."

"I think I have to side with Ben on this one," Grace added, climbing out of the passenger seat before Asher could insist on getting her door.

"How shocking," Asher said, poking her in the ribs with an elbow. "Grace, taking Ben's side, whyever might that be…"

Ben felt his cheeks going hot. He picked up his pace as he strode toward the hospital's door, glad for a couple of seconds to collect himself before they all headed inside. Worrying about Grace's possible crush on him wasn't important at the moment, however embarrassed he felt.

Today was about his cousin Reilly, his wife Lauren, and the beautiful twin girls she had just delivered a little early. After spending a week in the NICU, they were healthy enough to meet the family. As far as he knew, the rest of his brothers and his father were already here.

"Let's get going," he said, pausing as Asher and Grace came up beside him.

Just then, someone's phone rang.

"Ha!" Asher crowed as he ducked through the sliding door of the hospital.

"Hold on," Grace said, following him as she dug her phone out of her purse. "It's not Gabe, actually. Sorry, Asher."

"Hey, dad, what's up?" Grace said, tucking the phone into the crook of her neck as she ushered Asher and Ben to keep walking inside.

Ben opened his mouth to taunt his twin about the five dollars he owed, but promptly closed it again as he watched Grace's face fall.

"What do you mean, she's gone? When did this happen?" Grace was saying, her voice rising in volume with each word.

Asher stopped walking and turned back to his companions, his brow furrowing with concern as he shot Ben a questioning glance. Ben shrugged and placed a finger to his lips, though Grace was making no effort to avoid being heard.

"Last night? Do the local police know?" Grace continued, pacing back and forth in the hospital entranceway. "Of course that's what they think. Typical. I know Katie, and she wouldn't do that. I know she wouldn't. Well, tell Donald I'll call him, alright? We'll get someone on this. I just have to talk to Gabe."

Ben and Asher caught each other's eye. Apparently, whatever was going on was about to become FBS business.

Grace hung up the phone and rubbed at her temples.

"What's going on?" Ben asked.

"We're needed on a case?" Asher added.

Grace looked up at them, her blue eyes filling with tears.

"A family friend of mine, Katie Fairman, has disappeared on spring break," she choked out. "And I just know something terrible must have happened to her. You need to help me talk to Gabe. Please. We need to help her."

Without stopping to think about what he was doing, Ben stepped forward, enveloping Grace in his arms and holding her tight against his chest.

"Don't worry, Gracie," he said. "We'll find her. It's going to be okay."

* * *

Check out Ben and Grace's story in *Forged in Secrets!*

Keep reading to find out how to get your FREE prequel, *Forged in Darkness.*

If you enjoyed this book, please take a moment to leave a brief review — it helps more people to find my books. Thank you!

Get Your Free Prequel

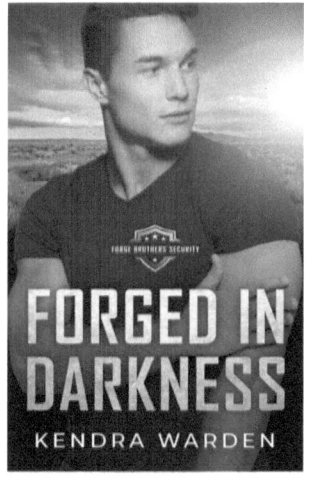

Find out how Reilly and Lauren met with a FREE novella!

Just head to www.kendrawarden.com/newsletter to sign up for my latest updates and download your copy. :)

About Forged in Secrets

Sometimes the devil lurks in paradise...

Office manager Grace Hinton is used to working behind the scenes at Forge Brothers Security. She knows that the team can't function without her, even if her long-time crush Benjamin Forge would never be willing to admit it. But when her childhood friend Katie goes missing on spring break, she can't bear to stay at her desk.

Solving a mystery at the beach surrounded by rowdy college students isn't exactly Ben's idea of a great time. He'd much rather hide in his computer cave with the air conditioning at full blast, but even he has to admit he could use some practice in the field—even if it means spending time with Grace and her limitless enthusiasm for driving him crazy.

As the puzzle behind Katie's disappearance begins to come together, they realize that even the darkest secrets can sometimes hide in plain sight.

Serve. Protect. Redeem.

About the Author

Kendra Warden writes romantic suspense with real danger and fearless faith. She lives in Ontario, Canada, with her husband, three young children, two cats, and a whole lot of books. She's passionate about (very) early mornings, long walks, and buffalo sauce.

https://www.kendrawarden.com